Melissa Wiesner's mother didn͏ TV as a child and, instead, made her play with paint, colourful pipe cleaners, random bits of fabric, and other crafty things. This set up Melissa for a lifetime of creative pursuits, and it was only a matter of time before things took a bookish turn. A night owl, Melissa began writing novels when her early-to-bed family retired for the evening. She is the author of emotional women's fiction and romantic comedies. Along with her charming husband and two adorable children, Melissa splits her time between the big city of Pittsburgh, Pennsylvania, and rural West Virginia.

You can learn more at:
MelissaWiesner.com
X **@Melissa_Wiesner**
Facebook **/MelissaWiesnerAuthor**
Instagram **@MelissaWiesnerAuthor**

THE
SECOND
CHANCE
YEAR

Melissa Wiesner

HEADLINE
ETERNAL

Reading group guide copyright © 2023 by
Melissa Wiesner and Hachette Book
Group, Inc.

The right of Melissa Wiesner to be identified as the Author of
the Work has been asserted by her in accordance with the
Copyright, Designs and Patents Act 1988.

Published by arrangement with Forever,
an imprint of Hachette Book Group.

First published in Great Britain in 2023
by HEADLINE ETERNAL
An imprint of HEADLINE PUBLISHING GROUP

1

Cataloguing in Publication Data is available from the British Library

ISBN 978 1 0354 0615 9

Offset in 10.45/14.96pt Sabon LT Std by Jouve (UK), Milton Keynes

Printed and bound in Great Britain by Clays Ltd, Elcograf S.p.A.

MIX
Paper | Supporting
responsible forestry
FSC® C104740

Headline's policy is to use papers that are natural, renewable and recyclable
products and made from wood grown in well-managed forests and other
controlled sources. The logging and manufacturing processes are expected
to conform to the environmental regulations of the country of origin.

HEADLINE PUBLISHING GROUP
An Hachette UK Company
Carmelite House
50 Victoria Embankment
London EC4Y 0DZ

www.headlineeternal.com
www.headline.co.uk
www.hachette.co.uk

*For all three of my wonderful moms,
Gloria, Sharon, and Lynn.*

Author's Note

This book contains scenes of sexual harassment in the workplace, which may be difficult subject matter for some readers. Please know that I did my absolute best to treat this topic with sensitivity.

Chapter 1

December

If the last year of my life were a season of the *Great British Bake Off*, I would've been sent home on the first episode. My performance in the signature challenge would've left the judges shaking their heads, my technical bake would've ended up raw in the middle, and my showstopper would've collapsed in a heap of gingerbread and shame.

So, when New Year's Eve of my Very Bad Year rolls around, all I want to do is sit on the couch with a bowl of buttercream icing in my lap and an episode of *The Golden Girls* on TV. But my best friend, Kasumi, has other plans.

"Come on, Sadie, it will be fun."

I peer at Kasumi from beneath the ball cap I've been wearing because I haven't washed my hair in three days. "Nothing that starts with 'come on, it will be fun' is *ever* fun."

"This will be, I promise." She snatches the plaid blanket I've wrapped around myself like a fluffy layer of fondant and throws it on the chair where I can't reach it.

"Hey," I protest, half-heartedly making a grab for it. Kasumi is just jealous because that blanket is my new best friend. We've been hanging out almost exclusively for months. We were going to paint each other's nails and have a pillow fight later.

Kasumi plops down on the other end of the couch. "My friend Devon rented an empty warehouse that he's turning into a giant New Year's Eve carnival. Picture acrobats hanging from the ceiling, magicians sawing people in half, and cotton candy cocktails. It will be epic."

"You lost me at *carnival*. You know how I feel about clowns." I open my phone to find an email about another pastry chef job that went to someone who isn't me, and my shoulders droop. "My New Year's plans include sitting on this couch and reading my rejection letters." I click over to Instagram, the only thing that can make me feel worse. "If I'm really feeling festive, I might creep on Alex's social media to obsess over the new woman he's dating."

Kasumi's face softens. "Oh, honey. You need to stop torturing yourself. At least quit following Alex on Instagram. Nothing good can come of this."

She's right, of course. It's been months since my boyfriend, Alex, and I broke up. But we were together for three years, and I thought it would be forever. But now he's on a tropical island with a pretty blond woman who looks fantastic in a bikini. And I'm…well, I'm eating Nutella straight from the jar. I mean, I have some standards; at least I'm using a spoon. But it's impossible not to feel gutted that Alex has moved on with his life while I clearly…haven't.

"I'm worried about you, Sadie. I can't remember the last time you went in the kitchen and baked something. Your relationship with this couch is growing deeply dysfunctional. Come to the party," Kasumi urges. "It will get you out of this rut. And I'll splash it all over Instagram to show Alex that you're not sitting home wallowing."

I eye her black tulle skirt, suspenders, and sparkly red-and-white–striped T-shirt. "I don't have anything to wear to a New Year's carnival costume party." When I lost my job as a pastry chef and had to move out of my apartment, I packed up almost everything I owned and had my brother, Owen, haul it out to Gotham Storage in Flatbush. For the past three months or so, I've been working as a barista, and I live in black T-shirts and jeans that hide the coffee stains.

"I knew you'd say that." Kasumi tosses her dark hair over her shoulder and grabs a tote bag from behind the couch. She dumps out the contents—sparkly gold minidress with a poufy A-line skirt, cropped red blazer, and sequined black top hat—flashing me a grin.

The thing is, a year ago, I would have loved a carnival-themed party with an over-the-top outfit. But that was before Xavier, my former boss and the executive chef of one of the most exclusive restaurants in town, threw one of his epic tantrums over some bad pâté and screamed at a line cook. I'd stepped in because honestly, it was pâté, not world peace hanging in the balance. If the pâté had been an isolated incident, I might've kept my job. But I had a history of refusing to stand down for bad behavior, and the pâté was the excuse Xavier needed to finally get rid of me.

Then, as icing on my crap-cake of a year, Alex broke up with me after I made a scene and told off one of his sexist coworkers outside a party with some of his clients. It wasn't the first time I'd done it, and for Alex, it was the last straw.

He couldn't have a girlfriend who was hurting his career prospects.

At the time, both those incidents had seemed justified. *Someone* had to speak up, right? And that someone was usually me. My mom used to tell me that my big mouth would get me into trouble someday. *Sadie, when are you going to learn not to be so abrasive all the time? You'll attract more flies with honey than with vinegar.*

Back then, I'd responded that no chef in her right mind wants to attract flies, it's a health code violation. But now, as I head into my third month on this borrowed couch, having put not only Alex's job prospects in jeopardy, but mine, too, I wonder if maybe my mom had a point. Maybe there was a better way to handle my boss and Alex's coworkers that wouldn't have left me single, homeless, and struggling to find a job.

As Kasumi holds up the gold dress, Jacob, my brother's best friend and the owner of the apartment where I'm currently crashing, walks in. Kasumi waves the sparkly frock in his direction like a road worker directing traffic. "Jacob. Hey, Jacob."

Jacob stumbles to a stop, blinks, and then pulls an enormous pair of black headphones from his ears, leaving them hanging around his neck. "Sorry? Did you say something?"

Kasumi neatly folds the dress and sets it on the pile. "Sadie and I were just talking about a carnival party my friend is throwing tonight." She cocks her head. "Don't you think she needs to go out and have some fun for once?"

Honestly, I don't know why she's asking Jacob. I'm pretty sure a carnival-themed party, or any party, really, is his worst nightmare. But then again, he's probably dying to get me off his couch, so he'd say yes if she suggested I bungee jump off the Brooklyn Bridge.

Jacob's dark eyes drift from Kasumi to the clothes on the coffee table. Finally, they settle on me. "Will there be clowns at this carnival?"

Kasumi rolls her eyes. "What is with the two of you and clowns?"

"Sadie is terrified of them."

I glance sharply at Jacob. Ever since my brother made us watch Stephen King's *It* when I was in sixth grade and Owen and Jacob were in fifth, I've been afraid of clowns. But I'm surprised that Jacob remembers that. I'm surprised he knows anything personal about me at all.

When I lost my apartment, the last person I expected to come to my rescue was Jacob. We're not exactly what you'd call friendly. He's so introverted and uptight, and I'm...well, a loudmouth. *Abrasive*, as they say. I can't imagine how it tortures him to have me in his space. But no matter what Jacob thinks of me, he's always had Owen's back, and I guess he didn't want my brother to get stuck with cramming me into his studio apartment when Jacob had a spare room he wasn't using anyway.

Kasumi looks him up and down. "What are you doing tonight? You could come along to the party to protect Sadie from the clowns." She gives me an eyebrow raise, which I know she thinks is subtle, but it's about as obvious as if she'd yanked down my neckline, hiked up my boobs, and shoved me in his direction.

A slow heat drifts across my cheeks, and *not* because I'm

interested in Jacob. Because— *Ew*. He's my little brother's best friend. The kid with the too-large glasses and pimples who I once caught flipping through my Victoria's Secret catalog. Who, along with my uber-nerd brother, never had a date to a high school dance because the two of them were glued to our basement computer writing bizarre ambient music and hacking the nuclear codes.

But Kasumi never knew Jacob as an awkward teenager, so her view of him is entirely different from mine. I mean, objectively, I can see the pimples *did* clear up, he shot up past six feet when I wasn't paying attention, and his clear-rimmed glasses are trendy now, probably from one of those indie eyewear brands. Plus, he's become so successful at composing his electronic music that he was able to afford to buy this bright, spacious apartment. But, still. He's *Jacob*.

He hesitates, and I can feel the weight of his gaze on me. If he were anyone else, I'd say he's considering coming to the party. But more likely, he's judging me and the glittery outfit Kasumi picked out, because Jacob would never deign to attend a theme party.

I smile to myself, trying to imagine him dressed up in a black jacket and sparkly top hat, waving a magic wand. But as my gaze settles on him, my amusement fades. A suit would highlight his tall, lean frame, and with his glasses and that razor stubble on his jaw, I think he could actually pull off sexy-magician. I realize I'm staring as soon as our eyes meet, but for some mystifying reason, I don't look away and neither does he. Even more inexplicably, my breath catches.

"So, are you coming or what?" Kasumi cuts in loudly.

Jacob breaks eye contact first, and my cheeks grow warmer. This is all Kasumi's fault for planting the seed of Jacob as a smokeshow in my clearly addled mind. "I'm sure Jacob has better things to do tonight," I stammer. "Some creepy sci-fi music to compose, or something?"

Jacob's eye gives a little twitch, but then he nods. "Yeah. I've got a deadline. You should go, though." He pulls his headphones back over his ears and turns back toward his bedroom. "I'll probably get more done with a little peace and quiet."

As he walks away, I haul myself up off the couch with a sudden urge to get out of here for a while. "Okay. Let's go to the party."

Kasumi jumps to her feet. "Yay!"

I grab the gold dress off the coffee table and head down the hall to get ready. As I pass Jacob's bedroom, I can hear him moving around, probably tinkering with his sound mixer or electronic keyboard or whatever other equipment he's got in there. I stop outside the door, recalling his hesitation at the party invitation and his dark eyes locked on mine. Will Jacob be here all by himself when the clock strikes midnight? Something about that leaves me as hollow as a cannoli without any filling. He always seems like such a loner, aside from his friendship with Owen. But could he actually be a little lonely? I picture sexy-magician Jacob, and my cheeks heat again. Maybe I should knock, apologize for my snarky comment, and see if he wants to come to the party after all.

As I hover there, debating, the door swings open, and

Jacob is towering over me. He takes a deep breath and lets it out slowly, as if to summon what little patience he has left. "Did you need something, Sadie?" He stares over my shoulder as if he could not be more over this conversation.

"Uh. No. Nope. Not at all." I back up a few steps. "I was just heading to my room. Just this way. Down the hall here." I gesture toward my bedroom door, which is, of course, unnecessary. It's his apartment; he knows where my room is. But he reduces me to this nervous babble. Every. Single. Time. "Okay, well. Have a good night."

And with that, I turn and flee.

Chapter 2

In retrospect, I probably should have passed on the buttered popcorn martini, but it seemed like a good idea at the time. I've downed three carnival cocktails at this party in the hopes that the alcohol would help fun-Sadie rise from the ashes of my Very Bad Year, but so far, all I feel is nauseated. For the past half hour, Kasumi's been dancing with a shirtless, tattooed sword-swallower, and there's a dirty joke in there somewhere that I don't even have the heart to make. I'm happy she's having fun, though, and I don't want to drag her away to deal with my attitude.

Kasumi's friend Devon really outdid himself on this party, and for a social media famous event planner, that's saying a lot. The steel beams of the warehouse ceiling are obscured by huge red-and-white–striped curtains that mimic a circus tent, and acrobats in sparkly leotards contort their bodies like rubber bands on long silks that hang above the dance floor. A DJ wearing a yellow cat-ear headband and furry gloves spins records from inside an old-fashioned lion's cage on red-painted wheels while partygoers pulsate to the beat.

I should be out there shimmying up against the strong man in the red leather bodysuit, or at least checking out the array of circus-themed baked goods to see how they compare to my own recipes. But I can't seem to move from my makeshift bench on the leg of a giant fiberglass elephant installation. This party feels like a metaphor for my life. Everyone is out there, living their best life, while I sit on the sidelines.

I know I ought to focus on the silver linings: I have a job at the café, even if it does pay a third of what I used to make at the restaurant, and I'm lucky that Jacob is letting me live rent-free in his spare bedroom. But none of it is what I imagined when I moved to New York with the dream of working my way up to executive pastry chef at a place like Xavier's, opening my own bakery, and catering buzzy events like this one. Nothing about my current life is going to prove to my parents they were wrong when they said I was wasting my time on culinary school and should go to college like my brother.

As I sink deeper into my pot de crème of self-pity, a red-wigged clown pops out from behind the elephant's trunk and cocks his head at me. It's irrational, I know, but my heart whirs like electric beaters set to high speed, and my breath grows shallow. The clown tiptoes closer in his gigantic red shoes and I jump to my feet and slowly back away. He gives me an exaggerated frown, and then raises his gloved hands to his mouth, miming the motion of pulling his lips into a smile. And then, oh God, he reaches for my mouth as if he's going to do the same to me.

I'll smile at you over my dead body.

I lurch backward, ready to bolt, but my shoulder blades hit the hard surface of the elephant's rump, and there's nowhere to run. The clown creeps toward me, slowly wiggling his fingers at my face. I look around wildly for help, but I'm alone in a dark corner with this bozo and suddenly it seems possible that my dead body could actually factor into this story.

My thoughts ricochet around in my head. If I scream, will anyone hear me? If I fight back will he overpower me? I am frozen, pinned against an elephant's ass. *Is this how it ends?*

At that moment, a couple comes strolling around the elephant's trunk, the taller man's arm around the shorter man's shoulder. I open my mouth to cry for help, but it comes out choked, and the sound is quickly swallowed up by the thumping bass of the dance music. I reach out an arm, almost in slow motion, to flag the couple down. They're my only hope. But oblivious to my plight, they only have eyes for each other, and they keep walking. *No*, I'd yell, if only I could form the words. As they pass by me and the clown, I see my chance slipping away.

And then a miracle happens. The shorter man, clearly tipsy, stumbles, and when he takes a step forward to catch himself, he trips over the clown's colossal shoe. His shoulder hits the clown squarely in the chest, and both the man and clown go flying sideways and sprawl on the floor in a heap.

I take off running, weaving in and out of the dancers until I've made it to the far end of the warehouse. Only then do I glance over my shoulder for signs of curly plastic hair or a bright red clown nose, but the pulsing strobe lights and bodies moving on the dance floor leave me disoriented. Swinging back around, I scan for an exit, and in front of me looms a purple-and-gold velvet tent. I duck inside and lean against a tent pole to catch my breath.

"Well, hello there," a deep voice intones.

"*Oh my God.*" I jump about a thousand feet into the air and spin around.

In the far corner of the tent is a tiny old woman in a scarlet-and-gold peasant dress with a matching scarf tied over her long graying hair. She sits behind a table covered in a gold cloth with a crystal ball resting in the center.

"And who are you?" the woman asks in a husky two-pack-a-day voice.

I open my mouth to spill the story of my Great Clown Getaway when a thought stops me in my tracks. "Wait. Aren't you a fortune teller?"

She nods in acknowledgment.

I prop my fists on my hips. "Then shouldn't you already know who I am?"

The woman folds her hands on the table. "I'm a fortune teller. Not a psychic. I need to consult the crystal ball."

At that moment, the lustrous orb in front of her seems to glow brighter, and I blink, wondering if maybe someone slipped something into my carnival cosmo when I wasn't looking.

"Would you like me to tell your fortune?" the woman asks.

Part of me knows this is completely bogus, but for a moment, I consider the offer anyway. What if someone had looked into a crystal ball last December and warned me about the terrible year I was about to have? Would I have done something differently?

I *know* I'm outspoken and quick to react if someone offends me. What if I'd reined it in? On those nights out with Alex, when his coworker was being a jerk, maybe I could have taken a deep breath and spoken calmly instead of telling him off in front of the whole bar. If I had, would Alex and I still be together? What if, instead of yelling at my boss when he was being a bully, I'd tried having a reasonable conversation with him? Would I still have my job at Xavier's and my cute studio apartment with the walk-in closet?

And would I still be on track to making my dreams a reality?

I sigh. None of this really matters. I don't need to see the future; I need to change the past. And that's not on the table...

Is it?

I eye the old woman's crystal ball. "Does that thing do any other tricks?"

Her eyes drift from the crystal ball to my face. "It's not an iPhone. You can't use it to watch TikTok videos."

"I know..." I sink down onto a tufted-velvet stool. "Look, the last year of my life sucked like a straw in a milkshake. I can't help thinking if I'd known what was coming, I would have made different choices. So, while knowing my fortune is fine and all...what I *really* need is a do-over of the last year."

"Ah, yes. I see." She nods sagely. "You're one of *those*."

"One of those...*what*?"

"One of those people who want to go back and meddle

with the past. It's not a good idea. I'm telling you"—she waves a crooked finger at me—"it never ends well."

A shiver runs up my spine, but I shake it off, keeping my eyes on the prize. "So, you're saying you can help me?"

The woman looks me up and down. Finally, she throws her hands up in the air. "Fine. I can grant you one wish. But before I do, you must be sure you want to go through with this. It may not turn out the way you think it will."

Goose bumps pop up on my skin, which is ridiculous because this whole thing is a total sham, and if I weren't slightly tipsy and there wasn't a clown stalking me, I'd be out of here. But for some reason, I find myself nodding anyway. "Yes. I want this."

The old woman sighs deeply. Then she slowly pulls a wooden box out from under the table and opens it. I sit up on my stool, trying to peer over the top. "Is that where the magic happens—?"

She holds up a hand, and I stop talking. Reaching into the box, the woman pulls out a ceramic bowl and several small glass jars full of what look like dried herbs in an array of colors. She tosses a handful of red herbs into the bowl, followed by green, then a pinch of blue and a dash of orange. Smashing it all together with a pestle, she grinds the colors into a maroon-colored powder that she pours into a small cloth bag.

"Now. Go to the bar and order a shot of vodka," she instructs me.

I wrinkle my nose. Vodka tastes like lighter fluid. "I'm really more of a tequila kind of girl. Do you think I could—"

The woman cuts me off with a wave of her hand. "Silence!"

I press my lips together, examining the bag full of powder. It occurs to me that the fortune teller might want me to pour that stuff in a shot of vodka and drink it. That's going to have to be a hard no, and not just because I don't like the taste of vodka. If I was worried about someone slipping something into my drink before...well. This is not a good idea. But I've come this far and I can't quite make myself get up and leave.

"Order a shot of *vodka*," she repeats. "Drink it. Then close your eyes, spin around three times, make your wish, and toss this powder in the air."

Even though the rational part of my brain is rolling around on the floor laughing at these instructions, I nod along, going over the steps in my head to make sure I have them straight. Vodka, spin, wish, powder...vodka, spin, wish, powder...Got it. "And then what happens next?"

"What do you think happens next?" She closes her eyes and shakes her head like I'm the dumbest person on the planet. "And then your wish comes true."

I feel like that answer only raises more questions, but I'm not sure it's appropriate to point it out when she's gone to all this trouble to mix up a potion for me. Instead, I gather up my bag of powder, shove it in my purse, and stand up. "Well, thanks for your help."

The fortune teller clears her throat and hitches her chin at a glass jar on the table. TIPS, the sign says. Right. I stuff a twenty I can't really afford into the jar.

"Good luck," she calls to me as I make my way out of the tent and back onto the dance floor.

Without the thick drapery muting the sound, heavy bass from the dance music reverberates through me. I stand at the edge of the crowd, watching bodies kaleidoscope around me and weighing my options. Am I really considering going through with this hokey directive from a fortune teller?

A pair of arms cinches around my shoulders, and my thoughts immediately fly to the creepy clown. I whirl around, but instead, I find Kasumi standing there with a happy grin on her face. "Sadie! I've been looking for you everywhere," she yells over the noise. "Isn't this party amazing?"

"Unbelievable," I yell back, patting my purse to make sure the powder is safely tucked inside. I don't want to have to explain what I've been doing.

"Guess who came tonight after their shift was over," Kasumi says. "Sonya and Marianne! We should all do shots!"

I smile weakly. Along with Kasumi, Sonya and Marianne both work at Xavier's. We were all friends when I was employed there, but ever since I got fired, I've been avoiding my former coworkers. I'm embarrassed to face them knowing I haven't been able to find another job as a pastry chef anywhere in the city. Xavier went out of his way to make it known that I'm difficult to work with, and even if another chef hasn't heard the rumors about me, they still want a reference from my former employer. I didn't just burn that marshmallow when I left Xavier's, I incinerated it.

"You know, I actually think I feel a migraine coming on," I improvise. "I'm going to head out."

"Oh no, I'm sorry." Kasumi's shoulders slump. "I'll ride home with you."

I shake my head. She's clearly having a blast, and I'd feel even worse if I ruined it for her. "No, you stay with Sonya and Marianne. It's not even midnight yet. I'm fine to get home by myself."

"Are you sure?" She glances over my shoulder at the dance floor, her forehead scrunched with uncertainty.

"Yes, absolutely." I pull her in for a hug. "Call me tomorrow."

I wade back into the crowd, making my way toward the exit. Near the coat check is one of the bars scattered around the periphery of the warehouse, and the line is unexpectedly short. I hesitate with my hand on my purse, eyeing the Grey Goose and Absolut bottles lined up on the shelf.

Should I?

What could it really hurt?

Before I lose my nerve, I order a shot and carry it to a darkish corner where couches and beanbag chairs are scattered around on the floor. A few couples are talking, or making out, but nobody even glances in my direction. I set my shot on a table and pour the colored powder into my hand.

This is it.

I'm ready.

In one swift motion, I toss back the vodka, feeling the burn all the way down, and then I whirl around in a circle once, twice, three times. Dizzy now, I stumble to a stop and send my wish into the universe. *Please give me a second chance. Please give me a do-over of the past year.* Eyes still squeezed tight, I toss the powder high into the air and feel it settle softly around me.

All the anxiety and angst of the past year seem to drain from my body, and a calm washes over me. The stale warehouse air shifts to a sultry, tropical breeze that teases my hair and warms my skin. I spread my arms wide, floating on the cloud of sensation and, in this moment, I believe in magic.

I slowly open my eyes, adjusting to the darkness. Is this it? Is it possible I've really changed the trajectory of my life? Will I have a chance to right my mistakes? I take a deep breath in, and then—

I scream at the top of my lungs.

The clown. The clown is standing in front of me, his too-wide painted-on eyes only inches from my face. He cocks his head, raising his hands in a questioning motion, as if to ask what the hell I'm doing. I blink as the throbbing beat of dance music works its way back into my consciousness. Suddenly, it hits me that the man wearing a red rubber nose and polka-dot coveralls is actually the rational person in this situation. What the hell *am* I doing? My heart drops to the vicinity of my stomach.

Before I can humiliate myself any further, I push past Bozo and make a break for the door.

Chapter 3

You'd think my night couldn't get any worse, but as soon as I get to the subway station, the digital display announces that the L train broke down inside the tunnel, and outbound service to Brooklyn has been suspended. There's no way I'll catch a cab on New Year's, so I end up walking an extra ten blocks in order to catch the M train.

On the ride home, reality sinks in. Am I so pathetic that I actually allowed myself to believe that an old lady shilling fortunes for tips could change my life for the better? I wish I could blame my complete break from reality on party drugs, but the truth is that even the alcohol wore off a while ago.

The train arrives at my stop, and I get off, swimming upstream through crowds of revelers carrying New Year's party hats, noise blowers, and bottles of champagne. Off to parties like the one I just fled. Out on the street, the buildings create a wind tunnel, pushing the cold December gale straight through my scarlet bolero jacket. But instead of shivering, my skin grows hot with humiliation. What if Sonya and Marianne had spotted me spinning around in the darkness like cake batter in a KitchenAid? Can you imagine what they'd tell everyone back at Xavier's about how poor Sadie has gone off the deep end?

My alternate route back to Jacob's takes me by my old apartment building, and I keep my head down because it hurts to gaze up at the second-story window that used to be mine. A few blocks later, Higher Grounds Coffee is closed up for the night, but I'll be there bright and early for my shift in the morning. As I approach Jacob's building, a text comes in from my dad.

Happy New Year. Did you look at those Brooklyn College brochures I sent you? You can't live on Jacob's couch forever.

I close my eyes with fresh humiliation. I'm not living on Jacob's *couch...*

I just spend a lot of time there.

Somehow, my dad always manages to make me feel like I've dumped salt instead of sugar into a batch of cookie dough, ruining everything. Despite some less-than-gentle prodding from my college-professor parents, I chose culinary school instead of the local university, and they've never gotten over it.

But maybe my dad's right. I can't stay at Jacob's forever and it's not like the pastry chef jobs are flying in. Sighing, I quickly fire off a text. *Maybe I'll check them out later this week.*

The second I hit send, I want to take it back.

Great! my dad replies. *Maybe this is all for the best. I'm proud of you.*

I stare at those last four words on my phone. I don't know

if either of my parents have ever said they were proud of me before. The fact that *this* is what it took depresses me.

I arrive at Jacob's building, an updated prewar with a doorman. As I step off the elevator onto his floor, I nearly crash into Jacob's next-door neighbor Paige and her boyfriend. When I first moved in, I couldn't help but notice Olivia Rodrigo playing constantly on repeat through our shared wall, and I pieced it together that Paige was going through a rough breakup. I could relate. One evening, after listening to a muffled version of "traitor" coming from the direction of the exposed brick for about six straight hours, I had a bottle of wine and a box of chocolates delivered to her apartment. In a happy turn of events, Paige and the long-haired delivery guy named Brandon really hit it off. Now, I have the pleasure of seeing them make out in the hall whenever I get off the elevator.

I clear my throat to let them know I'm standing here, but they don't bother looking embarrassed. Paige flashes me a grin and pulls Brandon onto the elevator. The doors aren't even closed before they're kissing again.

Seeing the two of them should make me hopeful. But selfishly, their happiness only depresses me more. Why can't I be like Paige? Why can't I seem to move on?

I enter Jacob's apartment quietly in case he went to bed already. Though he doesn't talk to me about his work, I've figured out his routine. When he has a big project on deadline, he might be up until all hours of the night, but once it's over, he'll crash early. I never quite know which one to expect, and either way, he's usually in his room with the door closed, so it never really makes much of a difference to me.

Although he and my brother were inseparable through-out my childhood, Jacob and I were never friends. He and Owen were the smart kids. The talented kids. The ones who took honors classes and competed for valedictorian and landed scholarships to Ivy League universities. While the only class I excelled in was home economics. By junior year, I'd grown so tired of my parents comparing me to my perfect brother that I quit trying to do well in school and started trying to have fun instead.

Jacob not only got straight As but was also some kind of musical prodigy, and he always looked down on me for being the Molly Ringwald to his Anthony Michael Hall. When I'd try to make conversation, Jacob would stare at me like I was the rat in biology lab: a radically different species, beneath him on the food chain, and with no future ahead of me. I can talk to pretty much anyone, but Jacob's quiet contempt would leave me babbling incoherently to fill the awkward silence.

To be honest, not much has changed. When I started crashing at Jacob's place a couple of months ago, I thought maybe we'd hang out. He's my brother's best friend, and Owen and I are super close now. But the first time I invited Jacob to watch a movie, he flinched like it would physically pain him to spend two hours on the couch with me, so I gave up.

Now, we've settled into a mostly comfortable routine where Jacob stays in his room, or strolls by with his head-phones on, and I stare into my pint of ice cream and pre-tend I don't notice. So, when I arrive home from my New Year's disaster and tiptoe into the apartment, I'm surprised to hear music floating down the hall from the living room. Maybe Jacob is still awake, and he's put a record on the turntable. But when I stop in the doorway, I realize the music is coming from the piano.

Jacob sits on the bench with his back to me, a single lamp in the corner casting shadows over the lacquered surface as his hands move gracefully across the keys. The song that drifts out is slow, and melancholy, and reminds me of snow falling in the woods or the empty city streets on my early-morning walk to work. I lean against the doorframe as the melody envelops me, and when the last note rings out, I swallow hard to quell the unexpected emotion burning in the back of my throat.

Jacob turns, and his face registers surprise. "Sadie," he says quietly, scrubbing a hand across his forehead as if he's trying to orient himself back into the present moment. Dazed, I kind of know how he feels.

"I didn't know you play the piano," I say, stepping into the room.

His lips quirk into a half smile. "Did you think the giant instrument in my living room was for holding potted plants?"

I shake my head ruefully. "I mean, I guess I'm aware that you can play. I've heard your electronic music, and I know you use keyboards and stuff. But I didn't know you played music like that." I wave my hand at the piano. "Did you write that song?"

His eye twitches, almost like he's surprised by the question, and inexplicably, a little hurt. Finally, he nods.

"It's beautiful."

Jacob looks down at his hands before meeting my eyes. "Thanks."

It dawns on me I've never really said anything nice about his music before. It's been in the background for my entire life, drifting up from the basement of my childhood or piped in as the soundtrack to whatever video game or other computer-y thing Owen was inventing when we were kids. I know Jacob's made a living doing this, but I guess he was always sort of background music in my life, too.

"You're home early," he says, reminding me that he wanted peace and quiet, and my presence brings him a considerable lack of both. He was probably looking forward to an evening alone. Except for work and an occasional lunch with Owen or Kasumi, I've basically been moping on his couch for the past few months. I'll bet he hears *The Golden Girls* soundtrack in his dreams. No wonder he never comes out here to play the piano.

My cheeks heat with shame. "I'm sorry to bother you." I take a step backward, but my heel catches on the throw rug, and I stumble.

Jacob stands and takes a few steps toward me, but I manage to grab the wall before I land on my ass like a creepy clown and humiliate myself further. "I'm fine, I'm fine," I mumble in embarrassment. Jacob watches me, probably to make sure I'm stable—literally and figuratively—and when I'm back on both feet, he moves to the couch. "You're not bothering me," he says, folding his long limbs into the cushion at one end. "How was the party?"

Just like everything else about this strange night, the question surprises me. Our interactions mostly consist of six-word conversations about who's buying milk. We don't talk like this. But maybe it's because it's the end of the old year and the start of a new one. Or maybe it's the late hour and the stillness of the room that masks the usual awkwardness between us. But something about the way he leaves space at the other end of the couch feels like it might be an invitation to sit down.

The last thing I want to do is slink to my bedroom and wallow in the mortification of my night. So, I slip out of my shoes and make my way over. "Kasumi was right. The party was epic."

"Yeah?" he prompts.

I hesitate. Does Jacob really want to hear about my night? He seems genuinely interested. Could he be feeling as lonely as I am?

I tell him about the sword-swallower and the popcorn martini, and by the time I get to the part where the clown cornered me, my night seems less dire and genuinely funny. Jacob throws his head back against the couch with laughter, and I clutch my stomach against the uncontrollable giggles. As our mirth slowly dies down, he lifts his head to look at me at the same time I shift my body in his direction. Our eyes meet, and my breath catches. He holds my gaze, and just like earlier in the day, an awareness stretches between us like taffy. My heart raps painfully against my sternum, and that same emotion he evoked when playing the piano washes over me. Some sort of longing I don't know what to do with, so I look away.

Jacob clears his throat, shifting in his seat. "So, if the party was epic, why were you home at eleven thirty?"

I grab a throw pillow and clutch it to my chest. "I don't know. I guess I wasn't in much of a party mood."

He rests a hand on the back of the couch, and my eyes are drawn to the muscles flexing in his forearm. It must be all that piano playing. "It's been a hard year for you," he says. "Maybe you didn't feel like you had much to celebrate."

Once again, I'm surprised that he seems to know me better than I realized. I mean, I guess he couldn't miss the pints of Ben & Jerry's piling up in the freezer, or my own Olivia Rodrigo playlist on repeat. But he's not poking fun at my misery like Owen does. He seems to understand that I've really been struggling. And that means a lot right now.

"I know I haven't exactly been easy to live with," I say. "And I'm not sure I ever told you how much I appreciate you letting me stay here until I get back on my feet." I trace a line of thread on the throw pillow with my finger. "If it weren't for you, I would've blown through my meager savings by now. And I guess I'm still foolish enough to hope that someday I'll get to use it to open my own bakery."

"Why is that foolish?" He shifts his body in my direction.

"I don't know. Maybe I should have gone to college. I could have an actual career right now, like Owen does."

"Now you sound like your parents," Jacob says. He's sat through enough Thatcher family dinners to know Owen is the golden boy with his 4.0 GPA and his computer science degrees, while I'm the black sheep who barely scraped by with Cs. By the age of sixteen, I could craft a quadruple layer cake with lemon curd filling and vanilla fondant flowers worthy of the *Great British Bake Off*. But maybe

I should have tried harder in school. Buttercream frosting was never going to impress my college-professor parents.

"Maybe they're right." I shrug. "I mean, I'm thirty years old."

Jacob squints at me. "Wait, Owen and I are thirty. I thought you were thirty-one."

I throw my hands in the air. "Jesus, Jacob, kick a girl when she's down, why don't you?"

His shoulders shake again, and it brings me unexpected pleasure. He's usually so serious and reserved, so *judging*, it feels like a victory to make him laugh.

"My point," I continue, "is that I'm too old for this. I'm too old to let my big mouth ruin my career and my relationships."

He considers that for a minute, regarding me across the couch cushions. "Nobody ever picked on Owen and me when we were kids," he finally says.

I look at him sideways. Where is he going with this?

"Because everyone in school knew you'd kick their ass if they tried." He gives me a lopsided smile.

I breathe out a tiny laugh. "I would have."

Jacob's dark eyes roam over me, his expression unreadable. "I wish you could see yourself the way I do. Because I don't see someone with a big mouth." In the dim lamplight, the two of us here with only this narrow space between us feels suddenly intimate. "I see someone who stands up to bullies. Who doesn't let bigger, more powerful people get away with treating someone badly."

And with that, the burning in the back of my throat is back. I look down at my hands.

He leans in. "If someone doesn't appreciate that... Well, they don't deserve you."

Is this... *Jacob*... I'm talking to? For once in my life, I am speechless.

And then suddenly, the world outside of Jacob's quiet apartment erupts into pandemonium. Pots and pans clang, noisemakers trumpet, and dozens of voices burst into cheers on the street below. From our view on the tenth floor, fireworks glitter and explode over the East River.

We sit up to gaze out at the city's celebration at the exact same time, and we're not at our own ends of the couch anymore, but sharing the middle cushion. I'm hyperaware of the heat radiating from him as my shoulder accidently brushes his.

"I guess it's midnight," I murmur.

"I guess so." He turns his head toward me, and our eyes lock. And... Oh my. I remember there's a way people traditionally ring in the New Year.

Does Jacob want me to kiss him? And more importantly— *Am I really thinking about kissing Jacob?*

"So, should we do something to mark the occasion?" I ask, my voice like fluffy meringue. "Goodbye, terrible year! Maybe high-five? Or we could bang some pots and pans? Or—" Did I mention I babble when I'm nervous? And in this moment, Jacob Gray is making me extremely nervous. "If you know the words to 'Auld Lang Syne' we could sing—"

"Sadie." Mercifully, Jacob cuts me off. "Do you want to high-five? Or"—his mouth twitches like he's trying not to smile—"sing 'Auld Lang Syne'?"

I bite my lip. "Not really."

"How about this instead?" Jacob takes me gently by the shoulders. "Happy New Year." He leans in, pressing a kiss to my cheek, and his lips are soft, and cool against my flushed face. He hesitates, and the roughness of his razor stubble brushes my jaw. Before I can overthink it, I slide my hand up to his chest and grasp a handful of his T-shirt. He freezes, mouth inches away, eyes searching mine. I reach up to slowly pull off his glasses and set them on the back of the couch.

"Happy New Year, Jacob," I murmur. And then I kiss him, tilting my head for better access to his mouth, coaxing it open to slide my tongue against his. Jacob plunges one hand into my hair and wraps the other around my waist, shifting until I'm pressed back against the arm of the couch. He leans over me, bending down to kiss my lips, my cheek, my neck. And then he's back to my mouth again, and *oh my God*, he's so good at this. How is he so good at this? How did I go all this time without noticing these broad shoulders and solid arms and those gorgeous musician's hands that are currently playing a concerto across my burning skin? I pull him closer and—

Somewhere far away, a key jiggles in a lock. A door creaks open and slams shut. And then, from down the hall, a horrible, irritating male voice calls out, "Yo, Jake!"

Chapter 4

I give Jacob's chest a hard shove and struggle to sit up. "It's *Owen*."

"Shit." Jacob dives to the other side of the couch, grabbing his glasses and flinging them on his face. He glances at me, reaches over to tug my dress back down over my knees, and then shifts his body so he's facing forward, legs crossed casually in front of him.

My brother strolls into the room, bypassing the two of us on the couch and heading for the kitchen where he opens the fridge and grabs a beer. "You ready to go, dude?"

"Uhhh...," Jacob says, straightening his glasses again.

Owen wanders back into the living room and plunks himself down on the piano bench across from us. "Interesting outfit, Sadie. What's that powder in your hair?"

I try not to be irritated with my brother for strolling in like he lives here. Jacob and Owen have twenty-five years of history, dating all the way back to kindergarten. After high school, they both attended college in Boston—Owen at MIT and Jacob at Berklee College of Music—then moved to New York together. Owen has a key to Jacob's place and lets himself in because Jacob is usually absorbed in his mixing board with headphones glued to his ears. It's never bothered me when Owen showed up unannounced before, but then again, I was never making out with his best friend before.

I flush at the memory but play it off as indignation over his comments about my outfit. "None of your beeswax," I say, showing off my maturity where my brother is concerned. "What are you doing here?"

Owen takes a swig of his beer. "I'm dragging Jacob out of his music studio to meet some people from AstRoBot for a drink at Blackbird." When Owen graduated from MIT, he was still a computer nerd. But then he got a job at a robotics start-up fueled by a gazillion dollars in venture capital, and suddenly he started wearing two-hundred-dollar hoodies, classic Vans, and beanie hats even in summer. Now, he hangs out in bars that serve cocktails made of charred persimmon and pickle juice, and where Pabst Blue Ribbon costs fifteen dollars a can.

I'm a little surprised that Jacob made late-night plans to go out for drinks with Owen's tech-bro friends. But if this night taught me anything, it's that I really don't know Jacob at all. Maybe I never did, and maybe...it wouldn't be the worst thing if I got to know him a little better.

Owen stands up. "I gotta go break the seal." He heads down the hall for the bathroom, leaving me alone with Jacob.

I jump up off the couch and turn to face him. "So..."

"Sadie..." He stands too, only inches away, and I have to tilt my head back to look at him. I'm painfully aware of how his T-shirt stretches across his chest, his long eyelashes cast shadows across his cheeks in the dim light, his lips are slightly swollen from kissing me.

I open my mouth to tell him that the past hour was the most fun I've had this year. That I actually feel something like my old self again. And to ask him if...maybe...he wants to hang out tomorrow. No pressure, just lunch, or a walk in the park or something...

But before I can say a word, he blurts out, "Sadie, I want to apologize."

"Wait." I stumble backward. "What?" *Apologize?*

He runs a hand through his hair, and the words come spilling out. "I didn't mean for any of this to happen. I mean, you came in here looking so sad, and I— Well. I—" He shakes his head, cursing under his breath. "I'm so sorry."

"You're sorry for—kissing me?"

"Yes, for..." He waves a hand at the couch. *For all of it.*

And then it dawns on me with complete clarity. He's not interested in me, and why would he be? I'm the sad girl in her bathrobe on his couch, eating cereal straight from the box and crying over episodes of *Queer Eye*. Jacob felt *sorry* for me, that's why this happened. Tonight was nothing but a pity kiss for Owen's pathetic sister.

My heart constricts in horror. What if I'd actually said that stuff about hanging out tomorrow? What if he turned around and told Owen? My brother would literally laugh so hard he'd pass out and need medical attention, and I'd have to move to a yurt in the desert for the rest of my life.

I press my hands to my cheeks. "Oh my God."

Jacob runs a hand through his hair. "I made a move on you when you were vulnerable."

Well, if I didn't feel pathetic before, boy, do I now.

"Sadie," he continues. "I'm really—"

"Stop saying you're sorry." I turn away because if I have to look at the mouth that was just pressed against mine telling me how deeply he regrets it, I might haul off and smack him.

"I understand if you don't want to forgive me right now."

"You want me to forgive you for kissing me."

"I—" He nods. "Yeah, I guess so."

God, I am such an idiot.

"Maybe we can pretend it never happened?" He shoves his hands in the pockets of his jeans. "It doesn't have to be weird, right?"

I push a lock of hair out of my face and come out with a palmful of red powder. This is the worst night of my entire life. And the real kicker is that Jacob is right. What was I thinking, making out with my brother's best friend—the owner of the apartment where I'm currently living because I'm homeless and underemployed—and thinking it could turn into anything less than a disaster? Could I possibly sabotage my life any further?

I stand up straight, determined to walk out of here with whatever teeny-tiny shred of dignity I have left. And then to wake up tomorrow and *get my shit together.* Maybe it really is time to look at those stupid college brochures my parents sent me. I mean, I'm running out of options here.

I glance up at Jacob and force myself to shrug. "Pretend *what* never happened?"

Relief flashes across his face. "We're good, right?"

"Yep!" I say, my voice like rainbow sprinkles. "Of course. Absolutely!" He looks at me sideways, and maybe I'm laying it on a bit thick. Suddenly, I am exhausted. "Have a good night, Jacob."

I head down the hall to do what I should have done hours ago. Climb into bed and pull the covers over my head.

Chapter 5

January

*B*ecause I've always been a glutton for punishment, I wake up with Jacob on my mind. If such a thing is possible, I am even more humiliated than I was last night. Here I was thinking he was lonely and wanted my company. Thinking we had a connection.

But no. The poor guy was just waiting for his night to start, and I showed up, pathetically covered in pixie dust and blabbering about my parental issues. He probably kissed me just to get me to stop talking.

And oh lord, what a kiss.

How am I supposed to live with him and pretend it didn't happen? I guess the silver lining is that Jacob succeeded in getting me off his couch because I will be hiding out in my room, so I never have to face him again.

I open my eyes and stare up at the ceiling. I have truly hit rock bottom. The star-shaped midcentury chandelier above my bed sways gently, as if it's nodding along to this assessment. A breeze from the window ruffles the curtain in agreement. I always leave it open a crack because the old radiator in the corner has one setting—broil—and otherwise I'll be roasting when I wake up. I roll to the left side of the bed to grab my phone, debating about whether or not I should call Kasumi and tell her about what happened with Jacob.

My hand fumbles in the air. There's no nightstand on the left side of the bed. There's only— *Oh my God, what is happening?*

I bolt upright.

There's *a man* sleeping on the other side of the bed, his back to me and the covers pulled up all the way to the crown of his head.

Panicked, I fling aside the duvet and jump to my feet. Did I sleep with Jacob last night? Maybe someone really did slip something in my drink at the carnival party. How can I not remember this? (Damn, if that kiss was any indication, I really *want* to remember this.)

And then I freeze.

The chandelier. I cried when I packed up that chandelier and Owen took it to storage in Flatbush.

The open window and the radiator that's channeling the surface of the sun. That shouldn't be here. Jacob's updated building has forced air heating.

I spin in a circle as the rest of the room comes into focus. The screen prints I bought at the Brooklyn Flea. My West Elm duvet. A black chef's coat with XAVIER's embroidered on the pocket, ready to wear to work.

This is my old apartment. The one I had to leave when I lost my job. *How the hell did I get here?*

My gaze flies to the door that leads out into the building's hallway. Maybe I got drunk and broke in last night?

Except, the door is neatly closed, and there's no sign of forced entry. Besides, if I'd broken in, my stuff wouldn't be here anymore. Someone else's stuff would be here. I reach out to touch the fabric of the chef's coat, right above where my name is embroidered. It's rough beneath my fingers, just like I remember it. No, I'm obviously hallucinating. I've finally cracked from the stress of the past year, and my brain has taken me back to the time before it all fell apart. I slap my hands over and over on my cheeks, hoping it will bring me back to reality, and when that doesn't work, I pinch my upper arms.

Should I call Owen, or my parents? If I tell them what's going on, they'll be here in less than two hours to take me to the hospital. I do another slow turn around the apartment as if looking for a portal that would lead me out of this alternate universe and back into Jacob's apartment. If Jacob is around here somewhere, *he* could take me to the hospital. But even in my addled state, that thought stops me. As if last night wasn't humiliating enough, now I have to find him and admit that kiss finally broke me.

I back up against the wall. No. Nope. I can't do it. Eventually, I'll come down from this trip like a club kid the morning after a rave, and I'll wake up on the floor of Jacob's spare bedroom, my throat parched and head pounding. Until then, I'll just wait it out here. But just as I'm about to settle in for the long haul, my gaze lands on the man in my bed. And at that moment, he sighs in his sleep and rolls over. The duvet slides off his bare shoulder, and—

My legs buckle, and I grab for the back of the couch to keep myself upright.

It's Alex.

Somehow, I've hallucinated not just my former apartment, but my former boyfriend sleeping in my bed. Before I can come to terms with this latest development, my phone buzzes on the coffee table in front of me and lights up with Kasumi's name.

And, suddenly, this absolutely bonkers situation comes into focus.

The carnival party. The fortune teller. My wish to go back and redo my terrible year.

Is it possible?

I grab the phone and run for the bathroom so I don't wake Alex.

"Sadie, where are you?" Kasumi demands after I've swiped to answer. "You were supposed to be here twenty minutes ago to prep the pastries for the New Year's brunch."

"I was supposed to be *where*?" I close the lid to the toilet and sit down.

"What do you mean, where? At work, Sadie. I covered for you and told Xavier the shipment of plums didn't come in for the stone fruit galette, so you ran out to buy some. But he's only going to accept that excuse for so long. So, get your butt over here."

I stare at the bathtub in front of me. I loved that giant soaking tub; it was one of the reasons I chose this apartment. But I shouldn't be here. This is not my apartment anymore. "Kasumi, did we go to a New Year's party last night?"

"What? Yes, of course we went to a New Year's party."

"And, um." I don't even know how to ask this. "Can you remind me of...where? Where the party was?"

There's silence at the other end of the phone. And then finally, "Sadie, are you okay? Did you get blackout drunk after you left last night or something? Where's Alex?"

"I'm fine, Alex is...here." Except Alex shouldn't be here. Alex is a hallucination. All of this is a hallucination. *Isn't it?* "Please, just tell me. Where was the party?"

"It was at the apartment of one of Alex's finance friends. Zach, or something? That guy hit on me and got creepy close when I came out of the bathroom, by the way."

I seize on the party at Zach's place. Okay, I was there. I remember it. Except that party was *last* New Year's Eve. A year ago. Not last night. Last night was the carnival party.

Is it possible the fortune teller and the acrobats and all the rest were just some vivid dream? But how could it be? It all feels too real. The smell of the warehouse and the taste of a sickly buttered popcorn cocktail and the feel of Jacob's stubble scraping my cheek as he kissed me. And there's no way I imagined the entire last year of my life. Getting fired. Moving in with Jacob. Working at Higher Grounds.

I drop my phone to my lap and click to my home screen to look at the date. And suddenly the room is spinning. Because though it's January first, just like I expected... It's January first, *twelve months ago*. The entire last year of my life is—gone.

Gone.

Just like I wished for.

I slap my face and pinch my arms again. Fortune tellers aren't real, and wishes don't come true. So, maybe this is a dream. Maybe I went to sleep last night, and I'm still sleeping, and any minute now my alarm will go off—

"Sadie?" Kasumi's voice carries up from the phone in my lap. "Are you there?"

Am I here? My gaze skates around the bathroom. The shower curtain with the watercolor print. The crack in the tile by the mirror. My eyeliner and lipstick on the counter, left there from when I did my makeup before Zach's party.

Surely, if this were a dream, or a hallucination, it wouldn't feel this real. Something would be hazy or out of place. That crack in the wall would be talking to me. Kasumi would suddenly turn into my mother. But none of those things are happening. It feels like an ordinary day in an ordinary apartment. They just happen to be the wrong day and the wrong apartment.

So, that leaves just one possible scenario.

Last night, I asked for a second chance, and today, it's January first of last year. Not only do I still have my apartment, but that man out there in the bed is still my boyfriend, and I have a job as an assistant pastry chef to get to. That old fortune teller with her colorful powder and her weird vodka spell came through for me, and this is my opportunity to do it all differently.

"Sadie?" Kasumi repeats, her voice rising now.

I lift the phone back to my ear. "Stall Xavier a little bit longer, okay? I'll be right there."

Chapter 6

*B*ack in the main room of my apartment, I'm faced with my first dilemma. In the second chance universe where I'm currently residing, Alex and I have been together this whole time. But according to my secret internal calendar, I haven't seen him in months, unless you count the Instagram photos that I spent too many hours dissecting.

Last night, I kissed someone else. It feels real to me, even if technically, it never happened. I'm still hurt that Alex broke up with me and started dating someone else. I feel disloyal to Alex that Jacob is still on my mind, and irrationally, I feel a little disloyal to Jacob, too. If you'd told me twenty-four hours ago that I'd wake up with Alex in my bed, my heart would have leaped with joy. But my entire world flipped like a pancake last night, and now I'm not sure which way is up.

I grab my uniform and carry it into the bathroom to change because I suddenly feel shy about stripping right there where Alex could roll over and see me. I'm sure it will just take a while to get used to having him back in my life.

After I brush my teeth and pull my hair into a ponytail, I tiptoe out to look for my shoes.

Alex is sitting up in bed, shirtless, with the duvet resting on his lap. My gaze traces his muscular torso down to the little strip of hair on his navel that disappears beneath the covers. My face heats up, and I'm sure I've turned bright red. If I remember correctly, Alex likes to sleep in the buff, which means if the duvet shifts, I'm going to get a front-row view of—

"Hey, babe. Off to work?" He stretches his arms above his head, and I look away.

It's not like I haven't seen him naked before. We dated for three years. But that was before he broke my heart, and I'm not sure I'm emotionally equipped for a peep show right now. Besides, I'm late for work, and if I plan to take this second chance seriously, I need to keep my job.

"Yep. Gotta go." I face away from him to put my shoes on, and then I search for my purse. Where would I have put that thing when I came home from the party last-night-slash-a-year-ago? "You have a key to lock up, right?" And then I stumble to a stop. We'd made kind of a big deal about exchanging keys to each other's places, going out to dinner, and toasting with cocktails. And I'd ugly cried when, a couple of years later, he gave my key back. "I mean, of course you have a key."

He looks at me sideways. "Don't worry, I'll lock up. Have a good day at work."

Am I supposed to kiss him now? Is this how we said an ordinary goodbye on an ordinary day? It's funny the things you forget. I hesitate before I finally settle on leaning over to give him a peck on the cheek. "You have a good day, too," I say.

"Hey." He takes my hand before I can step away from the bed. "Are you okay? You seem a little out of it."

In this moment, my brain is so fried you could serve it with toast and a side of potatoes. But I can't tell him any of that. "Of course! I'm fine. Just tired. It was—uh—a long night." About a year long, to be exact. I try to tug my hand away, but Alex holds on.

"Let's get dinner tonight. I'll meet you after work?"

I gaze across the rumpled duvet. The styling product Alex uses to tame his wavy blond hair rubbed off while he slept, and now his cowlick is sticking up in the back. Or maybe he isn't using that hair gel yet. In this time line, he's still a brand-new graduate of Columbia's MBA program, and he only started the investment banker job a few months ago. It's disorienting to catch a glimpse of him looking like the Alex I met three years ago. By the time we broke up, halfway into my Very Bad Year, he was wearing the same slicked-back hair and designer suits as the other guys at the firm.

I give his hand a squeeze, half expecting it to disappear in a puff of smoke. But Alex returns the pressure. He's really here. This is really happening.

"Sadie?" He nudges me.

I realize I'm staring dumbly at him. "Uh. Dinner? Sure. I'll text you when I get off," I say, and then flee the apartment.

There's no way I'm going to make it through a New Year's brunch at Xavier's restaurant without caffeine and food, so on the way to work, I stop at Higher Grounds. Zoe has the best coffee in Williamsburg. I should know—when

I worked here during my Very Bad Year, it took me three weeks to learn how to make it properly. The scones aren't great. I could make better ones in my sleep, but I'm so hungry I don't care.

When I walk in, the familiar scent of ground coffee, vanilla, and something that's unique to Higher Grounds envelops me, and it's strangely comforting in my familiar yet foreign new world. Zoe, the owner, stands behind the counter with her long black braids tied up off her face in a colorful wrap.

"Hi, Zoe," I say as I approach. "I'd kill for a latte and blueberry scone. To go, please. I'm already late for—" I abruptly stop talking. Because she's staring at me with her eyebrows knit together. And with good reason. I might have spent four months behind that counter, but I don't work here, and as far as everyone in the place is concerned, I *never* worked here. Zoe doesn't know me from Adam, and I'm talking to her like we're old friends.

"Have we met?" she asks, raising an eyebrow. "How do you know my name?"

"Oh, well..." How am I going to talk my way out of this? I give her my most sincere not-a-stalker smile. "I was in here a couple of months ago—" Zoe won't recall that far back, will she? Except she's one of those people who has an amazing talent for remembering customers and making them feel welcome. If we'd talked before, she'd know. "And...I *overheard* someone call you Zoe," I improvise. "And coincidentally, I had a—um—*a cat* named Zoe. She died." Oh great, now in one of my multiple lives, I have a dead cat. I hang my head, looking as sad as possible over my dearly departed pet and banking on the fact that Zoe will take pity on me. "So, that's how I knew your name, and obviously it stuck with me."

This is New York City, so I'm certainly not the strangest person to ever come into the café, but I'm willing to bet I'm the strangest person this week. I can almost see Zoe's brain working out how to handle me in the kindest way possible. "Oh...I'm honored to have had the same name as your...furry friend. Poor Zoe. How are you?"

"Holding up the best I can," I say. "It's hard when you lose a pet. They're like family." *Shut up, Sadie.*

"Yeah." She nods. "I'm so sorry. Remind me of your name again?"

"It's Sadie," I tell her, relieved that she seems to be playing along. "Sadie, sort of like"—I make air quotes with my fingers—"'Sadie, the Cat Lady.' That's me." Oh my God, it's that nervous babble again. Somebody please put me out of my misery.

Zoe backs away from me, and who could blame her? "Well, let me get you that latte."

When she turns to use the milk frother, I press my palms to my face and shake my head. Pretending I haven't lived through this year before is going to be more difficult than I expected. There are so many pitfalls. I'm really going to have to work harder to keep track of what I'm not supposed to know and learn to think before I talk. I should only be using the information I have to fix the things I messed up during my Very Bad Year.

It occurs to me that I should have paid attention to some hot stock tips or lottery numbers the last time around. But,

Oh, well. It's too late now. Besides, if I suddenly started buying tech stock, it would be even less plausible than this dead cat situation I've gotten myself into.

I glance to my left and find an older woman glaring at me. Mrs. Kaminski. No way am I acknowledging that we've met before. She loves to sit at the counter and bark orders at the staff. Zoe doesn't seem to mind, and sometimes she even gives her free coffee.

When my latte and scone are ready to go, I make sure to leave a big tip. Zoe earned it for putting up with me. I scarf down my sustenance on the four-block walk to Xavier's, and when I arrive, I slip in the back-alley door, mercifully undetected.

Kasumi is standing at one of the industrial metal worktables slicing strawberries to go on top of Xavier's pearled sugar and preserved lemon waffles. "Sadie," she whispers after I toss my purse in the staff break room and tie an apron around my waist. "Thank God you're here. Xavier is on a tear over something—who knows what?" She rolls her eyes because we're all used to Xavier's tantrums. "Are you okay? You were super weird on the phone this morning."

"Yeah, I'm fine. It's just—" For a wild second, I consider blurting out that a fortune teller sent me a year back in time to fix my messed-up life. Who wouldn't believe a story like that? Thankfully, I come to my senses. "It's just that I was a little hungover this morning."

"Yeah, me too. Alex's new friends can really drink, can't they?"

At the Wall Street investment banking firm where Alex has worked for the past few months, the motto seems to be

Work hard and play harder. I thought people in the restaurant industry were drinkers, but we've got nothing on those finance guys who toil until all hours and then drop hundreds of dollars a night at bougie bars with tufted leather seats and cigar rooms in back. None of that is really Alex's scene, but he's new at the firm and sometimes has to play the game.

"Alex is such a good guy," Kasumi muses, mirroring my thoughts. "I'm surprised he can spend so much time with those douchey finance-bros."

"I'm sorry about Zach hitting on you at the party," I say. Zach, the host of the New Year's party, just happens to be the guy who caused Alex's and my big breakup. Except I remind myself that technically *I* was the cause of our big breakup when I allowed myself to be baited into a very public argument with Zach in front of Alex and all of his coworkers. I don't know what I was thinking, but I won't let that happen again.

Before we can discuss the party anymore, Xavier bursts into the room. "Sadie," he roars. "Where were you?"

"Um." I look around wildly. Kasumi grabs a bag of plums that have been at the restaurant this whole time and shoves it across the table. "Plums!" I swing the bag in Xavier's direction. "The plums never arrived, and I know how you wanted stone fruit galettes on the menu today, so I ran to the Food Bazaar and grabbed some."

Xavier eyes the bag, probably looking for some way to find fault with it, and when he can't, he levels a glare at me. "Fine. Get to work rolling out the dough, and don't make it too thick."

I don't need Xavier to tell me how to do my job. I may

be a mess in other areas of my life, but I make a beautiful pâte brisée and can roll the dough perfectly thin with one hand tied behind my back. I was at the top of my class in culinary school before I spent four years as a prep cook at Jean-Georges. When I took this assistant job at Xavier's, I was lured by the opportunity to make a name for myself and, eventually, work my way up to executive pastry chef.

Xavier flounces out of the room to go berate the bar staff, and Kasumi shakes her head at the door he just exited. "What a dick."

I'm about to echo the sentiment because there's nothing I love more than a good old-fashioned Xavier-bashing. But at the last second, something stops me. This is my second chance. My opportunity to fix my mistakes and stop repeating the same old patterns. I don't want to start out trash-talking my boss, even if he deserves it. So instead, I just give her a shrug. "I'm sure he's stressed. It's been a busy week with the holidays and everything."

Kasumi's mouth drops open. "Did you just...*defend* Xavier?"

"No." Avoiding her eyes, I open a drawer and study the contents. "Of course not." I choose a rolling pin and pastry cutter, lining them up on the prep table in perfect parallel formation. "It's just that...well...I *was* the one who was late."

I don't need to look up to know she's gaping at me, and I can't blame her. I'd be gaping at me, too. But if I let Xavier get to me, I'll only regret it. Believe me, I've been there, and I'm not going back.

Instead, I keep my head down and focus on making the perfect dough.

Chapter 7

My stone fruit galettes turn out deliciously flaky with crusts rolled to perfection and the fruit just the right blend of tart and sweet. Though Xavier won't deign to admit I did a great job, the servers report that he was happy to stroll around the dining room collecting compliments and credit for my work.

By the time I hang up my apron and head out, my body feels like it's been run through the restaurant's industrial-grade dishwasher and wrung out to dry. The barista job I'd been working at Higher Grounds was always pretty chill except for the occasional morning and evening rush, and my back and feet aren't prepared to be thrown back into the chaos of a hectic restaurant kitchen.

I limp home in a daze, trying to ignore the blister on my heel from the chef's clogs I technically haven't worn in months. When I finally arrive at the front door of the building, I look through my purse for my apartment key, digging around in the side pockets for the purple unicorn keychain I picked up on impulse at the drugstore when I moved in. I can't find it anywhere, and I'm so tired I want to cry.

A shadow falls over me, and I squint into the late-afternoon sun to find Jacob standing on the sidewalk. "Sadie? What are you doing here?" He pushes his glasses higher on his nose, and my face flames. Out here on the street, and in broad daylight, I can't believe that I actually reached up and brazenly took those glasses off his face so I could—

"I lost my key," I blurt out. At least he's here to let me in. All I want to do is climb into the bathtub and— *Wait a minute.*

It's the memory of the bathtub that brings me back to reality. Jacob isn't going to let me into the apartment. *Because I don't live here.* I was so exhausted that my feet must've automatically turned off Bedford Avenue in the direction of Jacob's building. In the direction I've been used to walking for the past few months. What was I thinking? *My* place is actually ten blocks from here.

"Were you hoping to find Owen?" Jacob asks. "Does he have a spare key to your place?"

I nod stupidly. "Um, yeah, that's exactly why I'm here."

"I don't have any plans to see him today, but if you want to call him, you're welcome to come in and wait."

For a second, I am so tempted to take him up on his offer. This building, his apartment, it was my home for months. Inexplicably, I long for my little bedroom, the bright, spacious living room, and that plaid blanket on the couch.

Except that I never lived here. It was never my apartment, or my bedroom, and I've never been wrapped up in that plaid blanket. I never reached over and took those glasses off Jacob's face, or kissed him, or even had a conversation with him of any substance at all. I need to go home. My actual home. Ten blocks from here.

My hand closes around the key to my apartment, in the pocket where I tucked it this morning. It's attached to a lone silver ring, no purple unicorn in sight. "Oh, look! Never mind. I found my key after all." I hold it up.

"Oh," Jacob says, his voice dropping. "Great." I'm sure he's relieved he doesn't have to wait with me until my brother comes to the rescue. The slump in his shoulders is entirely my imagination.

I'm about to say goodbye and turn to leave, when something comes over me, and I stop right in front of him. It must be my complete shock and exhaustion because I blurt out, "How was your New Year's, Jacob?"

His eyebrows rise, and of course he's surprised that I asked. We're not friendly. We don't chitchat. He's my brother's friend and I'm his best friend's sister, and that's all we are to each other. It's all we've ever been.

Well, except that one time.

That one time technically he knows nothing about.

"Uh," he finally stammers. "It was quiet. I have a deadline for a project, so I mostly worked." He pauses for a minute as if he's waiting for me to give him the punch line. Otherwise, why would I be talking to him like this? When I don't say anything, he cocks his head and, in a slightly wary voice, asks, "How was *your* New Year's, Sadie?"

And just like that, I'm back there, with his body pressing against mine, his hand in my hair, his mouth on my neck. I pull my coat tightly around me against the January wind (sure, *that's* what's making me shiver) and look down at the pavement. "Oh, you know." I shrug. "Just a party with some of Alex's friends."

"Well, I hope it was a fun night."

It was, Jacob. It was so much fun. Until you told me it was all a horrible mistake.

For a second, I worry I've gone so far off the deep end that I've said it out loud. My gaze flies to his face, and he's looking at me like he's not sure what to make of me. I grasp for a subject change. "What are you working on? Your project with the deadline, I mean. What is it?"

Jacob shoves his gloved hands into the pockets of his charcoal peacoat, and I can't help but notice how perfectly it fits him across his broad shoulders. "Really?" he finally asks.

"Really, what?"

"Do you really want to know what I'm working on?"

If I close my eyes, I can still hear those beautiful, haunting notes from the song he played on the piano. The song he wrote. "I asked, didn't I?" It sounds more defensive than I intended, but that song brings up all kinds of feelings I don't want to think about. "I mean, yes," I say, more gently this time. "I want to know."

"Well…" He looks at me sideways. "It's the soundtrack for a film. Science fiction. Directed by Joshua James."

Now it's my turn. "Really?" Joshua James is legit famous. Not like Steven Spielberg famous, of course, but he's directed a bunch of award-winning sci-fi films.

"I take it that surprises you."

"No…," I protest. But then, "Well, okay, maybe a little." Joshua James films are less the alien-apocalypse type of sci-fi, and more the man-goes-out-into-the-universe-to-find-himself kind. The kind where a slightly aging heartthrob actor takes on a serious role to secure his legacy and generate Oscar buzz. It actually makes perfect sense. "An introspective Joshua James film seems like the right place for your music."

"Thanks?" Jacob looks at me with his brows knit together, and I get that this is all a bit astonishing. We've never had a conversation this long, or this personal.

Except that one time. That one time that never really happened.

Jacob adjusts the scarf around his neck, and lord, am I a sucker for a man in a peacoat with a well-placed scarf. Seriously, how did it take me this long to notice how attractive he is?

"So..." He looks down at me. Make that a sucker for a *tall* man in a peacoat and well-placed scarf. "I was going to run out for coffee before I get back to work. Um..." He cocks his head. "Do you want to come?"

I hesitate. Does he really want to hang out with me?

Probably not. Did you hear that pause before the *Do you want to come*? I'm standing here on his front step looking slightly unbalanced, half a mile from home. Jacob is just watching out for his best friend's sister. He feels sorry for me, again. But suddenly, I don't care why he's asking. I don't want to be alone right now in this strange time loop. And something about Jacob, my former-but-not-really roommate, comforts me right now.

"Sure. Where are you going? Higher Grounds?" I drop my apartment key back into my purse. Hopefully, Zoe's shift will be over. I'm not sure how I'd explain the cat thing to Jacob.

But he shakes his head. "I've walked by that place, but never tried it. Is that your favorite?"

Wait a minute. How is it possible Jacob has never been to Higher Grounds? When I worked there during my Very Bad Year, he used to come in all the time. I'd always assumed he was annoyed I'd gotten a job at his regular spot. He barely spoke three words to me, but sometimes he and Mrs. Kaminski used to chat for a minute. He was one of the few people she never barked at.

If it's January, and he's never been there, when did he become a regular? He wouldn't have started going to Higher Grounds because *I* worked there...would he?

My mind is spinning like a whisk in a bowl. But Jacob is still waiting for an answer, so I nod. "Yeah, it's great. Want to try it?"

We're mostly quiet on the walk over, but for once, it's companionable. Maybe I'm just too tired for awkwardness. When we arrive at Higher Grounds, I'm relieved to see that Zoe is gone for the day, although Mrs. Kaminski is still in her usual spot right next to the cash register, the best position to harass the customers and staff.

When she sees me, she yells, "Hey, it's Sadie, the Cat Lady!" and starts cackling. There's no way Jacob didn't hear, but she seems more off-her-rocker than even *I* do, so I doubt he thinks anything of it.

Luckily, Mrs. Kaminski goes back to antagonizing José Luis, the barista on duty this evening, and she doesn't say more about my cat fetish. José Luis is a design student at the Fashion Institute of Technology, and during my Very Bad Year, he used to work on his sketches when business was slow. One day, when he found out I was a former pastry chef, he drew a picture of me in a pink wedding-cake dress with piped-flower ruffles, macaron jewelry, and a strawberry cupcake hat. I wish I still had it. But like everything about the past year of my life, that sketch never existed.

Mercifully, I remember I'm not supposed to know José Luis, so when Jacob waves me to the counter in front of him, I stick to my coffee order.

"And your friend?" José Luis asks, giving Jacob a sly up-and-down glance. Am I the only one who never noticed that Jacob is a real snack?

Distracted, I mumble, "Café Americano, please," without thinking. As soon as the words are out of my mouth, I realize my mistake. I've made Jacob dozens of café Americanos. It's all he ever ordered when he came into Higher Grounds. But in *this* version of my year, he's never been here before, and I've never made him coffee before. How do I explain how I know this?

I peek up at him, and now he looks stunned. "How did you know that's my coffee order?"

"Oh, you know..." I look around the café for inspiration. "I guess..." Above the counter, Christmas lights twinkle, leftover decorations from the recent holiday. That's it. "Christmas! And Thanksgiving! When you come over for the holidays with my family, you always have a café Americano after dinner." I have literally no idea if this is true, but my parents have one of those fancy, pretentious espresso machines they like to break out when their intellectual friends come over, so it's *probably* true. It still doesn't explain why I would have paid any attention to his coffee preferences, when I barely paid any attention to him. But it's been a hard day, okay?

He nods, clearly still skeptical. But what else is he going to think? That I used to work here and make him drinks, and then I came back in time, and now I know things that I technically have no way of knowing?

Who would believe a story like that?

Jacob turns to Mrs. Kaminski and leans forward to peer into her empty coffee cup. "Can I get you anything?" he asks, and for a moment, her face registers surprise. I imagine mine looks the same.

Mrs. Kaminski always drinks plain black coffee, but now that Jacob's buying, she orders a Mediterranean veggie panini and an extra-large café mocha. Oh, and a brownie to go. Shrewd lady.

"That was nice of you," I murmur while we wait for our order.

He shrugs. "She seems like she just needs somebody to pay a little attention to her." And at that moment, my insides turn to custard. Mrs. Kaminski is a grumpy old bat. But I guess I never thought about the fact that she's really just lonely, and probably doesn't have anywhere else to spend her days.

While José Luis sets the espresso machine to drip and grabs the milk from the fridge under the counter, Jacob asks if I want to get a table. I'm about to say yes when my phone buzzes with a text. It's Alex. I told him I'd meet him for dinner after work.

I sigh, exhausted from keeping up this charade all day long. I know it will be good for Alex and me to get back to normal, but right now, it's the last thing I want to do.

"Everything okay?" Jacob asks.

"Yeah, I...I forgot I'm supposed to meet Alex." My shoulders droop. "He's waiting at my apartment."

If Jacob is disappointed, he doesn't show it. And to be honest, he's probably *not* disappointed. He has a Joshua James film score to compose, and my brother to meet for drinks, and a whole life he doesn't need to wish away.

Jacob approaches the counter. "Excuse me," he calls to José Luis. "Can we get those coffees to go?"

No, Jacob doesn't care one bit that I have to leave to meet Alex. But the real question is...why do I care? It must be because Jacob is familiar, and right now, I'm desperate for anyone who feels familiar. I peek up at him as José Luis hands over our paper cups. I know for a fact that Jacob wears blue flannel pajama pants and likes cold Thai noodles and tilts his head to the left when he kisses. While after all this time, my knowledge of Alex feels hazy. Dim. Like something from my past.

But the past is here, Alex is my boyfriend, and Jacob is...Jacob is Owen's friend. Nothing more. He made that sugar-crystal clear on his couch last night.

When we're back out on the street, I hold up my coffee in a little salute in Jacob's direction. "Thanks for this."

"Sure. It was—" He cocks his head like he's trying to work something out. "It was good to see you, Sadie."

"You too, Jacob." Reluctantly, I turn and head down the sidewalk. My aching body protests, and my feet scream obscenities, but I keep walking until I've dragged myself back home.

Back home, and back to the life that I wished for.

Chapter 8

February

I've never seen so many men in gray vests in my life. I'm at a downtown bar, meeting Alex for drinks after work, and this place is positively swimming in performance fleece. I actually grew a little disoriented and approached two other tall, sandy-haired men with their backs to me before I found Alex. It's casual Friday, and it seems that every Wall Street banker got the memo: pale button-up shirt, khaki trousers, and Patagonia vest. Oh, and since we're at a bar, an old-fashioned in hand.

I finally identify my gray vest–wearing boyfriend in a sea of gray vest–wearing boyfriends, and he stands to give me a hug. The place is crowded, so he offers me his stool and gets the bartender's attention to order a glass of my favorite sauvignon blanc. Alex has always been thoughtful like this, and it's one of the first things I loved about him. Like Kasumi said, he's a good guy. The dating scene in New York City can be a jungle, so finding someone who will buy you a drink without the expectation of getting your panties off is less common than you'd hope. Not that I can't buy a drink for myself, of course.

When I slide on to the barstool, I come face-to-face with Zach Templeton. If dating in New York is a jungle, then Zach is the king of gorillas. I'd say I don't know why Alex hangs out with him but they're coworkers who both started at the firm the same week, so he doesn't always have a choice. Apparently, it's part of the Wall Street culture to network over drinks.

Lately, I'm really not one to criticize Alex for sucking it up for the sake of professional harmony. I've been metaphorically covering my ears, squeezing my eyes shut, and singing "la, la, la" in order to ignore Xavier's bad behavior. I haven't told him off or made any big speeches in weeks. And I've stayed off his radar, which is not something I could say the last time around.

This whole second chance thing is still an adjustment, but I've started to get used to it. There are moments when I have the most intense sense of déjà vu, and then I realize that no, I don't have the feeling I've had this conversation before. I've *actually had* this conversation before. Which is how, as I take a sip of my wine, I know that Zach is about to say something to really irritate me.

He doesn't disappoint. "Is your cute little Japanese friend meeting you here?"

I may be learning to let things go, but I can't simply "la, la, la" my way through this conversation. "Please don't call her that. She has a name, and you've hung out with her enough times to know what it is." I pause, taking in his slicked-back hair and smirk. "Actually, never mind. Forget her name and forget she exists. Because you know what they say about not even if you were the last man on Earth—"

"Well," Alex cuts in, his voice a little too loud and overly cheerful. "It sounds like Kasumi probably isn't interested, so let's talk about something else. What are you baking at work these days, Sadie?"

I spin my chair away from Zach and focus on Alex. "I have a new recipe for lavender lemon tarts. And actually"— I pull a small pastry box from my bag with a smile—"you can let me know what you think."

Alex used to joke that our love story began over dessert. I met him on the subway when he was just starting out in the MBA program at Columbia, and I'd been at Xavier's for about a year. Xavier had sent me on an errand to deliver a cake I'd made for one of his VIP friends at a downtown office building. I was standing on the crowded subway, balancing the giant pastry box, and trying desperately not to pitch sideways into the lap of the old woman to my left. Alex was in the next row and spotted me swaying. He lunged to his feet, grabbed the box just as it began to tip, and offered me his seat. When I got off the train, Alex did too, carrying the pastry box for eight blocks until it was safely deposited at the VIP's office. I didn't learn until our second date that Alex had been going uptown, and that hadn't even been his stop.

In the early days, I showed my affection by dropping off treats when Alex was busy studying for finals or working on a big project. He'd text me selfies in return, photos of him biting into my desserts with silly notes like, *I love you berry much.* Or, *You're the icing on my cupcake, I'm muffin without you.*

"Where's mine?" Zach asks.

I give him an exaggerated shrug. "Sorry, I only brought one."

"It's cool," Zach says. "Bring me one next time."

I bite my tongue.

"Hey, Zach," Alex cuts in, probably to steer the conversation to safer topics again. "How's it going with the candidates for the financial consultant position? What do you think of that woman you interviewed yesterday?"

And then, I realize what's coming next. I sat in this same bar on this same day during my Very Bad Year, and I had a version of this conversation before. And it did not go well. Because if memory serves, then Zach is about to reply with...

"Eh. I don't know, man. She's smart, I'll give her that. Really qualified. But, based on her graduation date, I'd guess she's about thirty-two, thirty-three, maybe. No wedding ring, but when she clicked on her phone to look at her calendar, I could see from her lock screen that she has a boyfriend."

"So?" I ask, just like last time. "What does that have to do with her ability to do her job?"

And even though I know what to expect, I'm hoping that somehow the universe has shifted, and Zach isn't about to say what I think he's going to say.

Spoiler alert: He *is* about to say what I think he's going to say.

"Well, no offense," Zach says on cue. "But what's the point in hiring her if she's just going to get married, and then pregnant, and then quit to be a stay-at-home mom?"

It sounds just as terrible now as it did the first time. Maybe even worse. And I can remember that first time so clearly. For a moment, I was too stunned to say anything. And then I hopped off my barstool, got in his face, and yelled, "Are you kidding me? That's so fucking stupid."

Last time, Zach's eyes grew wide as he backed away from me like I was a zoo animal let out of my cage. Conversations around us trailed off, and someone muttered, "Whoa," as the other guys from Alex's firm looked over at us. And then Alex took me by the arm and murmured, "Sadie..."

"What?" I demanded louder. "You don't agree with that bullshit, do you?"

"No, of course not." Alex shot Zach a hard look. "Dude, tone it down, okay?" he murmured.

"Tone it down?" I looked back and forth between Alex and Zach. "How about, dude, don't have shitty, sexist attitudes about women in the first place? Ones that are probably *illegal*." My voice rose even higher, and I was attracting the attention of not just Alex's colleagues, but strangers across the bar, too.

I can still picture Zach turning bright red and then sort of purple. His gaze swept across the groups of people looking on. "It was a *joke*," he huffed.

I leveled a stare at him. "No, it wasn't."

"Okay," Alex cut in. "Zach and I can talk about this at the office tomorrow. Sadie, why don't we head out?" And that was when I noticed his clenched jaw and jerky movements as he pulled on his coat. He didn't look up as we walked past the other guys from his office, but I saw him flinch when a couple of them snickered.

I'll never forget the fight we had out on the sidewalk. It wasn't what I'd said, Alex insisted. Of course he agreed with me that Zach was an ass with antiquated attitudes about women. Of course he was going to discuss it with Zach tomorrow. "But Sadie, I wish you'd talked to me instead of making a scene in front of the entire bar." If the story got around to Dave, his boss—and I could bet it would get around to Dave—did I have any idea what this could do to his career?

"But if Dave doesn't agree with me," I argued, "he's as bad as Zach."

"Dave can agree with you and *still* not want his employees to make a public scene while half of Wall Street is watching. The whole firm's reputation is at stake."

A tiny part of me understood what he was saying. But the bigger part dug her heels in. "*You* didn't make a scene. *I* did."

I remember Alex shaking his head, shoulders drooping. "What you do reflects on me. It affects my career."

He hailed me a cab instead of suggesting we go back to his place. When I called him the next morning, Alex assured me things were fine, but his voice remained cold. Eventually, we moved past it, and everything seemed to go back to normal. But now I know that he never completely got over it, and I would only dig myself even deeper the next time we hung out with his work friends.

Now I know this was the beginning of the end for me and Alex.

But it's my second chance year, and it doesn't *have* to be the end. As Zach's shocking, obnoxious words come back to me, I realize I have a chance to do it differently.

I take a deep, cleansing breath. I count backward from

ten. I repeat *I will not cause a scene, I will not cause a scene* in my head like a mantra. But you know what? It's not as easy as it sounds. Because I really, really want to cause a scene. Zach's smug face is making my skin crawl, and his smirky smile is just begging for me to reach over and—

I spin in my chair and turn to Alex. And his words come back to me, too.

I wish you'd talked to me.

"Honey, can we go outside for a second?" Before he can respond, I slide off my stool, grab his hand, and drag him through the crowded bar toward the door.

"Jeez, Sadie," Alex says when we're out on the sidewalk. "What's so important that you couldn't just tell me inside?" Despite his fleece vest, Alex is obviously freezing, but my anger warms me.

"You're not going to let Zach get away with that, right?"

"Get away with what?" He looks confused. "The hiring thing? That's why we're out here in the cold? I'm sure he doesn't mean it. He was just joking."

I'm taken aback by this. Last time around, Alex said he agreed with me, he just didn't like how I delivered the message, loudly and in front of his colleagues. So, this time, I've done exactly what he asked me to do. I've pulled him aside to talk to him in private. I've kept my voice calm and even. I've made sure my bad behavior doesn't overshadow Zach's.

So, where is Alex's righteous indignation?

I blow out a breath, and it turns to frost in the air. "He *did* mean it. But even if it was just a joke, does that make it any better? Is discriminating against women supposed to be funny?"

Alex crosses his arms over his chest. "No, of course not."

"So, you'll talk to him about it? You'll make sure he hires the best person for the job? Regardless of her marriage prospects or childbearing abilities?" I can't help it; my voice gets a little snarky at that last part.

He holds out his hands, palms up. "I'm not on the hiring committee. It's not up to me."

My shoulders stiffen. Is he really trying to tell me that he can't do anything? "But you could at least have a conversation. Or you could talk to Dave about it." I pause, hearing the resentment in my voice. Maybe if I add a question at the end, it might not sound so abrasive. According to my mother, abrasive is *the worst*. "Can't you?"

Alex sighs. "It's not as easy as you make it sound." He looks past me at the taxis zipping by on the street. I wonder if he's wishing he could hop in one and get himself out of this conversation.

None of this is how I expected this to go *at all*. I pace across the sidewalk and then swing back around to face him. "If you don't do anything, you're protecting that old boys' club culture. If you're not part of the solution, you're part of the problem."

At this, Alex cocks his head and flashes me a grin, shoving his hands in his pockets. "Can I get that printed on a T-shirt?" His body language is channeling *Aw-shucks, give me a break, I'm a nice corn-fed Midwestern guy*. I've seen this work for him a million times. When we showed up at an off-Broadway play and realized we forgot our tickets at home. When he was trying to get a table at La Petite Poule and they were booked for weeks in advance.

But now he's using his charms on *me*.

I press my palms to my frozen cheeks. Last time around, Alex said he agreed with me. I've known him for three years and he's never, ever acted like Zach. Is it possible he's just not getting it? I try a different tack. "Think how this kind of thing affects me. I created these amazing lavender lemon tarts today, and the Earl Grey fig cake yesterday, and the basil ricotta macarons the day before that. You know who gets credit for all my hard work because I'm only an assistant? The executive pastry chef whose lemon tarts taste like hand soap. And you know why he has that job, and I don't? Let me introduce you to my friend, *Dick*."

Alex's eyes soften, and he grabs my hand, pulling me toward him. "I know you deserve that job. I'm sorry. I don't mean to make a joke of it." He wraps an arm around me.

I push a hand against his chest, searching his eyes. "The woman Zach interviewed—whoever she is—she might deserve the job, too."

He nods, his face earnest. "I hear what you're saying, and tomorrow I'll talk to Zach."

"Dave might be open to discussing this," I suggest gently. Alex has always had a close relationship with his boss. Dave took an interest in him at a networking event while Alex was still in grad school, and he was a big part of the reason Alex ended up on Wall Street.

"Maybe," Alex says slowly. His gaze slides to the door of the bar where three men in suits and wool coats step out onto the sidewalk, chuckling over someone's joke. I flinch as a couple of choice words drift my way. Those guys are not corn-fed Midwesterners and I'm pretty sure the cocks they're referring to have nothing to do with farm animals. As they head down the sidewalk, Alex looks back at me. "There's this whole culture in finance, and I'm still learning how to navigate it."

"I know," I say, squeezing his hand. The lines around his mouth deepen, and I'm sure he's thinking of his dad right now. Alex had always meant to get his graduate degree and then move back to Wisconsin to work in his dad's financial advising firm. But in the second-to-last semester of his MBA program, his dad died of a heart attack. All of a sudden, Alex's mom found herself alone and in need of money, so she sold her half of the business to her deceased husband's partner. Just like that, there was no family business for Alex to go back to.

When Dave and Alex hit it off over cocktails a few months later, I know Alex saw more than just an opportunity for a job. He saw an opportunity for a father figure.

The wind picks up, blowing through my dress, and Alex pulls me in for a hug. I decide not to push this anymore. I've managed to get my point across without making a scene, and Alex promised to talk to Zach. I won't have a lonely cab ride home or hear the coldness in Alex's voice tomorrow. And in a few months, Alex and I will still be together.

Everything is turning out exactly as I wished.

And if a tiny part of me feels as wobbly as a perfect batch of crème caramel, well, it's better than the alternative.

Chapter 9

March

I'm spreading ganache on a chocolate orange layer cake when Xavier comes tearing into the kitchen. "Sadie." He points a finger at me. "I need you to help the servers in the dining room tonight. We've got some VIPs who need extra attention. There's a server's shirt hanging in the break room."

"But"—I drop my spatula in the pot of chocolate—"I'm not a server. I don't know the specials or the wine selection, or—"

"Oh"—Xavier waves his hand as if he's shooing away a fly—"you'll be fine." And with those words, a version of this exact same conversation slowly comes back to me. I dig deep in my memory to recall what Xavier is going to say next. It dawns on me at the same moment the words come out of his mouth. "Just smile and help top off the water glasses."

Last time around, I'd slapped my hands down on the prep table, stood up to my full height, and told him that his words were insulting to the servers. *"And did you just tell me to smile? Really? Like I'm some sort of ornament?"*

He'd stormed out of the kitchen before I could say any more, and I went back to making my cakes.

Just like last time, I feel my palms hit the table and my mouth open, ready to tell Xavier exactly where he can shove his *smile*. But as the words are forming on my lips, I manage to grab Sadie of the past and yank her back from the edge of the cliff.

Not this time around. This is my second chance, and I'm not going to risk my job over this. "Um, excuse me, Xavier? Can I have a moment?"

Xavier has already moved on to berating the dishwasher for some spots on the water glasses, and I've interrupted him in his happy place. He swings back around to me. "What?"

I clear my throat. "I have four cakes to decorate for the lunch event tomorrow. If you need more help in the dining room, I'm wondering if Doug wouldn't mind." I gesture to our newest line cook. Doug has only been on the job for about a week, so he's mostly been training and doing a little light prep work. "It might be good experience for him to spend an evening in the front of the house."

Xavier looks Doug up and down. "He can do the cakes."

I can't help myself, and I blurt out, "*Doug* will do the cakes? He's been here a week. He doesn't have any training!"

Xavier turns to Doug. "Hey," he calls across the kitchen. "Doug. Can you finish making these cakes?"

"Uh—" Doug's voice cracks and he looks wildly around the room, probably for someone to save him. "Uh— Yes? I mean…" He clears his throat. "Yes. Of course."

"There you go," Xavier says, and then he spins on his heel and leaves the kitchen.

As soon as the door swings shut, Kasumi comes running over. "Oh my God. I can't believe that just happened."

"Right?" I say, pulling off my apron and slapping it on the table in front of me. "I mean, he told me to *smile*? What the hell? And I can't wait to see this shirt I'm supposed to wear." I stop muttering and look up to find Kasumi giving me the side-eye. "What? Why are you looking at me like that?"

"You're not actually going to let Doug make your cakes so you can go work the front of the house—are you?"

"Do I have a choice?"

"I don't know." Kasumi lifts a shoulder. "Maybe? I mean..." She trails off, giving me a sly smile. "You *are* the one who unionized our entire class to get the school to pay us for our internship hours."

I laugh at the memory. It was a culinary school requirement for students to gain experience in the school's restaurant, and it never sat right that we were required to work for free in order to earn our degrees. "Well, I couldn't have done it without your amazing social media campaign."

Kasumi and I met in culinary school a decade ago. We were partnered up during the first week of pastry class and immediately bonded over our assignment to make a lemon cake with yellow buttercream flowers. Kasumi had grown up poring over the beautiful photography in *Food & Wine* and *Bon Appétit*, and I'd secretly dreamed of designing celebrity wedding cakes. Together, we baked batches upon batches of lemon sponge, trying half a dozen different recipes until we'd settled on just the right blend of citrus and sweet. And then we spent another two days perfecting our rosettes until we felt our work was worthy of a spread in an upscale food magazine. Our instructor, an older man who'd been teaching at the school for decades longer than we'd been alive, called our work "adequate" and gave us a B-minus.

We were crushed.

And then Kasumi posted a photo of our creation on Instagram, and it got over ten thousand likes. When a local socialite reached out and asked us to make the cakes for her daughter's quinceañera, it was the first time I realized that maybe my parents were wrong. Maybe I really *was* good enough.

Kasumi and I sent the Instagram link with all the comments raving about our work to our professor, and he agreed to bump our grade up to an A-minus. Emboldened by our success, we decided to tackle the unpaid labor issue. I organized the students, and Kasumi ran a social media blitz. I'm proud to say that the students at the Northeastern Culinary Institute are now paid for their internship hours, and that Kasumi and I have been inseparable ever since.

Which is why it's so unsettling that's she's looking sideways at me like she doesn't quite know who I am. "You never put up with Xavier talking to you—or *anyone*—like that before."

I shrug and focus on rolling my apron in a ball, so I don't have to meet her eyes. "I'm not really sure what I'm supposed to do."

"Well, usually you tell him off or something. But—" She

stares at the industrial-grade oven behind me, shaking her head.

"But *what*?" I'm defensive because I know she's right. It goes against every instinct I have to stay quiet about this. But every time I'm tempted to open my mouth and tell Xavier where to shove his unreasonable demands, the *Golden Girls* theme song plays in my head. I don't want to go back there. I *can't* go back there.

I wish I could confess everything to Kasumi, but I honestly don't know how. She's been my best friend for ten years—eleven, if you count the one I'm living all over again—and I can usually talk to her about everything. But this second chance year goes beyond normal best friend problems. It's literally cosmic level.

I stand there, folding and unfolding my apron, and Kasumi watches me.

"Never mind," she finally says, grabbing a tray of vegetables and moving back to her prep space on the other side of the kitchen.

I put my head down and go to the break room to change into the server's uniform. And then I hand my cakes over to Doug and make my way out to the floor, just like Xavier told me to.

I am a terrible server. I get in the way, I accidently slosh water on some guy's lap, and I mess up the point-of-sale system, forgetting to add all the expensive bottles of wine to the bill. The real servers have to keep jumping in to fix my mistakes, and I can tell they're growing increasingly frustrated with me. I don't blame them. The only person who seems to enjoy my presence in the dining room is the older man who booked the VIP table. He's quite happy to request that I reach across the table to pour more wine, and I suspect it's so he can get a look down the front of the shirt Xavier picked out for me.

Even though the servers and I are friends when I'm in the kitchen, it's obvious they resent my presence in the dining room. At one point, after the water-in-lap incident, Marianne snaps, "What the hell are you doing here, Sadie?"

I honestly don't know how to answer that.

When the dining room finally clears out, I return to the kitchen, sweaty, exhausted, and with a deep appreciation for how hard the servers work. All I want to do is go home and fall into bed, but first, I need to check out Doug's handiwork.

He's nowhere to be seen, but I find Kasumi standing in front of the pastry prep table, her features arranged in an almost cartoonlike cringe. I follow her gaze to the chocolate-covered ... something ... on the table, and I gasp.

"Yeah." Kasumi nods in agreement.

"Are those my ... ?" I can't even finish the sentence.

"I'm afraid so."

"They're—"

"Awful?" she supplies helpfully.

Awful doesn't even begin to describe what Doug did with my cakes. Instead of four perfect cylinders coated in shiny chocolate ganache with a wave of delicate candied oranges frolicking across the top and down one side in a seemingly random but completely intentional manner, Doug has made...

Well.

Doug has made four enormous poop emojis.

"Oh my God," I wail. "I'm going to be here for hours fixing these."

Kasumi shakes her head. "I think the only way to fix these is to throw them in the Hudson River."

I sigh, exhausted to my bones, and begin a slow shuffle to the supply closet. "I guess I'll have to start over. Xavier needs them by eleven a.m. tomorrow."

"Do not despair, friend. The other sous chefs and I have your back." Kasumi takes my arm and leads me over to the speed rack. She waves her hand at twelve round pans, each containing one perfect layer of chocolate orange cake. "We made them when we saw the havoc Doug was wreaking. They won't be as good as yours, but they'll be edible. All you have to do is layer and decorate them."

I throw my arms around her. "Thank you. You're the best friend ever."

"It wasn't just me. Everyone pitched in. We've got to stick together in this business." She leans back from my embrace to look me in the eyes. "Is everything okay with you, Sadie?"

"Sure." For the second time today, and about the hundredth time since January first, I'm tempted to tell her about this wild second chance I've been given. But I have a mountain of cake decorating ahead of me, so instead, I give Kasumi a shrug. "Why wouldn't everything be okay?"

"You just don't seem like yourself." She bites her lip as if she's debating whether or not she should say the next thing. "A couple of months ago, you wouldn't have let Xavier get away with parading you in front of a table of VIPs just because they wanted to look at a nice face and a perky pair of tits."

"Oh my God, Kasumi." I turn and grab a pot from the rack, banging it on the stove with extra force. "That's not what happened tonight!" Except it's exactly what happened.

My face burns with humiliation. I keep my head bent over the pot as I measure out the chocolate squares and heavy whipping cream for another batch of ganache. Kasumi is silent, watching me, and then finally, she says, "I'm sorry, Sadie. I didn't mean to make you feel used. I'm just worried about you."

"I know." I pull the cakes Kasumi and the other sous chefs made from the rack. She's a good friend, and she's only saying what I would have said to someone in my position a year or two ago. But that was before I knew what it meant to lose everything.

I'll never forget the day I had to pack up my entire apartment and ask Owen to haul it out to storage. I love that apartment, and I was so happy the day I signed the lease. So excited to decorate it with a quirky mix of affordable IKEA furniture and vintage flea-market finds. So proud to show my parents that even if I was *just a baker* without a college degree, I could make it on my own.

And I'll never forget the mortification of ending up homeless, a charity case for my little brother's best friend. The desperation of looking for a job—*any* job—and fearing I'd never find work as a pastry chef again. I've been given a once-in-a-lifetime opportunity to hold on to everything I lost in my Very Bad Year. I can do this.

Ignoring the pie weights sitting on my chest, I turn back to Kasumi. "Thank you for being such a good friend."

"Do you want me to stay and help with the cakes?"

I shake my head. "No, it's late, and you've helped so much already." I give her one more hug. "Go home and get some sleep."

At the door, Kasumi pauses. "You know I'm always here for you, right? You can always talk to me."

"Thanks," I say with a forced smile and then turn back to the ganache. There's one thing I can't talk to *anyone* about. And in this moment, it makes me feel very, very alone.

Chapter 10

Thanks to my best friend and the other sous chefs, my new cakes are done in record time. I consider taking Kasumi up on her suggestion to tie a cement block to Doug's disasters and toss them in the river, *Sopranos*-style. But I can't bring myself to waste perfectly good food. They may look like something you'd avoid stepping on in Central Park, but I baked the cakes beneath that chocolate ganache mess, and I know they'll taste delicious. I find a couple of pastry boxes and pack them up in case I see any homeless people on my walk.

I've managed to unload three cakes by the time I'm nearing Higher Grounds. I slow my steps, noticing the light spilling from the window onto the sidewalk and music drifting out when someone opens the door. I forgot that on weekends they stay open late for singer-songwriters, open mics, and poetry events. On a whim, I go inside. My stomach is still uneasy from what happened at work earlier, and I don't really want to go home to an empty apartment to think about it.

Zoe is working today, and as I approach the counter, she calls out, "Hey, it's Sadie, the Cat Lady."

I cringe a little. "Oh, uh, you can just call me Sadie if you want."

"Okay, Sadie it is." She cocks her head, looking me up and down. "How are you holding up? I know you're missing little Zoe."

Oh God. Will I ever live this down? The thing about Zoe (the human) is that I know she's not making fun of me. She hardly even knows me, but if she thinks I'm devastated over my cat, then she's going to check in with me about it.

I take in her ripped jeans and worn green hoodie thrown over her Higher Grounds T-shirt, and all of a sudden, I'm overwhelmed by missing her, and this whole place. When I worked here, I was so depressed I definitely didn't appreciate it enough. Zoe is only about ten years older than me, but she's always been kind of a mom figure for everyone who comes into the café. She allows José Luis to do his schoolwork when business is slow and never cares if someone has to leave early for a doctor's appointment or to pick up their kids. And she does a lot to support the community: giving to school fundraisers, feeding homeless people, and making a space for local artists and performers. When I worked here during my Very Bad Year, Zoe would *never* have treated someone the way Xavier treated me today.

I have the strangest urge say thank you and give her a hug. She'd probably just hug me right back, but I've already drawn enough attention to myself.

"Uh, thanks for checking," I say. "But I'm really fine about...Zoe. The cat, I mean. I've definitely...moved on."

"Good." She gives me a smile. "So, can I get anything for you?"

I order a decaf cappuccino, dropping my remaining cake box on the counter so I can dig in my purse for my wallet.

"Ohhh, what's this?" Zoe hitches her chin at the box while she steams the milk.

"I'm an assistant pastry chef at Xavier's and this was, um...I guess you could call it leftovers." I open the box to give her a peek.

She blinks at the contents. "Oh my. You know what that sort of looks like...?"

"Oh yes. I'm aware," I say with a smile. I tell her the story about Doug taking over the cake decorating—leaving out the part about why I was unavailable—and soon, she's leaning on the counter laughing.

"I made all the components, though, so even though it looks like something you'd shovel out of a horse stall, it should still taste pretty good. Here"—I push the box in her direction—"try it."

"Yeah?" Zoe asks, grabbing a plate and a knife. I cut her a piece, and she takes a bite.

This is my favorite part of being a pastry chef. The moment when one of my creations hits someone's taste buds and their eyes go wide and then close as they savor the sweet and tangy layers of flavor. "Oh my God," Zoe says, shoveling another bite into her mouth. "This is amazing."

"Thanks." I grin with pleasure. I needed a little boost of appreciation today.

Zoe hands me my cappuccino, then closes up the box and slides it in my direction.

"Oh no," I say. "Keep it."

"Really? My wife is a total chocolate addict. She's going to be so happy."

In my Very Bad Year, I made Zoe's wife about a hundred café mochas when she came into the shop, and I'm aware of her affinity for chocolate. But of course, I can't admit this. Instead, I just smile and pick up my cappuccino.

"Hey," Zoe says as I turn to go. "I know you already have a job at Xavier's...but let me know if you'd be interested in a little side gig. The place that's been supplying our pastries has seriously decreased in quality." I can't tell her I've noticed, so I simply nod. "We have a whole commercial kitchen in the back that hardly ever gets used. And after tasting that cake, I'd be cool with you using your creativity to make whatever you want for us."

The suggestion shouldn't be as much of a surprise as it is. After all, I worked at Higher Grounds for months, and I was definitely aware that the pastries were subpar. Why didn't I ever offer to come up with something better?

Probably because I quit baking entirely when Xavier fired me. And I'm embarrassed to admit this, but I wonder if maybe I thought crafting muffins for a coffee shop was a little beneath me after working in high-end restaurant kitchens for most of my career.

I like the idea of helping Zoe out, though, and of having an opportunity to try some new recipes. Still, I hesitate. There are rumors that the executive pastry chef at Xavier's might be on his way out, in which case, I want that job. Should I be committing to a side project that will take up so much of my time?

"Just think about it," Zoe says, and I agree that I will.

I'm turning to leave when out of the corner of my eye, I

spot a familiar pair of glasses and a café Americano. The wearer of the glasses looks up at me.

It's Jacob, sitting at a table in the back corner of the café, to the left of the stage where a woman with pink hair is playing a song I've never heard before. Jacob lifts a hand in greeting, and it would be rude not to at least say hello.

I make my way over, and he stands when I arrive at the table. If he were anyone else, I'd assume they were moving in to hug me, but I know that's not the case with Jacob. He must generally stand for women, sort of as if we're in a Victorian-era period drama. I find myself charmed by the politeness of it all, and I wish I'd ordered a pot of Earl Grey instead of this cappuccino.

After we say hello, a beat passes, and he shifts his weight from one foot to the other. Is he going to ask me to sit? Does he not want me to sit? Are we going to stand here the whole time?

Finally, he seems to register the awkwardness, and he waves at the chair opposite of him. "Sorry, I didn't know if you wanted to stay, or—" He blows out a heavy breath. "Would you like to sit with me?"

I totally cannot read what he wants me to do here, but since I don't really feel like going home, I pull out a chair and drop into it.

"You're out late," I remark.

"Yeah, another deadline, so...caffeine." He lifts his coffee like he's toasting.

"The Joshua James film?"

"No, I finished that. This one is a little less glamorous. It's the soundtrack for a video game."

I nod. "It must be wild to hear your music all over the place. Just drifting in at the movies, or when Owen's playing a video game, or when you step on an elevator..."

"Oh no. Hold on right there." He lifts a hand to stop me. "I do *not* compose elevator music."

"You don't? But I thought sometimes you wrote that sort of slow, electronic stuff. Like what they play on elevators."

I've pained him here. I can tell by the way he looks at me as if half of him wants to laugh and the other half wants to cry. "Elevator music is bland instrumental arrangements of popular music meant to be listened to passively while you're shopping for paper towels."

I consider the music piped in at the grocery store. I've never really paid attention to it before, but now I kind of see what he means. "You mean, like, an electronic piano rendition of 'Gangsta's Paradise'?"

He's definitely trying not to laugh now. "Just like that, yes."

"And that's not what you do."

"No."

He's an artist, and I realize too late that I've probably insulted him. I might feel insulted in a similar situation. "Is this conversation sort of the equivalent of someone asking a pastry chef how she feels about Hostess cupcakes?"

"It is one hundred percent like that. Yes." He's smiling, so I know I haven't really offended him.

Still, I genuinely want to understand. "So, you compose your own original music. But you just do it with a computer program instead of with a piano."

"I compose with both. I do a lot of mixing and use

software for effects, but I also play a bunch of different instruments."

Onstage, the pink-haired singer starts playing an acoustic version of "Free Fallin'" and a young, bearded guy joins her on piano.

"Do you ever think about getting up there?" I ask.

"Uhhh..." He fiddles with the spoon on the saucer next to his cup. "The singer-songwriter thing really isn't my vibe."

"But *could* you do that if you wanted to?" I can't listen to a piano without thinking of the gorgeous song he played in his apartment. I'd love to hear it again, but technically, I'm not supposed to know it exists. With this time loop I'm in, maybe he hasn't even written it yet. Maybe it *doesn't* exist.

Jacob gazes at the singer. "Are you asking if I could get onstage, play the piano, and sing a Tom Petty song?" He nods. "Yes." Then, after a pause, "Are you asking if it's ever going to happen?" He looks down at his hands and shakes his head. "Not a chance."

And suddenly, it hits me. Jacob is *shy*. He's not uptight and judgmental like I've been assuming about him in my head for so long. He's just...painfully shy. Something about that realization has my heart doing all kinds of little flips in my chest.

"Jacob Gray," I tease. "Are you telling me that after all these years of playing music, you have stage fright?"

Two pink spots appear on his cheeks. "Let's just say I'm more of a composer than a performer."

I tend to be a talker, and it's in my nature to start firing questions at him. But something tells me that with Jacob, you've got to keep quiet and let him take his time if you want to get to the real heart of things. Silence stretches across the table while he traces the wood grain with a finger. Finally, he looks up at me. "Even though I know thousands of people watch the films or play video games with my music in it, at that point it's just a piece of someone else's project. But when I'm composing and playing it, it's *mine*, it's personal. I can't imagine getting up there with just an instrument, and being that..."

"Vulnerable?"

He looks up, right into my eyes. "Yeah. I guess... vulnerable."

"So, you never play for anyone? Ever?" I have a huskiness in my voice that wasn't there before.

"Well, my family. And obviously Owen, but he's basically family."

I don't know what I'm asking, exactly. Am I waiting to hear that I'm the only woman who's ever heard him play a sad, melancholy song on the piano? It's completely irrational that I'd want that. But the more I spend time talking with Jacob like this, the more bizarre it becomes that we've had such an intimate moment, and he's completely unaware. I know the weight of his body, the sound of that little satisfied growl in the back of his throat, the taste of his mouth pressed against mine. But none of it happened in his world. For twenty-something years, we were just acquaintances who never had much to say to each other. All of that changed for me, but in his mind, that's all we are.

The last chord of the pink-haired girl's song reverberates across the stage and out into the audience. When she puts down her guitar for a break, I push my chair back. "Well, I should go."

Jacob channels Mr. Darcy and politely stands up when I do. "Thanks for hanging out." He does that awkward shuffle again, a movement sort of like when you're about to hug someone before they leave. Without thinking, I reach out my arm to wrap it around his neck. His eyes go wide, and his back stiffens. Oh God, this is so awkward. He didn't mean to end this conversation in a hug, did he?

But then his hand slides around me, settling on the small of my back, and the other arm pulls me even closer. I feel his razor stubble scrape my cheek and hear his sharp intake of breath as he presses me against the hard muscles of his chest. I stay like that for a beat, and then one more, and he doesn't seem to be in a hurry to let me go, either.

Finally, we both pull away, and I peek up at him. His cheeks are flushed and eyes bright behind his glasses.

"It was nice to see you, Jacob." I can hear my voice shake at the end.

"You, too, Sadie." He gives me a crooked smile and looks away.

"Well, I should go." I repeat, slowly taking another step back. As I turn and head back across the café toward the door, I can still smell his cinnamony Jacob-scent, so familiar to me now. And just like that piano song he played on New Year's Eve, it lingers around me long after I've left.

Chapter 11

"What do you think—Thai or Indian?" Alex slides open a kitchen drawer and grabs a stack of take-out menus. With just the slightest push of his hand, the drawer slides back silently on its track, catching at the end so it doesn't slam into the frame like the ones in my apartment do. He holds out the crumpled, oil-stained papers, and I'm surprised he allowed them into this pristine space.

Unlike my place with its mismatched furniture, cluttered array of abandoned earrings and Post-it note grocery lists on the coffee table, and shoes spilling from the closet, Alex's brand-new downtown apartment is sleek and minimalist. Until last summer, he lived in student housing at Columbia with two other guys from his program, so this place is quite an upgrade, one he could afford thanks to his investment banker salary. It's a couple of blocks away from his Wall Street office building and around the corner from the high-end bars where they all like to hang out after work.

Alex hired his boss's decorator to furnish the place in dark leather, chrome, and mahogany, and when I brought in a bright orange throw pillow to add a pop of color to the couch, it mysteriously disappeared a couple of weeks later. Alex never seemed like the kind of guy to hang a blank canvas smeared with gray paint on his wall, let alone to call it art. But now that I've been to Zach's place for that New Year's party, it all makes a little more sense. If you switched around the floor plan and exchanged the dark gray canvas for a light gray one, this apartment could belong to any number of Alex's investment banker friends. They even share the same cleaning woman who makes the rounds once a week to keep their apartments looking as austere as the MoMA.

I choose Thai food, and Alex places our order, then hands me a glass of my favorite sauvignon blanc. He always keeps a couple of bottles in the wine fridge for me, even though he doesn't drink it, and he bought a set of stemless glasses when he noticed I prefer them. Aside from the orange pillow incident, Alex has always gone out of his way to make sure I'm comfortable here. I was charmed the first time I found my favorite shampoo and body wash in his shower, and he keeps the pantry stocked with flour and icing sugar even though it drives him crazy to watch me sprinkle it across his dark marble countertops like a snowstorm blowing across Mount Everest.

To be honest, I'm probably the reason he hired the cleaning woman.

Alex neatly stacks the menus back in the drawer and we settle on the couch with our drinks.

"Bake anything good this week?" Alex asks, taking a sip of the whiskey in his glass.

I tell him about my newest creation: mini saffron Bundt cakes covered in a rich chocolate coconut ganache and decorated with candied grapefruit peel. "I may just have one in my bag for you," I say. "For after dinner, of course."

Alex grins and runs his palm up my thigh. "I was thinking of a different kind of dessert."

I lean over to give him a quick kiss, but before he can tug me closer, I slip off the couch and grab my bag from the chair across the room. "I'll put this on the counter for you." I hold up the cake box.

His brow furrows, and I know he's probably wondering what's going on with me. Before my Very Bad Year ruined everything, our sex life was pretty great. In his version of reality, nothing should have changed. But ever since I woke up to find myself in this wild time loop, I've been hesitant when it comes to intimacy, and I can't quite explain why.

Maybe it's because I'm still getting used to having him around after all those months apart. Or maybe it's because I remember how much it hurt when he walked away.

Luckily, we've both been busy at work, and our schedules haven't matched up very well, so it hasn't been an issue yet. But I need to get past this before it becomes one. I cross the room back to Alex, reminding myself that this is my second chance year, and Alex won't be walking away again. I plan to do everything right this time around.

Just as I sit down and reach for Alex's hand, my phone rings, and the word *Home* pops up on the screen. I sigh, realizing my mistake. I'd mentioned to my mom that I'd be at Alex's tonight, and the surefire way to get my parents' attention is to mention Alex. I bet they've been waiting by the phone for the right time to call all evening.

"Hi, Sadie," my mom says after I've answered the phone. The volume of her voice rises and falls, probably because she has the phone set to speaker so my dad can participate. "Is Alex there?"

At least she gets straight to the point. *Where's Alex? How's Alex's high-powered job?* No sense in pretending they're interested in what's going on in my life. How much is there to say about brownies and cupcakes, anyway?

My mom is the dean of the literature department at Rutgers University and a renowned expert in nineteenth-century women's literature, and my dad literally wrote the textbook on ancient Greek translation. In my childhood, it was normal for me to come home from soccer practice to find my parents and their professor friends drinking red wine in the living room and discussing George Eliot's influence on modern feminism or the symbolism in Homer's *The Odyssey*.

With a whole alphabet of letters after their names, it was only natural my parents expected Owen and me to go to college and then graduate school. And in my brother, they got everything they ever wished for. He tested into the school's gifted program when he was in first grade, earned straight As all through middle and high school, and had his pick of Ivy League universities after graduation.

And then there was me.

Let's just say I was well into high school before I realized *The Odyssey* isn't part of the *Star Wars* trilogy. School just wasn't my thing, and I couldn't pretend it was.

I landed a job working the cash register at a bakery when I was fifteen, and that's where I found my passion. Bread, cookies, cakes, tarts, I loved them all equally. And when the head chef broke her femur in a fly-fishing accident and was laid up for a month, I got my big break in the kitchen. My parents indulged me for a while—after all, who doesn't love a three-tiered banana cake with hazelnut and chocolate frosting? But when I stopped thinking of baking as a hobby and started to believe it could be my career, they were devastated. You'd think I'd gone into the adult entertainment industry the way they still can't really talk about it. I'm pretty sure their favorite thing about me is my boyfriend.

"Alex is right here, Mom." I switch my phone to speaker and hand it to Alex, mouthing, "I'm sorry."

He grins and shakes his head like it's no big deal. I'm reminded of how lucky I am to have him back in my life.

"Alex, how are you, son?" my dad's voice cuts into my thoughts.

Alex leans over the phone. "I'm good, Jim. How are you?"

"Fine, fine." My dad clears his throat. "Listen, I was reading the *Wall Street Journal* this morning and stumbled upon a really interesting article—"

I snort and try to disguise it as a cough. My dad never had one bit of interest in the *Wall Street Journal* until I started dating Alex. Now he has a subscription and reads it over coffee every morning. Apparently, he was pleasantly surprised to discover the paper covers tech news as well as finance, so it's given him a lot to talk about with Owen as well as Alex.

But just try to get him to watch an episode of *Cupcake Wars*. Just try.

My dad doesn't seem to notice me snuffling on the other end of the phone, which is typical. "—and I wanted to ask you your thoughts on mortgage-backed securities..." He proceeds to launch into a description of an article that makes absolutely no sense to me, and probably doesn't make sense to him, either.

It shouldn't bother me that my dad is manufacturing reasons to bond with my boyfriend, but I can't help it. When Alex and I broke up during my Very Bad Year, my parents were absolutely devastated...Not because their daughter was heartbroken, but because she'd blown their shot at a son-in-law with an MBA who they could be proud of.

While Alex is patiently talking my dad through something or other—don't ask me what, I have no idea—I answer the door for our food delivery and dig through Alex's carefully ordered cabinets to set the dining table. Then I slosh more wine in my glass and top off Alex's whiskey. He's going to need it if this conversation goes on much longer. Finally, Alex manages to escape my dad's grip, and he slides into the chair across from me.

"Thanks for your patience with my parents." I flash a crooked smile and pass him a cardboard food container.

"It's fine." He shrugs and scoops rice onto his plate. "I enjoy discussing finance with your dad."

I'm pretty sure he's lying because only someone who enjoys suffering would enjoy discussing finance with my dad. But it means a lot that he'd make the effort. As I gaze across the table at my boyfriend's handsome face, I'm reminded again of how lucky I am to have this chance to hold our relationship together.

Alex recently took me to another event with his work friends, and for the most part, it went fine. Last time around, I remember that same dinner was awkward and tense, probably because everyone at the table had seen me blow up at Zach a few weeks earlier. But this time, I'd never blown up at Zach, and nobody had any idea that I'd wanted to. So, I spent most of the evening getting to know the other girlfriends and avoiding the side of the room where a couple of the most obnoxious guys had staked their claim. I talked to one woman about her career as a data analyst and another about being a nurse practitioner. Everyone was super interested to hear about my job as a pastry chef and what it's like to work for a guy they've seen as a guest judge on *Top Chef*. As we said our goodbyes, I realized I'd actually had fun. And then on the cab ride home, Alex gave me a long kiss and told me how happy he was that I came.

He definitely didn't say *that* the last time around.

So, I need to let go of the idea that this relationship is going to suddenly dissolve like cotton candy in a rainstorm. I'd overreacted during my Very Bad Year, and now I've learned how to handle things better. Which reminds me—

"Hey," I say to Alex. "I meant to ask you if you hired that woman for the financial consultant position. The really qualified one we talked about?"

"Uh, yeah." Alex spoons green curry onto his plate. "I believe her paperwork is still making its way through HR."

"Really?" I grin at him across the table. "You hired her?" *See?* This is the perfect example of how well my second chance year is going. I didn't *need* to blow up at Zach. All along, I should have calmly talked to Alex. "When does she start?"

"A couple of weeks, maybe." He looks up at the ceiling, trying to remember. "I'll have to check with Zach." His gaze slides to me. "How are things at your job?"

I chat for a bit, telling him about the new recipes I've been developing, and then I trail off, remembering all the other stuff.

"What is it?" he prompts, after a moment of silence.

"Well...something a little weird happened."

"Yeah?" He reaches across the table and takes my hand. "Tell me."

I don't know why I haven't told him about the party of VIPs and the guy who looked down my shirt yet. I guess I didn't want to admit how they treated me. It's humiliating, so I've been avoiding thinking about it at all. "I've never worked as a server, I had less than no clue what I was doing. So, it's not like I was adding any real value other than..." *Being a nice face and a perky pair of tits.* I cringe. "You know. Being a woman they could look at."

Alex narrows his eyes. "Did any of them touch you?"

"No...But I could *feel* their gazes. Especially the older guy, the high roller ordering all the expensive bottles."

"I'm sorry that happened to you." Alex sets his fork on his napkin. "It sounds like you were uncomfortable."

"Yes. *So* uncomfortable. But—" That powerless feeling rolls over me again. *This* is why I've avoided thinking about that night. "It's not even about that smarmy old guy, really. I may never even see him again. The part that really bothers me is that Xavier threw me to the wolves." And if he did it once, he could do it again.

Alex's face softens. "Come on. Come here." He takes my hand and tugs me over to the couch. When we're settled in the cushions, he turns to look at me. "I imagine patrons at high-end restaurants have a lot of unreasonable demands."

"Sure. Like gluten-free vegan cheesecake. Not..." I wave my hand across my chest. "You know."

"Is there any chance Xavier didn't know those clients would make you feel that way?" Alex cocks his head. "Maybe he needed more help in the dining room and thought you'd do a good job?"

I think back to my conversation with Xavier that night. Xavier didn't want Doug to work the front of the house, but is that because Doug is even less experienced at serving than I am? Or because men are never told to look pretty and *smile*? "I don't know."

"Did you talk to him about it?"

"Well...no." I can't imagine having a conversation about this with Xavier. Not in any version of reality.

"Maybe it wasn't about throwing you to the wolves." Alex holds out his hand, palm up. "Maybe it's about giving you more responsibility, more face time with clients. It could be a step toward that executive pastry chef position."

"Maybe?" I'm so used to thinking the worst about Xavier that I'd just assumed he sent me out to the dining room to amuse the creepy old guy. But I want to believe what Alex is saying. Maybe Xavier was testing whether I'm up for the promotion, and he had no idea that the old guy would act inappropriately. Maybe I'm jumping to conclusions instead of thinking things through. Just like I always do.

But the whole point of this second chance year is to change that. Look at how well it worked out for me when I talked to Alex instead of confronting Zach. So, maybe I should apply that same principle to Xavier. Maybe I shouldn't always be so quick to blow up as soon as something offends me.

Alex cups my cheek with his palm. "You deserve that job."

"Thanks. I *do* deserve that job." And for the first time, I'm buoyed by the hope I might actually get it.

"So." His lips curve into a crooked smile. "This seems like a good time to give you a present."

I gaze across the cushions, eyes wide. "What's the occasion?" It's not my birthday until June.

"Do I need an occasion?" He stands up. "Wait here. I also have something important to ask you." And then Alex gives me a wink and disappears into his bedroom.

For a fleeting moment, my imagination goes wild. Is it possible Alex is about to *propose*? I rub my sweaty hands on my jeans. A proposal definitely didn't happen last time around. It's been three years, and we've had a few "someday" conversations, but nothing more specific than that. If you'd told me when I was on Jacob's couch with Blanche, Sophia, Dorothy, and Rose that someday, I'd be sitting in Alex's apartment on the brink of a proposal, I would have felt like I'd won a James Beard Award and the title of Star Baker all rolled into one.

But now, well…I'm excited. But it's more of a muted excitement. A winning-the-pie-baking-contest-at-the-county-fair kind of excitement. It's not that I don't want Alex to propose. But I'm still adjusting to the whole second chance year thing.

Maybe I need a little break from excitement.

Alex returns from the bedroom, not with the little blue box I've been imagining, but with a bunch of shopping bags. Relief fills me like crème pâtissière fills an éclair. But I don't have time to analyze my reaction because he's setting the bags on the table in front of me. "I hope you don't mind, but I snooped in your closet last time I was over to see what sizes to buy."

My gaze skims over the labels. *Dolce & Gabbana. Chanel. Prada.*

My mouth drops open. "What *is* all this?" Peeking inside a Dolce & Gabbana bag, I find a neatly folded garment made of silk and lace. My first thought is *lingerie*, but reaching in, I pull out a classic little black dress with a lace appliqué around the neckline. It's gorgeous, and from the way the fabric slides against my skin, obviously incredibly expensive.

Alex hands me another bag, and inside, I find a pair of black Louboutin pumps with the signature red soles. "These are…amazing." I meet his eyes, searching for an explanation. "And, I mean, I do love shoes. But Alex—you know I'm a chef. I'm not sure I'll have a lot of occasions to wear something like this."

"Of course I know you're a chef," he says with a smile and an amused roll of his eyes. "And I know you'd never buy anything like this for yourself. But there will be a lot more events for my job in the coming months. And wives"—he clears his throat—"and girlfriends are often invited along. I wanted you to have some special things to wear."

My gaze sweeps across the shopping bags full of clothes, shoes, and I'm pretty sure I see the straps of a handbag or two peeking out. And realization dawns. Alex may not be planning to ask me to marry him today, but he's clearly setting things in motion, starting with these clothes befitting a Wall Street wife. I know I should be ecstatic that we're moving in this direction, but all this high-end fashion probably costs as much as I make in three months at the restaurant. And I'm not sure any of it really suits me.

It's a bit overwhelming.

You wanted to be with Alex, a little voice reminds me, one that sounds an awful lot like an old lady fortune teller. *This is what it means to be with Alex.* And I know it's true.

So, I *ooh* and *ahh*, and smile, and I press my hand to my heart as I sift through the contents of the shopping bags. And by the time Alex hands me the last box holding a simple platinum necklace with a solitaire diamond pendant, I've gotten into the spirit of things. Because, my God, this stuff really *is* beautiful, and Alex can't stop grinning at me.

I stand and wrap my arms around him. "Thank you."

"I'm really happy that you're making an effort with my colleagues, Sadie."

"Dinner the other day was fun. I really liked everyone." Okay, that may be an exaggeration. I will never, ever like Zach, but I also don't need to make a big thing of it.

"I'm so glad," Alex says, tightening his arms around me.

"Because that's related to what I wanted to ask you. Dave mentioned he and his wife would like to get to know my girlfriend, and I was wondering if it would be okay for me to schedule a dinner."

His shoulders tense and eyebrows knit together, and I realize how much this means to him. The designer clothes and bags and shoes aren't just about impressing some Wall Street colleagues. They're about impressing Dave, who filled a hole in his life when his dad died. And then it dawns on me that the job, the apartment, his relationship with Dave, they're a new start for Alex after the bottom fell out of his world.

It's not that different from my own second chance year if you really think about it.

"I'd love to meet Dave and his wife."

And with that, I shove the last of my worries aside. My career is on track and there's a chance I could land that executive pastry chef position. I'm still living in my apartment, and I can afford to pay the rent. And as the cherry, whipped cream, and sprinkles on top, I have a great guy who wants me to be a part of his exciting new life.

It's all coming together just like I wanted it to.

Chapter 12

April

I'm testing a new recipe for brioche doughnuts with coffee cream when Xavier bursts into the kitchen. "Sadie," he says. "I need you to help out in the dining room again. Rob Thurmond is bringing in some VIPs again tonight, and he specifically requested you."

At this point, I've worked out that Rob is the creepy older guy who looked down my shirt a couple of weeks ago. Apparently, I made an impression. I sort of wish it had been a water-spilled-in-his-lap kind of impression. Maybe I can ask to be on hot coffee duty today.

I take off my apron, remembering the promotion. I'm doing this for the promotion. At least I finished making the pink lemonade angel food cakes earlier today. All Doug has to do is plate the slices and drizzle strawberry chardonnay sauce on top. Surely he can manage that. "Okay, I'll need another server's shirt."

Xavier blinks, and I wonder if he's surprised I'd go along so willingly. Unbelievably, he gives me a pat on the shoulder. And then, even stranger, he actually says the words *thank you*. Right to my face.

"Um. You're welcome."

He turns to leave, but at the last second, spins back around. "I received a lot of compliments on the white peach and basil hand pies last night, and I know that was your concept."

Truly shocked now, I can only nod.

"I'm sure you heard rumors that there may be some staffing changes later this year. I've got my eye on you for any openings." With that, he marches out of the kitchen, snapping at a server who had the nerve to get in his way.

I stare after him as the door separating the kitchen from the dining room swings shut. Did he just imply that I'm up for the executive pastry chef position? I feel a smile pulling at my lips as I look around to see if anyone else can confirm what he said. Kasumi stands at the far end of the kitchen by the industrial-sized sink. The wide-eyed expression on her face mirrors the surprise I'm feeling. But instead of returning my grin, she gives a tiny, incredulous shake of her head and turns around to rinse the cutting board she's holding.

I change in the break room, and head out into the dining area. Everything goes smoothly for most of the evening. While my presence is not actually helpful to the other servers, at least I manage to steer clear of being a liability. I stick to pouring coffee and water and avoid anything where taking orders or entering them into the computer is involved. I'm clearing dessert plates, hoping that maybe I managed to make it through the night without any disasters, when something brushes the back of my leg. It must be the angle

I'm leaning over the table to reach for a stray dessert fork. Maybe I've bumped the arm of someone's chair. But then whatever is touching my leg starts to slide from my upper thigh to my ass. I look down, and my eyes lock on the florid face of Rob Thurmond. He grins up at me.

I jerk back, away from the hand and its creepy owner, and the stack of plates I'm holding teeters, topples, and hits the floor with the unmistakable crash of china on slate tile.

"Oh, for God's sake. It's Sadie again," Marianne mutters to the other servers.

My cheeks flush so hot, I know they must be as red as the strawberry chardonnay sauce that's now smeared across the floor. I turn and flee the dining room, leaving the pile of broken plates for the servers to clean up. I know they'll be even more annoyed with me than they already are. But I don't care. I dart into the break room, yanking off my server's shirt and pulling on the sweatshirt I'd worn on my walk to the restaurant earlier. I'm grateful it's oversized, and long enough to skim my thighs.

I know Rob is the one who should feel ashamed, and that I ought to march into Xavier's office and tell him exactly what happened. But somehow, I'm the one who's red-faced and burning with humiliation, and I know I'll never say a word. I stuff the server's shirt into the garbage can, going over and over the events in my head. Did Rob think I was flirting when he told that dumb joke and I forced a smile? Maybe I leaned too close when I was pouring his water? One of my buttons came undone halfway through the night. Why didn't I check them before I went out there?

I'm angry that these thoughts even cross my mind because I know they're not rational. If Kasumi was the one who had her ass grabbed, I'd tell her that none of it was her fault. But I can't seem to give myself the same grace.

I just want to get out of here.

Thankfully, everyone seems too distracted by my mess in the dining room to notice me darting across the kitchen. I'm halfway to the door when I pass by my prep table and spot the doughnuts I'd been working on earlier. Someone packed them up neatly in a box. On a whim, I grab it and head out the door.

Outside on Bedford Avenue, the evening air cools my flushed skin, and by the time I've walked a half dozen blocks to Higher Grounds, I feel slightly less heated. Zoe has the café open late tonight, and the warm glow in the window beckons me.

Along with Zoe, José Luis is on duty tonight. Since business is slow, he sits in his usual spot behind the counter with a sketchbook propped on his leg.

"Hey, Sadie." Zoe gives me a grin as I walk in. "Good to see you."

I plunk the pastry box on the counter. "These are for you."

She raises her eyebrows and flips open the lid. "Ooooh." Out of the box, she pulls a tender brioche doughnut stuffed with the lightest, fluffiest coffee cream you could imagine. "This looks amazing."

José Luis hops off his stool to peer over her shoulder. "Yum."

Even Mrs. Kaminski seems to be slightly impressed. I put a napkin in front of her and place a doughnut on top.

"For me?" She blinks at the doughnut, and in the next second, she's devouring it. Powdered sugar drops on her navy cardigan.

"I'll do it," I tell Zoe. "If you want me to bake for you, I can come in twice a week. I'll stock the freezer with pastries—croissants, muffins, scones. All you'll have to do is pull them out and bake them. And then I'll make a couple of new desserts each week—cakes and tarts, things that are a bit more labor intensive that you'll want to serve fresh."

"You're hired," Mrs. Kaminski mutters with coffee cream on her chin.

"What she said," Zoe says with a laugh. "If you agree to what we can pay, of course."

I nod. Whatever Zoe can pay me is going straight into my Someday Bakery fund. If I could eventually work for myself, I wouldn't have to put up with anyone else's bullshit. Or roving hands.

"Welcome to the team." Zoe holds out her hand to shake on it, and her smile is infectious. "When can you start?"

Mrs. Kaminski climbs off her chair, brushing crumbs from her palms. "Sadie the Cat Lady," she says, pointing to me. "Wait here." Then she turns her shaking, mottled finger to José Luis. "You, young man. Come with me."

José Luis looks to Zoe for guidance, but she just shrugs. "You heard the woman."

He rounds the counter and follows Mrs. Kaminski as

she slowly shuffles to the front door, leaning heavily on her cane. Once they've disappeared outside, I turn to Zoe.

"Where do you think they're going?"

"No idea. That woman is eccentric."

I hang out at the counter, chatting with Zoe about baking supplies and the bulk cost of flour. A couple of minutes later, a cool breeze blows into the café as the door swings open. Mrs. Kaminski lumbers back in with José Luis balancing a cardboard box in his hands. The box appears to be moving, and I swear I hear something thumping around in there.

Once Mrs. Kaminski is safely inside, José Luis closes the door and sets the box on a table. "I'm not sure what's going on here," he confides, backing away. The box is definitely moving. And thumping. And then it lets out a high-pitched yowl.

"*What* is in that box?" Zoe demands, approaching it slowly. At that moment, a tiny, furry little black arm pops out the top of the box where the two flaps are folded together. Zoe lets out a startled shriek and jumps backward.

"Oh, stop being so dramatic." Mrs. Kaminski rolls her eyes. "It's a cat. For Sadie the Cat Lady."

"It's a *what*? For *who*?" I ask, eyes wide.

"It's a cat. I found it in the alley." She pokes at the box with her cane. "They won't let me keep a cat in my building, so I brought it for you."

I stand there, dumbfounded. "I can't take home a..." My voice trails off, because of course I can take home a cat. I told Zoe that my cat died and implied I was devastated. What would it look like if I refused this one?

But...I can't *actually* have a cat. Can I? I shake my head. I have enough trouble taking care of myself. How am I going to take responsibility for another creature?

The box rustles again, and through the flaps in the lid, a little black head pops out. The cat looks around and then lets out a tiny, plaintive *meow*.

"Oh my God, that thing is so freaking cute." José Luis presses his palms to his cheeks. "I'm *dying*."

I have to admit the cat really is freaking cute. *But I cannot take it home.* I seize on the opportunity José Luis presented. "It seems like José Luis has really fallen in love. Maybe he should take the little guy."

"Oh, I can't have a pet." He shakes his head sadly. "I live in campus housing. A girl down the hall won a fish at Coney Island, and she got in major trouble when the RA found out. I can't imagine what they'd do if I got caught harboring an illegal mammal."

The cat meows again, José Luis coos, and even Zoe gives a little "awwwww." She turns to me. "You really can't take him?"

Mrs. Kaminski huffs, looking extremely put out. "I thought you were a cat lady," she accuses.

"I am! I mean, I love cats. Love them! But..." *But what?* How am I going to get out of this? I wring my hands. "But...I gave away all my cat supplies when little, uh, Zoe passed. It was too painful to keep them around. So."

Mrs. Kaminski thumps her cane on the floor. We all jump, including the cat. "Young man." She waves a finger at José Luis. "Carry this cat home for Sadie." The finger swings to me. "You stop at the twenty-four-hour grocery for supplies on your way. They'll have enough to tide you over until you can get to a pet store tomorrow."

I look to Zoe, hoping maybe she'll take my side. But she just shrugs. "Do you mind helping Sadie, José Luis?"

"Of course not."

And just like that, I'm a brand-new cat mom.

José Luis deposits me, my cat supplies, and the cardboard box containing my new furry friend in the center of my studio apartment. "Text some photos, okay?" He scribbles his number on a Post-it on my desk, and then he's gone.

I set up the litter box behind the toilet in the bathroom and then pour some dry cat food in a bowl. "Here, kitty." I put the bowl down next to the box and flip open the lid. The cat's head pops up, its little nose working to sniff out the food. In the next moment, it hops out of the box, scurries to the bowl, and basically inhales the food. About two seconds later, the food is gone, and the cat turns to me and meows. Demanding more, I suppose. I measure out another scoop and add a bowl of water next to it. Then I settle into the couch to watch, and this time, the cat eats at a slightly more reasonable pace. I feel bad for the little thing. It must have been starving. When the second bowl of food is gone, the cat licks its paw and then immediately turns its gaze on me.

"Hi," I say. "How are you? What's your name?" Not surprisingly, the cat doesn't answer, but it does succeed in making me wonder if I've actually managed to turn into a cat lady.

The cat licks its paw again, and then walks in my direction. In one swift move, it jumps up on the couch, climbs onto me, and settles, Sphinx-like, on my chest. A moment later, the purr turns on. I look down into its little face. "You *are* pretty freaking cute, you know?" I hold my hand out, and it rubs its soft cheek against my fingers, purring louder.

In that moment, my shoulders finally release the tension they've been holding all night, and my back sinks into the couch cushions. I close my eyes, feeling the vibration in my chest. And, for the first time since Rob Thurmond put his hand on me, I feel like maybe I'm going to be okay.

Chapter 13

May

When I open my apartment door, the last person I expect to see standing there is Jacob.

Oh," I say, startled. "Hi."

"Hey." He clears his throat. "Owen invited me for brunch. I hope that's okay."

My hand unconsciously flies to my hair, which, of course, I didn't wash today. I silently curse my brother. *Thanks for the warning, Owen.* We have a standing monthly brunch date, and it would have been nice if he'd told me he'd invited a friend. But I can't really be mad. Jacob has been tagging along for our entire lives, and Owen would never in a million years consider that I'd want advance notice. If my brother suspected that I'd go out of my way to look nice for Jacob, he'd probably think I'd been huffing nitrous oxide from the whipped cream canister.

"Yeah, of course. He's not here yet." I swing the door wider. "Do you want to come in?"

Jacob eases past me into the apartment. I turn around, and my spacious studio seems rather cramped with this tall, broad-shouldered man taking up the center of the room.

My jacket is over by the window, and there's no way to grab it without brushing past him. I try, though, and he steps aside, but in the wrong direction, so I crash right into him.

"Sorry," he mutters, taking a step backward.

"Um, I just need my..." I point to the hook on the wall, and he grabs my jacket. Except he's not just handing it to me, he's holding it open to help me put it on. I'm charmed by this gesture, except it means I need to walk over to where he's standing. It seems safer over here.

Jacob takes a seat on the couch while I turn around to tidy up my apartment and discreetly check that I didn't leave any underwear on the floor. As I smooth the duvet and fluff the pillows on the bed, I'm hyperaware of his every move, and it leaves me flustered. For most of my life, I just kind of looked past Jacob without really seeing him. But now I can't seem to stop noticing all the little details of him. The scar on his chin from when Owen crashed into him on a bike in sixth grade. How he ducks his head at first, and then raises his gaze to meet mine. The way his fingers are always tapping out a melody on his leg as if they can't stop. Does he know he does that?

I'm saved from examining the warmth spreading over me by my brother's arrival. He flops down on the couch next to Jacob at the same moment my new cat crawls out from under the bed and yells at them.

"Hey, when did you get a cat?" Owen asks.

"A couple of weeks ago."

Jacob puts his fist down for him to sniff, and the cat pounces on Jacob's fingers. Jacob smiles and playfully uses his hand to wrestle with the little guy. My cat rolls around on the floor in raptures, then gets up and runs across the room. He pivots, darting back to pounce on Jacob's shoelace. Jacob lifts his foot so the cat can swat at the dangling string. "What's his name?"

Despite the fact that I'm deeply devoted to him, I don't have a name for my furry friend yet. "I don't know."

Owen squints at me. "You haven't named him yet?"

I drop my hands to my hips. "It's a lot of responsibility, Owen. I've been waiting for the perfect name to come along. Something that really captures his personality."

"Giocoso," Jacob murmurs, wrestling with the cat again.

"What?"

Jacob looks up. "His personality. Giocoso. It's a term in music that means 'playful' or 'joyful.'"

I look back and forth between Jacob and the cat. "That's perfect. I love it. I'll call him Giocoso, and he can be Gio for short." True to his new name, Giocoso races back and forth across the room and then pounces on the shoelace again. I glance down at the couch to find Jacob looking at me with sort of a half smile on his face.

"Where did you get him?" Owen asks. We never had pets as kids. Our parents didn't want the mess or responsibility of caring for creatures besides me and Owen.

"It's kind of a long story. There's a café where I've been doing some baking. An old lady there gave him to me."

Jacob looks up. "Mrs. Kaminski?"

"Yeah, how did you know?"

"She calls you Sadie the Cat Lady."

I guess Jacob *did* notice Mrs. Kaminski muttering at me that one day. "Yeah, that's uh . . . a long story, too."

Owen looks back and forth between me and Jacob. "Who is this Mrs. Kaminski? And how do you two know her?" I realize this must come as a bit of a surprise to my brother, who has no idea that Jacob and I have even had a conversation when he wasn't around, other than a bit of small talk at my parents' house at Thanksgiving.

Jacob ignores Owen's question, sitting up straight in his seat. "Wait, *you're* the new baker at Higher Grounds? Their scones are amazing now."

I smile shyly. "Thank you."

Owen shakes his head. "So, you're baking at some café now? What happened to Xavier's?"

"I'm still working at Xavier's." I turn around to look for my purse. "This is just a side gig." I returned to Xavier's for my shift the day after the Rob incident, and nobody seemed to have noticed that I'd taken off early the night before. Xavier hasn't asked me to help out as a server again, and if he does, I'll have to fake an illness and go home. Actually, I won't have to fake it. I will actually be ill.

"Why are you doing this?" Owen asks. "For your Some-day Bakery fund?"

"Every bit helps."

"Well, if you'd let me invest a little, it would help a whole lot faster. And you wouldn't have to work two jobs."

I sigh because I am both moved and exasperated by this offer. In the tech world, a guy with Owen's skills is in high demand, and with all his bonuses and promotions, he's recently found himself with more money than he knows what to do with. Other than his expensive hoodie habit and penchant for pretentious cocktails, he's not really a spender. It's not the first time he's offered to help me out, but I'd rather bake Twinkies for the rest of my life than take money from Owen. "Thanks, buddy, but I can't."

It's his turn to sigh in exasperation. "Why not?"

"Well, first of all, what would Mom and Dad think if I took my little brother's savings to fund my cupcake hobby?"

"Who cares what they think?"

I roll my eyes. "Easy for you to say, Golden Boy."

"Whatever. Work your two jobs, then. Where is this Higher Ground place, anyway?"

"Bedford Avenue," Jacob says. "Past that liquor store you like."

"So…" Owen points at Jacob. "You're hanging out at the café where Sadie is working?"

Jacob shrugs. "They have good coffee."

I'm not sure what the look Owen gives Jacob is about. It's sort of an eyeroll and headshake all packed into one. Jacob just shrugs again.

We head out for breakfast at the Buttered Biscuit, Owen's and my favorite diner. It's such a dive that even the Brooklyn hipsters don't ironically hang out there, but the pancakes are thin and crepe-like with crispy, butter-fried edges, and the eggs are perfectly cooked. Growing up, breakfast at Owen's and my house consisted of sugar-free Muesli with skim milk or low-fat yogurt. So, in adulthood, we've both developed a thing for greasy, fried hangover breakfasts, and we try to meet at the Biscuit every month. Despite the fact that I find my little brother generally annoying and gross, I also kind of adore him, so it's nice to have this time to catch up.

I ask about the robot he's building at work because I'm

still trying to grasp the intricacies of AI and computer vision. Owen eventually gives up trying to explain and tells Jacob and me about an idea he has for a video game design instead. I know as much about video games as I do about robots, but it sounds like a good idea, and Jacob agrees.

Now that I'm paying attention, I notice that Owen and Jacob's friendship is actually very sweet. Maybe it's because they've known each other since they were nerdy little boys, but there's none of that manly bro-stuff happening here that I've seen with other guys. Alex and his friends might talk about real things that are important to them, but I've never witnessed it. Mostly, it's a lot of shit-talking and one-upping each other.

But Jacob and Owen actually know what's going on in each other's lives, and they talk about it as if it's not just an opportunity for a punch line, but something that really matters. Sure, they make jokes at each other's expense too, but the ribbing doesn't dominate the conversation. I'm suddenly really glad that my brother has had this enduring friendship for the past two and a half decades.

"So, how are things going with Olivia Rodrigo?" Owen asks Jacob when we've exhausted the video game conversation.

Jacob leans on the table and puts his head in his hands, shaking it back and forth.

"Olivia Rodrigo?" I look from my brother to Jacob and back. "The pop singer?" I'm very familiar with Olivia Rodrigo. The songs "traitor" and "good 4 u" got me through the worst of my Very Bad Year. "Are you doing a music project with *Olivia Rodrigo*?"

"I wish," Jacob mutters, and it's muffled since his face is still buried in his palms. He finally lifts his head. "The woman in the apartment next door is going through a bad breakup. She and this jerk have been on and off for months. When they're *on*, I hear them fighting, and when they're *off*, she plays Olivia Rodrigo on repeat until they get back together."

"It's *very* loud," Owen adds.

"I obviously hate the fighting," Jacob says. "But the constant Olivia Rodrigo tunes are messing with my own music." He drops his head back in his hands and sings a couple of lines from "drivers license." "Over and over and over," he laments.

A shiver goes up my spine because not only did Jacob just sing, totally off the cuff, which I now know is *not* something he'd do in front of just anyone, but his voice is beautiful. Warm and deep and almost haunting, just like that song he played on the piano. It's perfectly on pitch, even though he's slumped over the table, with a little rasp at the end. The constellation of feelings this revelation evokes must be playing across my face, because Owen is giving me the side-eye.

I look away and rearrange my silverware. "So, I guess that must be annoying."

Jacob lifts his head again. "I mean, it's kind of a catchy song. Great bridge. It might not be a problem if her apartment didn't share a wall with my music studio. It's impossible to get any work done."

For about the hundredth time since I started this second chance year, a vague memory from my Very Bad Year begins to take shape. Paige. The next-door neighbor. When I'd moved into Jacob's guest room, Olivia Rodrigo was also playing on repeat. I guess I'd caught Paige on an off period of her relationship, too. I hadn't really minded the music because who was I to judge someone for their reaction to a bad breakup? But I'd felt bad for her.

"Wine and chocolate," I blurt out. I'd ordered it from a local shop and had it sent to her apartment. She'd fallen for the long-haired bike messenger who'd delivered it to her door, and that was the end of the on-and-off jerk for good.

"Wine and chocolate?" Jacob repeats.

"Go online to the Goat and Grape's website and have some wine and chocolate delivered. It will cheer her up."

Jacob looks skeptical, but he pulls out his phone.

"Trust me."

While Jacob spends a few minutes typing in his phone, another realization from my Very Bad Year works its way into my consciousness. Jacob said his studio butted up against Paige's apartment. But the room that shared a wall with Paige was the second bedroom. It was the guest room where *I'd* stayed. Jacob had his studio equipment in his own bedroom. Did he move it out of the guest room so I could have that space?

When I'd arrived to stay with Jacob, there was furniture in the guest room—a bed, side table, dresser. He even had a couple of succulents on the windowsill, and I remember the screen prints on the walls were from a Brooklyn artist that I admire. Had Jacob furnished that room for me?

I shrug off this ridiculous train of thought. Jacob obviously moved his studio out of the guest room because of the noise from Paige's. He didn't rearrange his entire apartment so his best friend's sister could spend months sitting on his couch eating Nutella from the jar and watching eighties sitcoms.

"Done." Jacob looks up from his phone. "You really think this will help her to feel better?"

I nod, remembering Paige and Brandon making out in the hallway. "I'm sure of it."

Chapter 14

"Smile, Sadie!" Kasumi flops down on the bed next to me, phone in her outstretched hand, and presses her cheek to mine. I look up from my copy of *Baker's Monthly* magazine, flash a smile at the camera, and then go back to flipping pages.

I'm used to Kasumi Instagramming her every move, and mine along with it.

"Look," she says, cuddling up next to me. "Your almond raspberry torte with the edible flowers has over twenty thousand likes."

"Really?" I lean over to look. "Wow, that's *amazing*." Kasumi took a gorgeous photo of my cake, and it honestly looks more professional than anything in this magazine I'm reading. I can't believe she managed that with an iPhone in Xavier's ugly kitchen, especially given the horrible fluorescent lighting. "You're really good at this."

"Why thank you." Kasumi grins. "When you open your bakery, I'll do your social media."

"I'm not sure I'll be able to afford you." I take the phone and scroll back through her Instagram feed. Of course I follow her, and I've seen these photos before. There are dozens of images of my cakes and tarts, all expertly photographed and edited to look like she'd spent days on styling and lighting. And then scattered among my baked goods are other food shots—dishes she and the other sous chefs made at Xavier's, but also casual photos of ingredients, too. A toppling pile of carrots, deliciously fresh and vibrant, showcased on a simple white plate. Three perfectly fat cherries lined up across a metal prep table.

Plus, there are dozens of pictures of Kasumi and her friends looking youthful and vibrant, but still natural at the same time. A group of Xavier's kitchen staff makes faces at the camera. One of the prep cooks scatters fresh herbs on a plate. Looking at these photos, I realize that Kasumi is a talented chef, but she's never really been passionate about cooking. Even back in culinary school, she was always more interested in styling and presentation.

"You should do social media professionally," I tell her, handing back the phone.

"That would be amazing," Kasumi says, her voice wistful.

I sit up. "Seriously, Kasumi. Why *don't* you?" In just the minute I was watching, my cake racked up another hundred likes. "You're easily as good at this as your friend, what's his name…Devon?" Devon, the social media influencer who hosted the carnival-themed New Year's party. But I can't mention that, of course. Because that party won't happen for about seven more months. "You're basically doing it professionally anyway," I point out. "You're just not getting paid for it. And you're handing Xavier all that free promotion."

She bites her lip. "I do think about it sometimes. I just can't imagine putting up with Xavier's bullshit forever, you know?" She hops off the bed and crosses the room to open the fridge. "Or the sexism of restaurant work in general."

Sometimes, I can still feel Rob's hand sliding up my thigh. I shudder at the memory and push it out of my head. "I know what you mean."

"Do you?" There's something in the tone of her voice, an edge to it, that has me sitting up straighter. "It seems like it doesn't bother you that much."

"What do you mean by that?"

Kasumi pops the top on a can of seltzer. "Nothing...it's just..." She sinks back down on the bed. "You didn't used to put up with all the bullying. But lately, it seems like you're okay going along with it. We've all kind of noticed."

I toss my magazine on the bed next to me. "Who is 'we'? The servers? Because I didn't ask to be sent out on the floor with them, you know."

"But you didn't push back, either."

I slide off the bed and pace across the room. "You know it's not that easy to push back. All I've ever wanted to do is be a pastry chef. I need this job. If I lose this job, I could be blackballed by the whole industry." I turn to her with my hands on my hips. "Xavier might be a dick, but he's a dick with a lot of influence."

Kasumi shakes her head. "That would never happen."

It did happen! I want to scream. *It did happen, and I lost everything!* But I can't. Because it didn't happen in Kasumi's reality, in my current reality. It happened in my Very Bad Year. The year I'm doing everything I possibly can to keep from repeating. "You have no idea what could happen."

Kasumi sighs. "I don't want to fight with you about this. You're my best friend. I'm just worried. You don't seem quite like *you* anymore."

"I'm still me." I drop my arms from their defensive position. "Maybe I'm just the *me* who's grown up a little. The *me* who realized you can't cause a scene every time you don't like something. You have to pick your battles."

Kasumi gazes across the room, her brows knit together. After a beat, she seems to shake it off, jumping to her feet.

"You know what? I'm sorry I brought it up." She heads for my walk-in closet. "Let's figure out what we're going to wear to Sonya's thirtieth birthday party. Her boyfriend rented out the entire rooftop deck at the Hotel Budapest. It's going to be epic."

Kasumi flings the closet door open and then reels backward. "Holy shit."

"What?" I hurry to her side. "Is it a cockroach? I *hate* cockroaches."

"No." She looks at me, wide-eyed. "It's half of Madison Avenue taking up residence in your closet." She waves her hand at the heap of high-end shopping bags piled on the floor.

"Oh, yeah. That." I haven't exactly gotten around to putting away the clothes Alex bought me. When I came home the night he gave them to me, I chucked the bags in my closet and have been ignoring them ever since.

Kasumi is gaping at me. "Are you a Kardashian? Do you have a secret shopping addiction? What's happening here?"

She grabs a handful of bags and drags them out into the room.

"Alex bought them." I clear my throat. "He, uh, he wanted me to have some nice things to wear to his work events."

Kasumi's mouth forms into a silent *ohhhh*. She surveys the high-end labels scattered all over my floor. "Well, that's very...sweet."

"Yeah, it *is* sweet, right?" Why do I sound like I'm trying to convince myself? "It's just..." I trail off.

The truth is these clothes aren't me. Other than a Diane von Furstenberg wrap dress I pulled out for one of Alex's after-work happy hours, I can't really see myself wearing any of this stuff. The Louboutins may be gorgeous, but there is a very good chance I will fall over in them. And where am I going to carry a Prada bag? The Food Bazaar? Yoga class? Even to an event like Sonya's birthday party, I'm much more comfortable in a dress from a Williamsburg boutique and a quirky pair of earrings I bought at the Brooklyn Flea.

"It's just that you might have wanted to pick out your own clothes?" Kasumi fills in the blank.

"Well," I say, trying for upbeat. "These are the latest styles."

"You have your own style." She tilts her head, studying me. "Alex used to like it."

I feel a flush creep up my cheeks. Kasumi is only saying exactly what I was thinking a minute ago. But I find myself going on the defensive again. "All the Wall Street women dress like this, so Alex wants me to feel like I fit in when we hang out with them."

Kasumi is giving me that look again. The one like she's about to say something that I'm not going to like. Luckily, Gio chooses this moment to hop off the bed and delicately weave his way through the designer bags on my floor. He sniffs around, finally choosing Armani. The thick paper crinkles as he settles on top, tucking his front paws beneath him.

Kasumi holds up her phone and starts circling Gio, snapping photos. "This one is going on Instagram for sure."

When the photo shoot is over, we gather the shopping bags and line them up neatly on the closet floor where I know I'll probably go on ignoring them for a while.

"So," Kasumi says, flipping through my clothes on the hangers. "What are you going to wear to Sonya's party?" She pulls out my favorite pink slip dress and holds it up in front of her. "How about this one?"

Suddenly, I have a flashback to Kasumi standing in the exact same position with a sparkly gold minidress in her hands. Or maybe it's actually a flash-*forward*, since technically that New Year's Eve carnival party is seven months away. But either way, I'm reminded of what a good friend she's been to me, and suddenly, my throat is burning. I throw my arms around her, hoping she doesn't notice my eyes growing wet. "I love you, Kasumi," I say against her hair.

"I love you, too, silly," she says in return. "Now, let's pick out which photo of Gio we're going to post on Instagram. I have the perfect label for it." She pulls back from our hug and gives me a wink. "I'll call it 'Haute Cat-ure.'"

Chapter 15

June

I'm arranging a tray of candied pear and walnut muffins in Higher Grounds' display case when Jacob walks in. Hearing the bell on the door, Mrs. Kaminski turns in her chair to get a look at him, and then she shakes her head. "You again."

Zoe smiles. "Be nice, Mrs. Kaminski."

"It's lovely to see you, Mrs. Kaminski." Jacob's Victorian-era manners apparently extend to grumpy old ladies, because he's unfailingly polite to Mrs. Kaminski, even when she snipes at him.

"You only come in when that girl is here," she accuses.

"Which girl?" Jacob gazes around the half-full café.

"Sadie the Cat Lady." Mrs. Kaminski humphs. I'd think she's jealous, except there's nothing about me and Jacob to be jealous of.

Jacob's cheeks turn a little pink, and he lifts his gaze to mine. I swear my insides begin to caramelize.

Nothing to be jealous of at all.

He clears his throat. "If I don't come in on the day she bakes, everything will be gone."

Which is true, of course, and a totally reasonable explanation. Much more reasonable than thinking he comes in here to see me. That would not be reasonable at all, and therefore I am not thinking it. At all.

I hand Jacob a muffin and put another in front of Mrs. Kaminski, because he always buys her one.

"Thank you," she says primly, folding a napkin on her lap.

Jacob takes the seat next to Mrs. Kaminski, and I grind the espresso for his café Americano. Technically, I'm not a barista here, but Zoe's hands are full, and I know how to make all these drinks from when I worked here during my Very Bad Year. This time around, Zoe was super-impressed when I made a pot of coffee because it usually takes people two weeks to learn how to do it up to her standards. I obviously don't mention that in an alternate universe, it actually took me three weeks.

"How's the video game music coming?" I ask, setting Jacob's drink in front of him.

"Just finished earlier this week. Owen came over last night with a bottle of whiskey to celebrate." He winces and runs a hand through his hair. The couple of days of stubble on his jaw and purple circles under his eyes scream *hangover*.

"Do you need another one of these?" I gesture at his coffee.

He smiles. "No, I'm good."

"Well, if Owen is as hungover as you are when he comes over later today, I'll be sure to turn the lights on really bright and talk loudly. Maybe I'll find an excuse to use the blender."

"He deserves it." Jacob nods. "He's a bad influence."

"Who's Owen?" Mrs. Kaminski demands.

"My brother," I say at the same time Jacob says, "my oldest friend."

"Is he as good-looking as you are?" she asks Jacob.

"Uh…" He rubs his jaw. "I'm not sure I'm qualified to answer that."

She turns to me. "Is he as good-looking as Jacob?"

I am not about to comment on how good-looking Jacob is, either. But luckily, we're comparing him to my brother, so I have an easy way out. "No, Owen's an ugly troll," I say, and Jacob laughs.

"Well, bring him in here, and I'll be the judge."

For a moment, I'm really tempted by this. I'd love to hear Mrs. Kaminski tell my brother he'd be handsome if only he'd take off that stupid hat. But Owen has started calling me Sadie the Cat Lady thanks to Jacob spilling the beans, and I don't need Mrs. Kaminski giving my brother any more ammunition.

"So, you're hanging out with Owen tonight?" Jacob pops a bite of his candied pear and walnut muffin into his mouth, and I love the way his eyes close, just briefly, with pleasure.

"Yeah, we're going to watch the *Antiques Roadshow* and make fun of all the ugly artifacts people bring in for appraisal. You want to come?" The invitation pops out, surprising me a little, but not completely. I've never asked him to hang out before, but we weren't friends before. And now…well, it seems like maybe we are.

"I'd love to, but I have—" He stops talking, and then, "I have other plans."

I will not ask if he was about to say he has a date.

"But I wish I could come." It sounds like he actually *does* wish he could come, so he must not have a date. Because who would want to hang out with me and Owen and nineteenth-century candy dishes worth a stupid amount of money if they had something fun to do, like go on a date?

"I'm asking because Owen left his wallet at my place last night," Jacob says. "Can I give it to you?"

"Sure, but I can't promise I won't go on a shopping spree with all his credit cards."

"Once it's out of my possession, I take no responsibility for what happens to it." Jacob grins. "Let me run home and get it."

I slide the last plate of muffins into the display case. "Actually, I'm done here." I pull my apron over my head. "I can walk with you."

We say goodbye to Zoe and Mrs. Kaminski, and the few blocks to Jacob's place pass quickly. In the lobby, I realize that even though this building is as familiar to me as my own, it's supposed to be the first time I've been inside. I play dumb on the elevator, asking which floor to push, and again when Jacob waves me to go first into the hall. He leads me to his apartment and is pulling out his key when the neighbor's door swings open and Paige steps out.

"Jacob! Hi!" Paige walks over, arms outstretched, and gives Jacob a hug.

Huh. Since when do Paige and Jacob hug?

Hi." Paige turns to me. "I'm Paige."

Jacob clears his throat. "Sorry. Sadie, this is Paige. Paige, this is Owen's sister, Sadie."

"Oh! It's so nice to meet you, Sadie!" At that, she leans over and gives me a hug, too. Maybe she's just a hugger. I try to remember if that was the case in my first go-around. "I adore your brother."

"Oh, you know Owen?" I ask, straining to piece all of this together. When I lived here during my Very Bad Year, I was the only one acquainted with Paige, and only because I...

Oh.

Only because I sent her wine and chocolate.

The wine and chocolate I encouraged *Jacob* to send her, just a couple of weeks ago. When I sent it, she came over to say thank you, and we chatted for a bit. So, she must have done the same with Jacob.

"Yeah, I know Owen." Paige laughs. "And I'm ready to kill him for bringing that bottle of whiskey last night. I've never had such a killer hangover."

Okay, so clearly, she and Jacob didn't just chat, they also hung out drinking. I wonder if Brandon was there, too.

"Oh man." I wrinkle my nose. "Yeah, I avoid the stuff. I hope you'll be okay. Maybe Brandon can bring you some soup or something."

Both Paige and Jacob look at me sideways, and it's a look I've gotten used to in the past few months. I'm not supposed to know anything about Paige and Brandon. As far as anyone around me knows, I never lived here in Jacob's building, so I've never actually seen Paige and Brandon making out in the halls. All of that happened during my Very Bad Year, which never *actually* happened.

I can't believe I've done this again. How am I going to explain that I know about Brandon? I can't pull another Sadie the Cat Lady and make up an outrageous story like I did with Zoe.

But then Jacob says, "What are you talking about? Who's Brandon?"

Paige's brows knit together. "I don't think I know anyone named Brandon."

How can she not know anyone named Brandon?

And then it hits me. Paige met Brandon because I'd sent her a package and he'd delivered it. But if Jacob sent the package, that small change could have altered everything that followed. The wine and chocolate could have been delivered by *anyone*. And obviously, that anyone wasn't Brandon, because Paige doesn't know a Brandon. She's not dating a Brandon.

And she's drinking whiskey with Jacob and hugging him in the hall. Is it possible that Paige and Jacob are dating?

This train of thought goes careening off a cliff when Paige smiles at Jacob and says, "Don't worry, I'm going to take some Tylenol and have a nap. I'll be totally good for dinner later."

Yep. I guess it's possible. And mystery solved about Jacob's plans tonight.

That's when I realize that it's not only the trajectory of *my* life that I'm altering in this strange second chance year. There's a domino effect for everyone around me. What if Brandon is missing out on the love of his life because Jacob sent Paige the package and I didn't? What if my actions are screwing up everybody's lives?

But short of finding Brandon and dragging him to Paige's door, there's not much I can do to fix this. And who knows? Maybe Paige is the love of Jacob's life, and not Brandon's after all.

And if that thought bothers me more than it should… Well, there's not much I can do to fix that either.

Chapter 16

"Sadie," Xavier says, as I put the last touches on a six-layer mimosa cake with chocolate drizzle and candied orange peel. "I need you to stay late tonight. Rob Thurmond and his group just came in, and he specifically requested you."

I wonder how he managed that, since I doubt Rob even knows my name. Did he call me *the girl whose ass I grabbed*? I can still picture that smarmy grin as I backed away from him in disgust. There's no way I'm letting him within ten feet of my ass again. Or any other part of me.

"I'm sorry, Xavier, but I can't." I set my pastry bag on the counter and push the champagne confection in his direction, hoping to distract him with his own reflection in the perfect mirror glaze. "I just finished up here, and I have something I really can't get out of."

"What is it?" he demands, not even glancing at the masterpiece before him.

It's none of your business doesn't seem like the smart response, even if it would feel really good to say it. I search for an excuse that Xavier would deem worthy of bailing on Rob Thurmond. *Volunteering at the soup kitchen?* No.

Visiting my sick grandma? Unlikely. *Emergency brain surgery?* He'd want me to reschedule.

What if I just went ahead and told Xavier the truth about Rob? Alex suggested that maybe Xavier doesn't know his VIP client is a creep with roving hands. As mortifying as it would be to have to admit what happened to me, maybe it's the right thing to do?

But just as I'm opening my mouth to speak up, Xavier cuts in. "Rob and I have been friends for twenty-five years, and he's a huge supporter of my restaurant. So, don't drop any plates like you did last time."

My mouth snaps shut. Why would Xavier ever believe the word of an assistant over his longtime friend and patron? I know exactly how this will play out. Rob will deny anything happened, and Xavier will fire me. And I'll be right back where I started.

I can't work that party, though. Not just because my skin crawls at the idea of Rob Thurmond's hot, sweaty face. I'm meeting Alex and his boss, Dave, for dinner tonight, and Alex is waiting for me at the bar next door. But I don't think *a date with my boyfriend* is going to cut it with Xavier as far as excuses go.

Luckily, I remember that Xavier loves anything to do with rich people and their money. "Actually," I tell him, "I'm having dinner with one of the managing directors at Wright and Moore. They're a top investment banking firm on Wall Street…"

"I know who they are." Xavier rolls his eyes.

"I thought it would be a good opportunity to talk up the restaurant. Maybe invite him to come out for dinner sometime. He does a lot of entertaining clients, obviously, so I plan to assure him the chef's table is always available."

Xavier's eyebrows raise. "Good thinking, Sadie." He might actually look a little impressed. "I knew my instincts about you were right." With that, he finally spares a glance at my cake. "Hmmm." He purses his lips, and I brace myself. Finally, he murmurs, "Very nice. Great work."

Whew.

As soon as Xavier heads out into the dining room to make a show of greeting Rob and his guests in an artificially enthusiastic voice, I run for the break room to grab the garment bag out of my locker and change into my designer dress and heels.

I hurry next door where Alex is waiting for me at the bar. As soon as he spots me standing in the doorway, his gaze sweeps down to my feet and then to the top of my head. I can tell by how his face lights up that he approves of my outfit. I've chosen a classic little black dress by Celine and paired it with the diamond pendant necklace and the Louboutin pumps. Since I had to work earlier, I didn't have time to do anything with my hair except pull it into a super quick French twist, but I decide it gives me a *Breakfast at Tiffany's* vibe. I try out a smoldering look on Alex, channeling Audrey Hepburn, and several people glance up from their drinks to admire me.

Maybe there really is *something to these fancy, expensive clothes and accessories.*

But before that thought has time to fully form, I step off the mat at the bar's entrance and onto the wood floor. Unaccustomed to towering four inches higher than its usual latitude, my heel slips, and my ankle twists, and I go flying into the lap of an older gentleman at a nearby table. My elbow hits his drink and sends it toppling to the floor.

"Oh my God, I'm so sorry." I grasp at the table, trying to stand in my heels without slipping in whiskey or stabbing the man in the eye with my black clutch. As I flail around, two strong hands hook under my armpits and haul me to my feet. I look up to find Alex standing above me, his expression unreadable.

I would kill to be in my pajamas right now.

"I'm so sorry," I repeat, this time partly for Alex's benefit.

"Are you okay?" he asks, checking my ankle for injuries and my dress for whiskey stains, thankfully finding neither.

"Yes, just mortified."

After Alex sorts out the man and his spilled drink, we climb in an Uber headed into Manhattan. I start to reassure Alex I won't repeat the same scenario in front of his boss, but then I trail off because I really shouldn't be making promises in four-inch heels. Alex gives me a crooked smile and a shake of his head, which is probably the only response I can reasonably expect. I wonder if he's regretting buying these shoes. And then I wonder if it would be too much trouble to ask the driver to stop at T.J.Maxx so I can buy a pair of sneakers.

Instead, I gaze out the window as the Upper West Side rolls by, a neighborhood we used to frequent when we started dating, but I haven't visited since Alex was a student at Columbia. I remember our carefree days walking down Broadway to grab falafel at our favorite hole-in-the-wall before heading over to Central Park to eat it by the

Reservoir. We'd end up back in Alex's fifth-floor walk-up, making out on his futon and drinking the eight-dollar bottle of Merlot we'd picked up at the liquor store down the street.

These days, Alex is obviously a downtown-high-rise-with-all-the-amenities kind of guy, and when we arrive at the restaurant, he goes to the bar to get me a glass of champagne. But when he presses a kiss to my temple and tells me he's glad I'm here, that familiar affection spreads across me.

"How was your day?" Alex asks as we sip our drinks.

I lean back against the leather banquette, finally feeling my shoulders relax, and glad to be off my feet. "Just more of the same from Xavier. He wanted me to stay and wait on that creepy guy I told you about. The only thing that got me out of it was name-dropping your company and hinting that we might bring your boss there someday."

"You won't be working for Xavier forever, Sadie." Alex takes my hand. "And I know you're going to be great at whatever you do next."

I give his hand a squeeze in return, and when I excuse myself to run to the bathroom a few minutes later, I stop in the hallway to send him a punny text. *You bake my life a butter place.* Just like old times.

I return to the bar just as Alex's boss and his wife walk in. Dave and Melinda are a middle-aged couple, attractive in that way people are when they have plenty of money for personal trainers and hair stylists and bespoke suits. Though Dave and Alex greet each other with a handshake, Dave gives Alex an extra pat on the back, and Alex's face lights up. There's a warmth to their exchange that hints at a personal relationship, and I'm reminded that Alex didn't always plan to be an investment banker.

Ever since the third grade when he was asked to write an essay about what he wanted to be when he grew up, Alex expected to become a financial adviser and work in his dad's company back in Wisconsin. Charlie Martin was the kind of guy who coached his kids' soccer games, took them camping in the summer, and went out of his way to make it home each night by six so he could have dinner with his family. Alex adored him. When Charlie died unexpectedly at the age of fifty-eight, and Alex's mom sold the company, Alex's whole life changed in an instant.

I know how important this meeting is for Alex. So, I turn to Dave and Melinda and give them my most charming smile. We head for the table, and I take careful steps, determined not to trip over my shoes or fall in any other laps.

Dave pulls my chair out for me, and once we settle into our seats, he orders a bottle of red for the table. "So, Sadie," he says, leaning back in his chair once he's swirled, tasted, and approved the wine. "Alex tells me you're a pastry chef."

I nod. "I've worked at Xavier's for about four years."

"Oh, how fascinating." Melinda presses her left hand on Dave's arm, and her enormous diamond ring twinkles. "Honey, Xavier was the chef who did the menu for Steve's fiftieth birthday party, remember?" She turns to me. "Dave's brother. His wife hosted a dinner party for his birthday last August. The food was wonderful."

"Sadie probably made the pastries for that party." Alex looks down at me with a proud grin. "She's basically

Xavier's right-hand woman. You won't find better desserts at any restaurant in the city." He stretches an arm behind the back of my chair, and I lean into him. Melinda and Dave exchange a smile as if they're charmed by our young love. Pleasing Dave means so much to Alex, so for his sake, I'm thrilled this seems to be going well.

We chitchat about Dave and Melinda's latest vacation, and then Dave and Alex break off to talk about some client or other. Melinda turns to me. "Beautiful bag." She strokes my Chanel clutch with appreciation.

"Oh, thanks." I pick it up and then set it back on the table. "It was a gift from Alex."

She nods with a tinkly little laugh. "Of course. You've got to make sure you enjoy the perks of the job, after all."

I'm not sure what to say to that since it's not like I was expecting lavish gifts just because Alex works in finance. But maybe after you've been married to an investment banker for a couple of decades, you grow accustomed to designer fashion. Under the table, I wiggle my toes in my high heels, counting the minutes until I can get my feet out of them. But, who knows? Maybe someday, I'll run a mile in these shoes.

"Well, the perks of my job aren't quite as nice as Alex's," I say with a laugh. "My shapeless chef's coat and ugly clogs are examples A and B."

Melinda looks at her husband and Alex deep in their conversation about a merger. "At a certain point, his job becomes your job too, though, doesn't it?" It's not really a question, more of a statement she expects I'll agree with.

"Um...does it?" I murmur.

"Well, surely you've noticed the long hours of an

investment banker." She takes a sip of her wine. "Dave was on a conference call when I went into labor with our first child. He sat in the corner of the hospital room with a laptop and his phone, closing a deal, while I started pushing."

"Oh wow. That must have been upsetting for you."

"I was disappointed of course." Melinda shrugs. "But he did what he had to do."

Okay. I can't say I'd be quite so forgiving. But I'm not planning to push out a baby anytime soon, either. "Alex and I are nowhere near having children."

"I certainly don't mean to make assumptions about your relationship." She leans in with a conspiratorial smile. "But from the way Dave says Alex talks about you, his intentions are quite evident."

I blink. Alex discussed our future at work? I try to imagine him and the other guys sitting around the boardroom at Wright and Moore dissecting their relationships like they're the four women on an episode of *Sex and the City*. Except that Dave is solidly on the Mr. Big end of the spectrum, and I'm having trouble picturing Zach using any form of communication that doesn't involve fist bumps.

"It's important to understand that the demands on Alex won't ease once he's promoted to a vice president at the firm. And those demands will extend to his wife." Melinda gives me a pointed look. "Women who go into these relationships believing that their career will be of equal importance, that there will be a division of labor at home or in child-rearing…" She shakes her head. "Well, they end up very disappointed."

I nod slowly, letting that sink in. So, this explains all

the relationship talk. I'm being vetted to make sure I won't freak out if Alex blows off our honeymoon for a merger negotiation or holds a conference call while our baby is crowning. This dinner is the beginning of my induction into the world of Wall Street wives. And my job description seems very clear. Smile, support your husband, and keep your complaints to yourself.

But don't worry, there will be presents. Lots of presents.

On the Uber ride home, I want to talk to Alex about my conversation with Melinda, but he fields a call from a client that sounds important. My phone buzzes as well, and I open a text from my mother. *Hope dinner with Alex's boss is going well!* She follows the message with a long string of heart emojis, which, honestly, is a little strange coming from a woman with a PhD in English literature. *We can't wait to see you soon!*

I don't know why I tell her about things like this dinner with Alex's boss. I only end up annoyed by her reactions. But then I pause with my thumbs on the keypad of my phone, shaking my head.

Actually, I *do* know why I tell her. Because this is the one part of my life that will get her attention. For years, I tried cakes and pastries. She might walk right past *me* in the kitchen, but who wouldn't stop for a five-layer strawberry coconut cake with mascarpone filling? That backfired on me, though, when my desire to turn baking into a career became an even bigger disappointment than my abysmal high school grades. But once Alex came into the picture, I started getting more phone calls from her than I had since I moved away from home.

It's hard to understand why my well-educated and hard-working mother is more interested in talking to me about my boyfriend than my career. But my parents see Alex's job as investment banker as respectable, while they've never viewed baking as anything more than a hobby. I wonder what they'd think if I announced I planned to give it all up to become a Wall Street wife.

Our car turns south on the ramp to the FDR, and out the window, the lights of the city sparkle on the East River. Rain begins to fall, the sound drowning out Alex's voice reassuring the client he'll send over a spreadsheet as soon as he gets back to his apartment.

I swipe at my mom's message to delete the whole damn thing from my phone, but I can't delete the reality that my parents will never take me seriously. It echoes in my head, mingling with Melinda's warning that my career will always take a back seat to Alex's.

I glance down at my dress, and those maddening shoes, and my unease spreads like overcrowded cookie dough in a pan. Would Alex really expect me to give up baking, or view his career as more important than mine?

I shake my head. Melinda was speaking from her own experience, but that doesn't mean my relationship will be the same. I open my purse to shove my phone in, but that teeny-tiny clutch will barely hold a Band-Aid. Instead, I turn it off and spend the rest of the ride home staring out the window at the rain hitting the sidewalk.

Chapter 17

July

The yelling reverberates all the way down the block. I stop in my tracks, thinking I've stumbled into the middle of a robbery, or at least two angry cats fighting over a subway rat. But as I inch my way down the alley, approaching the back door of Xavier's restaurant, I can begin to decipher words among the jumbled garble of grunts and curses.

Sigh.

It's just Xavier throwing another tantrum. To be honest, I'd prefer a robbery. Or a rat.

I tiptoe in the back door where I find the staff standing in a circle, staring at a large baking pan on top of a prep table. Whatever is on that pan is pink, jiggly, and Spam-like. At the sight of it, that déjà vu feeling washes over me.

Kasumi catches my eye from across the table and shakes her head. I slowly make my way around until I'm standing next to her. "What's going on?" I ask under my breath.

"Somebody took that pan out of the refrigerator last night, and they forgot to put it back," she whispers. "It's hours of work and expensive ingredients, ruined."

I peer over her shoulder at the prep table. Xavier and I were two of the last people in the kitchen yesterday. Xavier was taking an inventory of produce he wanted to pick up at the farmers market this morning while I finished the piping on a citrus chiffon cake. I'd stayed in my corner by the sink, hoping not to draw attention to myself, because he was in another one of his moods, frustrated because he couldn't find the leeks. He'd even...

Oh no.

He'd even unloaded half the refrigerator onto the prep tables to look for them. I'd left soon after, but I'm willing to bet he forgot to put that tray back when he was done.

"It was Xavier," I blurt out, before I can stop myself. Luckily, Xavier is still ranting, so he doesn't hear me.

Kasumi does, though. She turns to me with eyes wide. "What?"

I lower my voice. "I saw Xavier take that pan out last night. I bet he left it there by mistake." The minute the words are out of my mouth, I wish I could take them back. Because I realize why this is all so familiar. I've seen that pink slop before. I've had this conversation before.

"You've got to say something," Kasumi whispers.

I back away slowly. "Oh, hell no." I've managed to keep my head down for all these months. Not only have I kept my job, but I'm a contender for that executive pastry chef position. Xavier has complimented my desserts multiple times, implying the job could be mine. And I want it.

The prestige something like that could bring when I start my own bakery would be huge. And the significant raise would mean I could save a lot more money. Not to mention that it would feel really good to tell my parents I'd earned a promotion like that. I've made it this far. I've put up with all this shit. I deserve that promotion, and I'm not about to blow it.

I turn to hide in the staff break room until Xavier runs out of steam, but Kasumi grabs my arm. "He's blaming Samantha for this. You have to speak up."

Xavier's wrath is directed at a brand-new line cook straight out of culinary school. She's holding back tears as he hurls insults in her direction, with words like *useless* and *incompetent* playing on repeat. Even if that poor girl *had* left the tray on the counter, nobody deserves to be treated that way. In another year, in another life, I'd let Xavier know exactly what I think of his behavior.

But I can't.

I can't because this is the pâté incident. This is the day I was fired during my Very Bad Year. I lost my job, my apartment, everything, over a pile of pink slop. I shake my head. Absolutely not. I am not doing it again.

"Sadie," Kasumi hisses. "He's going to fire Samantha over a mistake *he* made. We have to say something."

Kasumi's right. But if I speak up, I'll be right back where I was last time around. Out of a job, and then soon I'll be homeless. I can't go back there. Can't handle the depression, the hopelessness, the feeling that life was carrying on for everyone but me. And where would I live? Jacob just got Olivia Rodrigo out of his life, why would he allow her back in?

"If we stick together, I bet he'll back down," Kasumi murmurs to me. And before I can stop her, she stands up straight and calls out, "Excuse me, sir!" across the kitchen. "Sadie and I have something to tell you."

Xavier levels an angry glare in our direction. *"What."*

Kasumi takes a deep breath. "We don't think it was Samantha who left that pâté on the counter."

"Well, then, who did it?"

My chest squeezes painfully. I press a hand there. Why is it suddenly so hard to suck air in my lungs? If I don't sit down, I think I might pass out. Or throw up. Or both. I pull my arm from Kasumi's grasp. "I'm not even sure that's what I saw," I whisper in her ear. "Can we just let it go?"

Her mouth drops open, and her eyes go wide. And before she can say another word, I flee to the break room and slam the door shut.

I sit on a bench and bend forward, putting my head between my knees like they do in the movies, and taking shallow, gasping breaths. After a few minutes like this, my chest stops squeezing and my heart slows down. I sit up, and just as I do, the door flings open.

Kasumi marches in so ferociously that the breeze of her anger blows past me. She bangs open her locker and snatches her chef's coat from the hook.

"Did Xavier fire Samantha?" I whisper.

She whirls around, hands on her hips, and gives me the most contemptuous stare I've ever seen. "No, Xavier didn't fire Samantha."

I blow out a relieved sigh. "Oh good."

She turns back to her locker, grabs her purse off the shelf, and haphazardly stuffs her chef's coat inside. Then she tosses it over her shoulder with one arm of the coat still trailing over the side. "Xavier fired *me*."

Chapter 18

I stand outside Kasumi's apartment building holding an overstuffed pastry box like a white flag. Kasumi hasn't answered my calls or texts in over a week, so I baked a double batch of her favorite chocolate croissants and came over here. But now that I'm outside her door, I'm not really sure what to do. I try texting her again—*Hey, I'm here at your building. Can we talk?*—but she doesn't reply.

I press the buzzer for apartment number three, and her roommate answers.

"Adrianna, it's Sadie. Can you buzz me in?"

There's a long moment of silence, and I can imagine Kasumi and Adrianna whispering about what to do. Then the static of the intercom comes through the speaker, and a slightly fuzzy version of Adrianna's voice says, "Sorry, Kasumi's not here."

Defeated, I set the pastry box on the step. *I brought croissants*, I text. *I'm leaving them on your step.* Then I head down the block. Right before I cross the street, I glance over my shoulder at Kasumi's building. The door opens, and her head pops out. She looks left and right, and then she grabs the box off the step.

"Hey!" I take off running so I can catch her before she disappears back inside. "Kasumi, wait."

She hesitates, biting her lip, and for a second, I think she's going to act like she doesn't hear me. Her hand grasps the door handle, but to my relief, she turns around and takes a step back outside. "What do you want, Sadie?"

I come to a stop in front of her stoop, panting from my sprint down the sidewalk. "Can I talk to you? Please?"

"Fine." She shifts the pastry box under her arm. "Talk."

"I'm so sorry about what happened last week," I say, still slightly out of breath. "I can't believe Xavier fired you. Maybe if we go tell him that it was all a mistake..."

"It wasn't a mistake," Kasumi says sharply. "And I'm not going to say it was. I'm not going to kiss up to him or apologize or pretend that I was in the wrong when I wasn't."

"Okay, maybe *I* can talk to him." I've been sucking up to Xavier for months in order to keep my job, and the last thing I expected was for my best friend to get sacked instead of me. So, if it will fix this mess, I'll happily show up in Xavier's office to remind him he was robbed of the head judge position on *Top Chef*, his braised short ribs are the best in all five boroughs, and *Oh, by the way, can Kasumi have her job back?*

If I get him in the right mood, maybe it could work.

But Kasumi's eyes narrow and her head swings back and forth. "I'm not going back there."

"But—" I start to argue. Even a lot of well-paid restaurant workers live paycheck to paycheck in New York. What if Kasumi can't pay her rent? Or she loses her apartment? What if Xavier blackballs her, and she can't find another job?

My breath catches.

What if instead of *my* Very Bad Year, this has turned into *Kasumi's* Very Bad Year?

"Listen, Kasumi." I climb the steps to her door two at a time until I'm standing in front of her. "If you won't go back to Xavier's, do you need help with money or anything until you find a new job?" I tried not to dip into my nest egg during my own Very Bad Year, but this is different. I can't let Kasumi end up homeless because she landed upside-down in my time loop.

For a second, her face softens. "No. I don't want to take your money, Sadie."

"But how will you afford to pay your rent?"

"I'll be fine." Kasumi shrugs. "I have a couple of things in the works."

I wait, hoping she'll say more, but she just moves the pastry box to her other hand and reaches for the door handle. "Well, I've got to go."

I shift my weight nervously. I know she's still mad, but we've been friends for over a decade. "Are we still—do you think we can still hang out?"

Kasumi sighs. "I don't know." She swings back around to face me. "It's not just this thing at Xavier's. You've changed. Maybe the pressure from your parents has finally gotten to you. Or maybe it's Alex's new job with all those finance-bros that's making you care more about superficial stuff instead of what actually matters."

"What?" I stumble back against the stair railing. "Alex's job has nothing to do with it." But a little part of me can see how she might think it does. Until Alex started working at Wright and Moore, he never used to hang out with guys who made inappropriate, sexist comments and hit on us at parties. The few times Zach slithered around during my Very Bad Year, I shut him down. But in my second chance year, I've been putting up with him. I've been putting up with a lot of things that make me uneasy.

Confusion curls in my gut like a Swiss roll and suddenly, I'm overwhelmed by the desire to tell Kasumi everything. Maybe if she knew how things went wrong during my Very Bad Year, she'd understand. "Actually, Kasumi, the thing is…" I raise my eyes to meet her gaze. "Do you believe in the supernatural? Like, magic and wishes…things like that?"

Kasumi stares at me like I've just told her I've given up chocolate.

"Look, I know it sounds far-fetched." I take a deep breath. "But the thing is that about seven months ago, I met this fortune teller, and she—"

"Are you serious?" Kasumi cuts me off. "I just lost my job, and I'm trying to talk to you about our friendship, and you're going on about fortune tellers?"

Oh God. This isn't going well. "No, that's not what I'm doing—" Except that's exactly what I'm doing. "It's just that—"

Kasumi shakes her head. "I really do have to go." She

looks down at the pastry box in her hands, a frown creasing her brow. "Thanks for the croissants." And before I can say another word, she turns and disappears into her building.

Why did I think this was a good idea?

I slowly turn and start walking for home. And because the universe likes to kick me when I'm down, my phone buzzes with my mom's name. I swipe to answer.

"Hi, honey, what are you up to?" she asks.

"Oh...I just left Kasumi's apartment."

"Well tell her hi from me," my mom says, showing she wasn't really listening.

"Okay, I will. Next time I see her. Because I just *left*."

But my mom forges on. "I'm calling to let you know that your dad and I would like to come into the city for dinner with you and Owen next month." Owen and I grew up in New Brunswick, New Jersey. It's not a bad drive into the city, so my parents come for dinner every now and then. My mom names a date, and I check my calendar. It's during the week, so I shouldn't have a problem getting the time off.

That thought gives me a great idea. "Hey," I say. "Do you want to eat at Xavier's?"

I've worked there for four years, but my parents have never been. Despite his general assholery, Xavier is a fantastic chef, and the restaurant is gorgeous. It might be nice for my mom and dad to finally see where I work. To show them it's not a random hole-in-the-wall, but the kind of place people book months in advance. I could make a special dessert for their visit. And Xavier's bullying only happens behind closed doors. In public, he's the picture of the generous, charismatic celebrity chef. He'll come out in the dining room and absolutely charm my parents.

"Oh no, honey. That's okay. Your dad has already booked a table at Russo's."

Russo's? I nearly choke. Russo's is one of those New York restaurants that's been around for decades. It was probably the place to be back in the forties and fifties when Frank Sinatra was friends with the owner. But now it's a sad, dated restaurant that serves overcooked spaghetti and soggy cheesecake to tourists, charging them a boatload because the place is "iconic."

"Mom, you don't want to go to Russo's, believe me. The food there is not good."

"Don't be such a snob, Sadie," she snaps. "It's on your dad's bucket list. Let him have this."

I'm the snob? They're the ones who can't even admit to their college-professor friends what their daughter does for a living. I once overheard them tell someone at a party that I'm working in a restaurant while I look into master's programs. I don't even have an undergraduate degree.

Yet I keep trying. "Okay, well, maybe I'll make some special desserts. We could go back to my place after."

"Sure," she says, and through the phone, I hear her typing on her computer. My mom isn't listening again. But she agreed to the plan, and right now, that feels like a victory.

Chapter 19

I stand in the doorway of my apartment with a towel on my head, another one wrapped around my body, and a very annoyed man in a suit glaring at me from the hall. "Oh my gosh, is it seven p.m. already?"

Alex brushes past me into the apartment. "Seven oh five, actually. You don't look even *close* to ready."

We're supposed to be at a cocktail party for a new client at Alex's firm in twenty-five minutes. I can't believe I totally lost track of time. I was at Higher Grounds making lemon blueberry scones, and then someone called and asked Zoe if they could order two dozen muffins for tomorrow morning. I already had half the ingredients on the prep table, so I said yes. And then all of a sudden, it was 6:30 p.m.

"I'm sorry! I got caught up at Higher Grounds. A last-minute order for muffins. Here, have a lemon blueberry scone while you wait."

Alex drops the bag on the coffee table without even peeking inside and sits down on the couch with a huff. "Please just hurry."

"Okay. Sorry." I run for the bathroom, where I grab the

hair dryer and point it at my head. When I turn it off, Alex is swearing.

"What? What is it?" I dart back out into the main room just in time to see Alex pushing Gio off his lap.

"This cat is getting fur all over me," he grumbles.

"Sorry, he's aggressively affectionate. It means he likes you." I grab Gio off the couch and put him on the bed.

"I'd prefer he liked me from across the room," Alex mutters. He takes one more swipe at his sleeve and pulls out his phone, sighing at the time.

I remind myself that Alex is only grumpy because he's annoyed that I'm late. "Okay. I just need to get dressed, and then I'll be ready."

I grab the first dress I find on a hanger in my closet—the pink slip dress—and Alex looks up and says, "Can you wear one of the designer ones I bought you?"

I tense up at this. I know Alex bought me those clothes specifically for these work events, but something about him dictating my outfits doesn't sit right with me. I'm tempted to pretend I didn't hear, and passive aggressively wear the pink one, but at the last moment, something stops me. That's how the old Sadie would have reacted. Instead, I slowly count backward from ten. Alex is a good guy who wants me by my side for important events. Why am I being so resistant?

I put on a black Dolce & Gabbana dress and, even though I've been on my feet all day, I brave the Louboutins again. "What do you think?"

The smile that lights up Alex's face has me wondering why I ever thought of arguing with him. Still, when I stop in the bathroom before we head out and I see my favorite pair of dangly thrift-store earrings hanging by the mirror, I throw them on at the last second.

We take a cab to the party, which is on the rooftop deck of a swanky financial district office building that belongs to Alex's new client. When we arrive, the sun is just beginning to set. To our left, beyond the glass-and-chrome skyscrapers, the sky is lit up with streaks of amber and indigo. To our right, the lights of the Brooklyn Bridge glitter in the distance.

Something about that view is so familiar that I stumble to a stop in my four-inch heels, and Alex reaches out to grab my arm before I fall over. I've been on this rooftop before. I've been to this *party* before.

I wasn't wearing haute couture then, because Alex never bought me these expensive clothes during my Very Bad Year. And I didn't arrive with him at the start of the party. Instead, I'd come at the end, just as the guests were trickling out. At the time, I hadn't realized that spouses and partners were even invited to attend. I was there to meet Alex for a late dinner after the party had already wound down. Looking back from the perspective of my second chance year, it's clear that by this point in my Very Bad Year, Alex wasn't as serious about our relationship.

Of course he wasn't, I realize as I watch servers hand off glasses of champagne to men in bespoke suits and women wearing diamonds that cost more than the GDP of some small countries. I wasn't biting my tongue and trying to fit in back then. I was speaking my mind when guys like Zach made outdated, sexist jokes about women. And slowly, Alex had started to pull away.

Now, as Zach crosses my line of vision, headed to the bar, another memory begins to form. A crude joke from Zach. A sharp response from me. A fight with Alex out on the sidewalk.

This is the night Alex and I broke up.

The memory leaves me shaken. I'm about to take a moment to collect myself in the ladies' room when Alex slips an arm around my shoulders and presses a kiss to my cheek. "I'm so glad you're here. You look beautiful."

I smile up at him. It doesn't matter what happened last time around. Alex and I are fine now.

We grab our drinks and make the rounds. The upside of being kind of a big mouth is that I'm not shy, and I'm comfortable talking to all kinds of people. It also helps that I work for Xavier. He's been on *Top Chef* and the Food Network, and he has a best-selling cookbook, so people want the inside story of what it's like to work for him. Mostly, I do a lot of lying about how great it is.

After Alex has done a sufficient amount of schmoozing, we make our way to a circle of outdoor couches arranged under a string of twinkling lights. A group of people from his office are sitting around with cocktails in their hands, and Alex and I take the last two seats. Alex immediately gets sucked into a conversation about finance-related things that are completely over my head, so I introduce myself to the man sitting on the other side of me.

He gives me a firm handshake and tells me his name is Brett.

"I don't think we've met before, have we?" I ask. By this point, I know most of Alex's coworkers.

"No, I'd definitely remember meeting *you*." He flashes his perfectly straight, white teeth, and I almost expect them to glint with a cartoony sparkle. Is he hitting on me? Because I'm pretty sure he saw me sit down with my boyfriend.

Brett tells me he's a recent hire at Alex's company, and then launches into a ten-minute monologue about all the firms that were competing for him. Finally, he seems to remember that conversations are supposed to go two ways, because he asks me, "So, what do you do, Sadie?"

"I work at Xavier's. It's a restaurant in Williamsburg."

He nods. "Yeah, I've heard of Xavier's. Never been, though." He gives me a shrug. "To be honest, I don't make it out of Manhattan much, unless I'm headed to the Hamptons."

Right. "Sorry to hear that, Brett."

"But you never know," he continues. "With the right motivation, I might be convinced to come out and try it." He gives me a meaningful look, and I stare back at him.

If Brett is expecting me to convince him to come out to Xavier's, he's going to be waiting a very long time.

Brett finally breaks the silence. "I'm not surprised you're in the restaurant business."

"Really?" I'm at the edge of my seat to see where he's going with this.

"Yeah." He flashes me another glinty grin. "You seem like you'd do really well in the kind of job where you work for tips."

Wow.

"Well!" I keep my voice sugary sweet. "It's nice to meet

you, Brett." I shift in my seat so I can angle my arm into Alex's side and press my knee against his. He keeps talking to the guy to his right, so I give him a good jab with my elbow. Finally, Alex seems to realize that I want his attention. He turns and puts an arm around me. "I think my girlfriend is trying to tell me something," Alex says to the guy he's been talking to, and they both laugh. "Do you need another drink, honey?"

"Yes. I definitely need another drink."

We head to the bar and order cocktails. "Well, I met the new guy, Brett," I tell Alex, rolling my eyes. "He seems like a real charmer."

Alex shrugs. "He's not so bad when you get to know him."

I have a flash of Kasumi rebuking me for putting up with Alex's finance-bro friends. I can almost hear her muttering, *On what planet would Brett ever be* not so bad? And damn it. I miss her.

I look out across the rooftop, scanning the party guests. "Is that new woman here?" I ask Alex. "The one you hired a couple of months back?" Most of the women I meet at these events are girlfriends or wives. It's nice to remember that in addition to Brett, they recently hired a qualified woman, too.

"Um, no." Alex's gaze slides over my shoulder to the view of the skyline.

"Oh, too bad. Why didn't she come?"

"Uh, not sure," he says, turning to take our drinks from the bartender.

I cock my head, trying to meet his gaze. "Maybe I'll meet her next time."

"Maybe." Alex hands me my drink, but still doesn't make eye contact. I watch him scan the crowd, almost like he's looking for someone to save him. It takes a minute, but when it comes to me, a knot forms in my gut.

"I'm not going to meet her, am I?" I slowly shake my head. "Because you didn't actually hire her."

Alex sets his old-fashioned down on the bar. "Look..."

"Oh God." I didn't think it could get worse, but it just got worse. "You hired Brett instead, didn't you?"

Alex clears his throat. "There were a lot of factors that went into the decision."

I cross my arms over my chest. "Did you even talk to Zach about hiring her? Or was that just something you said to get me to be quiet?"

Alex sighs like he wishes he could get me to be quiet right now. "I'm doing what I can, but there's only so much I have control over. You don't know what the culture is like in an industry like finance."

"Right," I say. "I have no idea about sexist workplaces. Are you kidding? I've spent my entire career in restaurant kitchens where women are treated like second-class citizens. But just because something is 'the culture' doesn't mean you just sit down and accept it."

I can still feel Rob Thurmond's hand on my ass. How many times did those other men around the table look the other way and let him get away with touching women like that? With treating women like that? Maybe they even did it themselves because "the culture" told them it was okay. I look at Alex. "You have the power to push back and change things."

Alex scrubs a hand through his hair, leaving it sticking out on one side. I'd normally fix it for him because I know he'd hate to look messy at a work event. But right now, all I can think is *Good*.

"When you're a professional, there are conventions you follow," he says. "You can't just make a scene if you don't like how something is done." He glances around us, probably to make sure *we're* not making a scene.

Right now, I'm beyond caring about scenes. "I'm sorry, can we go back a minute? What do you mean by 'when you're a professional'?"

"I—" Alex stalls, and he seems to realize what he's said.

"You mean like you have a real job and I don't."

"I didn't mean it like that."

"What did you mean?"

He presses on his temples as if that might hold back his frustration. Then he drops his hands to his side and turns to me with his eyes flashing. "You make *pastries*, Sadie. You're very good at it. But it's not the same. I'm dealing with millions of dollars of my clients' money on a daily basis."

I stumble backward in the Louboutins and—*seriously, fuck these shoes*—almost end up on my ass. "Honestly, Alex. In all these years, I had no idea this is what you thought of my job." I slap my designer purse down on the bar. "Is that what the clothes, jewelry, and everything is about? If we were to get more serious, were you expecting that I'd give up being a pastry chef to be your Wall Street wife?"

A muscle twitches in his jaw. "I didn't expect you to give

it up. But there are all sorts of ways you can bake without having to work all the time."

"So, you're saying I could bake as . . . a hobby." My stomach churns like I swallowed a ball of raw sourdough, and I'm overcome by a feeling of déjà vu. This time, it's not because I've been at this party before, or because I've had this conversation with Alex before. It's because I've had a version of this fight with my parents a thousand times since I was a kid. I never thought that Alex felt the same way.

No wonder my parents love him so much.

My feet are killing me from standing in these heels, the lace on my dress is making me itch, and I'm too tired to argue anymore. "Okay, I'm going."

"Sadie, wait." Alex shifts his body so he's between me and the door. "I'm sorry. Please don't leave."

I hesitate, and he flashes me that Midwestern farm boy grin. The one he uses to charm people into doing things for him. The one that gets him out of trouble. The one that dismisses all of my feelings.

"Come on," he says buoyantly. "Let's get another drink and enjoy this beautiful night."

I close my eyes. I don't know what I'm doing here. In this conversation, this party. In this second chance year. It was supposed to be different. Why does it seem like I just keep making mistakes?

"I can't do this."

Alex's smile fades. "What does that mean?"

"This isn't working anymore." I pull my hand from his and pick up my purse. "I should go."

"Wait." His spine goes straight. "Are you breaking up with me?"

"I..." I hesitate. After everything I did to hold on to this relationship, *am* I breaking up with him? "I think I am."

Alex shakes his head. "You're not seriously going to end this relationship over a silly hiring issue at my company, are you?"

And right there lies the problem. That's what he thinks this is about.

"I'm sorry, Alex." I don't fit into this world, and maybe I never will. With that, I kick off my shoes, turn toward the door, and hobble slowly across the roof deck with as much grace as I can muster.

Chapter 20

August

Needless to say, I'm not looking forward to dinner with my parents. The memory of their disappointment at my inability to hold on to a great guy is still raw from the first time around. When Alex and I broke up during my Very Bad Year, my dad couldn't speak for over an hour, and I'm pretty sure my mom cried in the bathroom. I'm not in the mood to sit through round two of that scenario, especially because they'll try to convince me to get back together with him.

I'm feeling vulnerable enough that I just might do it.

In a complete reversal from my Very Bad Year, Alex has been calling and begging me to get back together with him. So far, I've been muting his calls and sending him to voicemail. But I loved him for years, and I admit that when I hear that familiar voice asking for a second chance, it's hard to not be swayed. So, when I find my parents' table at Russo's and my dad's first question is, "Where's Alex?" I avoid eye contact and mumble that he had to work.

It's not a total lie. I mean, Alex probably *is* at work.

Luckily, Owen shows up before they can ask any more

questions. "Hey," my brother says, coming up to the table from behind me. My mom jumps up to give him a hug, and then instead of sitting down, she reaches for someone else.

"You brought Jacob! How wonderful to see you, honey!"

I spin in my seat as Jacob is released from my mom's embrace and leans over to shake my dad's hand. Owen grabs the seat at the head of the table, which means Jacob ends up directly across from me.

"Hey, Sadie," he says, ducking his head. It's a sign of his shyness that, in the past, I might have dismissed as weird. But now I know better. It's almost like he needs a moment to work up to it, and then his eyes slowly drift to mine.

Jacob is one of those guys who unfairly has eyelashes for days, and I don't know how he avoids them brushing against his glasses when he blinks. He hasn't shaved today, and my gaze drops to his jaw. The memory of his bristled cheek marking my skin as his mouth moved across my neck sends a shiver through me. How is it possible that I can have such a visceral reaction to an experience that doesn't exist for him?

Jacob looks at me sideways, probably because I'm staring at him with a blush working its way across my cheeks. I blink and force a smile that aspires for casual but probably lands somewhere closer to clownish. The server comes to the rescue before I can pull out my nervous babble, thank God. She drops the menus on the table and asks if we're interested in seeing the wine list.

"Yes, we're absolutely interested in wine." It's my only hope of getting through this dinner.

Once we've ordered our wilted salads and soggy pasta—if

the kitchen staff at Xavier's could see me at Russo's, I'd never live it down—my mom starts fussing over Jacob.

"Oh, honey." She presses a hand to his arm. "We saw *Black Moon* on the day it came out. And as soon as I heard the opening music, I would have recognized it as yours anywhere."

Black Moon is a sci-fi film that came out recently. I've seen the posters on bus stops around the city. I guess Jacob composed the music.

My dad laughs. "When the credits rolled at the end, Fran told everyone in the theater that the music composer is our *second son*."

Jacob's an only child, and both his parents are human rights lawyers who are always traveling to far-off ends of the earth. Growing up, he spent as much time at our house as he did at his own.

My mom pats him on the hand. "You were writing music at our house when you were eight years old."

Jacob gives my parents a shy smile. "It all started on that old Mac in your basement."

"We're so proud of you. The piano in the scene where the astronaut finally meets his father..." She presses a hand to her heart, eyes tearing up.

I rearrange my silverware on my napkin, throat tightening. I'm not surprised that my mom and dad have kept up with Jacob's career. They've been bragging about his accomplishments since we were kids. After all, he competed with Owen for the top spot in their high school class, attended the most prestigious music school in the country, and now he works as a composer. Who wouldn't be proud of all that? But maybe this is why I kept my distance from him when we were younger. Because it only highlighted how little interest my parents take in *me*. Their actual offspring.

But I'm not a kid anymore. My parents' interest in Jacob over me certainly isn't Jacob's fault, and holding on to this grudge is immature and petty. Especially because Jacob is my friend now. So, when my mom pauses to flag down the server for a glass of iced tea, I lean across the table. "Congratulations on *Black Moon*, Jacob."

"Thanks."

"You didn't tell me you had another Joshua James film coming out."

He rubs his hand across the stubble on his chin. "I guess I've had my mind on my next project."

"I'm always sharing *my* work with you," I tease him. Jacob's become a regular at Higher Grounds these past few months. Mrs. Kaminski pulled another chair up to the counter for him, and she hisses at anyone else who tries to sit there. "Maybe we should go see it this weekend."

"We?" His eyebrows shoot up. "Like, you and me?"

"Yeah, you and me." For a moment, I think back to that day we ran into Paige in the hallway of their apartment building. They seemed to be pretty friendly then. Had that been a date? And have they had any more since? Maybe Jacob feels awkward because he thinks I just asked him out. Except he's my brother's best friend, of course Jacob doesn't think I asked him out. I give his foot a light kick under the table, just like I would to Owen. "Let's go see your film. Then when we get dinner afterwards, I promise I won't announce that you're my *second brother* to the whole restaurant."

"Yeah." His gaze slides to mine. "I'm... definitely not your brother." There's an intensity in his voice that has my breath catching in my throat.

"So," Owen interrupts from the end of the table. "I have some news."

We all look up, and I brace myself because I remember Owen's news from my Very Bad Year. While I'm happy for him, I'm also aware that my parents' outsized reactions are going to rapidly kill my goodwill.

"You're looking at the new CTO of AstRoBot," Owen announces.

My mom gasps. "Oh, Owen, that's wonderful!"

"Well done, son!" My dad claps Owen on the back.

Jacob grins at him. "Nice work."

"This calls for champagne!" My mom waves her arms to flag down the server like she's lost at sea. "My son just got a huge promotion," my mom hollers at the server, and at everyone else within a mile of our table. "We'll need some bubbly over here."

"Congratulations, Owen," I murmur. I love my brother, and it's not that I begrudge him this attention. It's that just once, I'd love for my parents to fawn over me this way. Watching them treat Owen's promotion like it's the Nobel Prize, when they didn't even come to my culinary school graduation, is a kick in the gut.

Once the champagne is poured, my brother launches into an explanation of the challenges of applying computer vision to moving objects. My dad wouldn't understand a word unless it was recited in ancient Greek, but he's on the edge of his seat. After a while, though, my mom's eyes start to glaze over, so she turns to me and Jacob.

"Fran," Jacob says. "Did Sadie tell you she's the new pastry chef at a café in Williamsburg? There's a line out the door in the mornings, and you have to show up before noon or everything will be gone."

"No, she didn't tell me."

Jacob grins at me. "Her pastries are amazing. Café business must have doubled since Sadie took over."

I flash him a grateful smile.

My mom looks back and forth between me and Jacob. "What happened to Xavier's?"

I shrug. "I'm still at Xavier's. This is a side gig, on my days off."

"What's this about Sadie having a second job?" my dad cuts in, finally giving up on whatever computer-y things Owen was talking about.

Jacob repeats what he told my mom.

"Huh," my dad says, exchanging a glance with my mom that I can't quite interpret. "And you're making a solid income there?"

I shrug. "I do okay." Zoe can't afford to pay much, but I enjoy hanging out at Higher Grounds and trying new recipes. And it's all going into my Someday Bakery fund, so I don't really mind. "Why?"

"I'm wondering if you could consider leaving Xavier's."

I study my dad's face. Where is he going with this? Why would he encourage me to leave a stable job to work for myself? I've been talking about opening my own bakery for the past twenty years; is it possible that my parents were really listening? That they might actually be ready to support this dream? "Oh, I'm not sure I'm quite there yet." I give my parents a smile. "But hopefully someday."

"Well, play with the numbers," my dad says. "If this café job is flexible and could cover your rent, this might be an excellent time to think about going back to school. Your mom and I would be willing to help you out with other expenses, and Brooklyn College is actually very affordable."

I stare at them, speechless. I can't believe we're talking about this. After I was fired during my Very Bad Year, my parents kept pushing me to enroll in college classes. And, okay, I hated it, but I kind of understood. I was homeless and living at Jacob's at the time. I'd told myself that my parents were just looking out for me, encouraging me to have a backup plan. *But I have a good job in my field.* Why would they be pushing this unless they truly don't respect my work at all? It shouldn't surprise me, but somehow it always does.

"What are you talking about?" I manage to sputter. "What would I even study at Brooklyn College?"

"There are all sorts of options." My mom gives me an encouraging smile. "With your outgoing personality, you'd be great at teaching. Or something in sales and marketing, maybe."

I stare down at the table, shaking my head. How long have they been waiting for an opportunity to spring this on me? When my dad texted me about Brooklyn College during my Very Bad Year, he'd said, *This is all for the best.*

Maybe my parents were secretly glad I'd lost my job because it gave them leverage to push me back to school.

"You could check out the catalog," my dad chimes in. "See what interests you."

"Unless the catalog is from Williams Sonoma, I doubt anything will interest me."

"Well, talk it through with Alex. See what he thinks."

My head snaps up as resentment rolls over me. "Who cares what Alex thinks?"

My dad sits back in his chair. "I assume you and Alex talk about major life decisions with each other."

"I'm not going to Brooklyn College. Or any college. There." I wave my hand in the air. "Major life decision decided. And I'm not going to talk it over with Alex because Alex and I broke up." It's a stupid move to blurt it out without thinking, but I get a perverse satisfaction from seeing the shock on my parents' faces. Across the table, Jacob sits up straighter in his chair.

"You broke up with Alex?" Owen lowers his fork to his plate. "When?"

"Uh, a couple of weeks ago."

My mom sighs, setting her water glass down on the table with more force than necessary. "Oh, Sadie. What did you do this time?"

"Me? Why do you assume it's *my* fault?"

"Because you're the one who's always so impulsive. Always making wild declarations and causing scenes."

"Well, for your information"—I cross my arms over my chest like a petulant teenager, because that's what being with my parents reduces me to— "you can't blame this on my big mouth."

"So, what happened?" my dad demands.

I hesitate. If I tell them what really happened, they *will* blame my big mouth. They'll say I should have stayed out of Alex's work concerns and kept my opinions to myself. And who knows? Maybe they're right.

"Listen," Owen cuts in. "Maybe we should talk about this another time, when we've all had some time to process it."

I'm both grateful for my brother and annoyed that he has to step in so our parents will leave me alone. Ever since he got his graduate degree and landed his tech job, they've treated him like an adult, asking for his opinion and respecting his boundaries. While I'm still the screwup kid who needs to get her life together.

Sometimes I wonder if that will ever change.

I shove my plate of penne alla vodka to the side, having lost what little appetite I had to begin with. The server comes to remove it, and while she's reaching between me and my dad, Jacob leans in and murmurs, "Are you okay?"

I just shake my head and look away.

Owen makes a valiant effort to lighten the mood, steering the conversation toward a funny story about a robot accidently driving through a wall at work, and Jacob eggs him on with uncharacteristically booming laughter. I appreciate their efforts, but my dad's face is as hard as a burned loaf of bread, and my mom keeps sighing and shaking her head like I've brought pumpkin pie to a summer party. It would be too much for anyone to overcome.

Once again, I've ruined a perfectly good dinner with my wild declarations and impulsivity.

The server stops by with dessert menus, and my mom puts up a hand to refuse hers. "Thank you, but I'm afraid I've lost my appetite. I've got a terrible headache."

That's when I remember I baked for everyone. "We were going to have dessert at my place, remember? I made a flourless chocolate cake with raspberry coulis, and white chocolate basil macarons." I look back and forth between my parents. "You still want to come for dessert, right?"

They exchange a glance, and then my dad shakes his head. "I think it's going to have to be another time."

"But—" I walked all the way to the gourmet food store in Greenpoint for Tahitian vanilla beans. I spent all day baking in my tiny studio kitchenette. I macerated two pounds of raspberries. But it's going to have to be another time? "Maybe you could come back to my apartment and take some with you? For later?" I can hear the longing in my voice. *Please say yes. Please make an effort because it's important to me.*

"Your mother isn't feeling well, Sadie," my dad snaps, like I'm selfish for asking.

"Okay." All of a sudden, my throat is burning, and my eyes are dangerously close to spilling over. "Maybe another time." I focus on my hands folded on the table, because if I have to make eye contact with anyone, I'm definitely going to cry.

The server is mercifully quick with the bill, and soon we're outside on the sidewalk.

"Where are you parked?" Owen asks. My dad names a

parking garage a couple of blocks away, and it's decided that Owen will walk my parents there.

"Thanks for coming," I murmur, because that's what I'm supposed to say, and then I give my parents half-hearted hugs, because that's what I'm supposed to do. "I'll see you later."

I stuff my hands into the pockets of my dress and hurry down the sidewalk toward the subway station. I don't want to give Jacob the chance to say goodbye to my parents or we'll end up on the same train back to Brooklyn. It's times like these that I'm grateful for the anonymity of New York City. I don't have to put on a brave face, and nobody will even blink if I'm crying on the subway.

As soon as I've crossed the street to the next block, the tears spill over. It's not just my parents' disappointment that hurts. It's Kasumi's silence, and my breakup with Alex, and Rob-fucking-Thurmond. It's everything that was supposed to turn out right this time around and somehow went as upside-down as a pineapple cake.

Chapter 21

I'm almost to the subway when Jacob's voice reverberates down the block from somewhere behind me, calling my name. I pick up my pace, pretending I don't hear him. I can't take Jacob seeing me with my swollen nose and mascara dripping down my face, on top of everything else. But he says my name again, only a couple of feet away now, and his footsteps thump on the pavement. *"Sadie, wait."*

"What is it, Jacob?" I swipe at my wet cheeks with the palm of my hand.

He brushes past me, putting a gentle hand on my arm. "Hey."

Stumbling to a stop, I stare over his shoulder. "Did you need something?"

Jacob shifts his body in the direction of my gaze until he appears in my line of vision. "I came to see if you're okay, but I guess it's pretty obvious that you're not."

"I'm fine. I just want to go home." Alone. Pulling my hand into the sleeve of my jacket, I use it to swipe at my eyes.

Jacob cocks his head, looking me over, and then turns to a nearby hot dog vendor. He asks for a bottle of water and a handful of napkins, leaving a few dollars in return. Shifting the bottle of water so it's under one arm, he hands me the napkins. When I've mopped up most of the tears and mascara, he opens the water and holds it out to me. "I'm going the same direction. Let me ride with you and make sure you get there okay."

Behind his glasses, Jacob's eyes are bittersweet chocolate, and all my desire to be alone melts away. I nod, wiping my cheeks one last time. "Thanks."

We walk to the train without talking. I don't want to discuss my feelings or rehash our disastrous dinner, so I appreciate that Jacob doesn't always need to fill the silence.

When we get off the train at our stop in Williamsburg, the crowd surges onto the subway platform. Jacob tucks my hand into the crook of his arm, so we stay together. When we're out of the crush, I should let go, but I don't. There's something comforting about holding on to this solid man, something comforting about his warm scent that calls to mind his peaceful, quiet apartment in the days when I lived there during my Very Bad Year. Jacob glances at my hand on his arm and keeps walking.

Once we're out on the street, it's a short walk to my building. After I fish my key out of my purse, I look up at Jacob. "So, I don't know if I mentioned that there's cake in here. If somebody doesn't help me, there's a very good chance I'll eat it all by myself."

Jacob's lips curve into a smile. "You had me at chocolate raspberry."

Five minutes later, Jacob is settled on my couch with a plate of flourless chocolate cake and a side of macarons. I sit on the bed across from him and take a bite of my own piece. It's perfect—a dense, rich layer of fudge with tart raspberry puree running through the center. "Hmmm. Not bad."

"Are you kidding?" he says. "It's delicious, as usual. I think I've gained ten pounds since you started baking at Higher Grounds." He pats his flat stomach for emphasis.

"You have not. Besides, you don't even eat that much. Mrs. Kaminski eats her own scone and then pilfers yours when she thinks nobody's watching." I know he sees her and pretends he doesn't.

We chat for a bit about Mrs. Kaminski and everyone at Higher Grounds. José Luis ended up sketching me in the cake-dress after all, except this time, Gio is in the picture, weaving around my legs. I had it framed, and now it hangs next to the bed. Jacob pulls his phone from his pocket to show me a sketch José Luis drew of him wearing a suit made of piano keys. "I hung it in my music studio."

"It looks just like you."

Jacob swipes through the photos to show me one more. "Last week when you were at Xavier's, José Luis sketched Mrs. Kaminski doing a Gene Kelly *Singin' in the Rain*–style dance with her cane." He flashes me a grin that's layered with affection. "She said it was the onions in her sandwich, but I honestly think she teared up."

I smile back at him, and it occurs to me that I felt alone when I left my parents back at the restaurant, but I'm not. I've built myself this quirky little family at Higher Grounds, and they mean a lot to me. I don't know how I didn't see them for who they really are during my Very Bad Year. My gaze drifts to Jacob. I don't know how I didn't see him, either.

I hop up off the bed. "Do you want more cake?"

His smile says he does. I refill his plate and sit back on the bed. "Thanks for this, Jacob."

"For what? Coming over and eating all your cake?"

I laugh. "Yes, actually. Thanks for coming over and eating all my cake. And..." I lift a shoulder. "Thanks for cheering me up. I felt pretty awful earlier, and now...I don't."

"Seriously, your parents really missed out on this." He lifts his plate. "And I'm sorry they're so wrapped up in their idea of what success looks like that they can't see how talented you are."

The back of my throat feels like raw sugar, and my eyes sting. I look away and grasp for a subject change because if I don't, I'll start crying again. "So, what about your parents? They're attorneys, right?"

He nods. "Yep. Human rights."

"How do they feel about you being a musician? Didn't they want you to go to law school or something?"

"Well..." Jacob shrugs, his face turning thoughtful. "It probably won't come as a surprise to you that I was a really shy kid."

"Not a huge surprise, no."

"My parents are the complete opposite. They've never been afraid to stand up for what they believe, to challenge the system, or defend someone who's powerless. It's why they're so good at what they do." He cocks his head and gazes across the space between us. "You kind of remind me of them, actually."

"*Me?*" Jacob's parents sound amazing, while I'm pretty much a mess.

"When we were kids, you were always standing up to bullies and looking out for the quiet, shy, weird kids." He gives me a self-deprecating smile. "Like me and Owen."

I'm not sure what to say to that. I remember Jacob telling me this once before, on New Year's Eve during my Very Bad Year. In school, I had a pretty easy time of it. Socially, anyway. But my brother was the classic nerd: supersmart and really into computers, he wore glasses like Jacob, and although he's over six feet now, he didn't hit a growth spurt until senior year. So, I got used to defending him. When I discovered that bullies will back down if you stand up to them, I decided to use my powers for good and help out other vulnerable kids on the playground, too.

But that was a long time ago.

"So, your parents didn't care if you became a lawyer because you were shy?"

"Sort of. When I was about five they sent me to a child psychologist because they were worried I wasn't making any friends. She was trained as a music therapist and had all these instruments in her office. I got really into them, and around the same time, you guys moved to town and the teacher sat Owen at my table. He was the same kind of weird as me, and well...you know the rest."

"And now you're wildly successful, so your parents must be very pleased."

He sets his fork on his plate. "I'm not sure I'd say I'm wildly successful. I'm lucky that I get paid to write and play music, and I'm one of the rare people who can live off my passion. That's all I can really ask for."

As Jacob leans back on my couch and props one foot on

his opposite knee, I'm struck by his quiet confidence. How is it possible that I ever thought this man was weird or awkward? He knows exactly who he is, and he doesn't need to apologize or change to please anyone. I wish I could be more like that.

Jacob slowly lowers his plate to the coffee table, and I realize I'm staring. He gazes back at me, and there's something charged in the air between us. My heart rattles in my chest, and his breath hitches, telling me he feels it too.

At that moment, Gio wanders out of the closet and hops up on the couch, breaking the spell. I'm not sure if I'm glad about that or not. Jacob reaches out to scratch him between his ears and, sensing an easy mark, Gio rubs his head on Jacob's leg.

"Oh, sorry about the cat fur," I say, setting my plate on the side table. "I can get him off you."

"It's fine." Jacob smiles as Gio turns up the purr. "How's it going, living with Giocoso?"

"He's the love of my life, and no man will ever live up to him."

Jacob's face turns serious. "I'm sorry about Alex. You guys were together a long time."

"Three years."

"You want to talk about it?" Jacob leans forward, resting his elbows on his knees, and Gio wanders off to check out his food bowl.

I stare down at my hands. I'm not even sure what to say about what went wrong with Alex. What went wrong with everything. "Have you ever wished for something so badly, only to finally get it and realize it's maybe not what you wanted after all?"

Jacob is silent for a moment, lips pressed together. "At least," he finally says in a low voice. "You can say you tried. Whatever it is. You gave it a shot."

"I guess. But I should have it all together by now. Like Owen does...and you."

He lets out a small laugh, shaking his head, and he seems almost bitter. "I've wanted the same thing all my life. But..." His expression darkens. "I've never had the courage to reach out and grab it."

Our eyes meet, and I don't think we're talking about his music anymore. The heat that was rising between us all evening suddenly cranks up to a broil. "Why not?" I manage.

Jacob lifts a shoulder. "I guess it's easier to hold on to hope than it is to try and fail." His face is tipped up at me, dark hair tousled and slanting across his forehead, one lock teasing the top edge of his glasses.

And— *Oh my.*

I don't *want* to be talking about his music anymore.

"But you could try and *not* fail," I whisper. I grab one hand with the other to stop them from shaking. "How will you ever know?"

He pauses, and my heart is pounding so loudly, I'm sure he can hear it.

And then he stands up from the couch.

Crosses the room.

Sinks down on the bed next to me.

Slides one hand behind my head.

And he kisses me.

Chapter 22

It's gentle at first. Our mouths come together, apart, back together again. He slides a hand up to my cheek and sits back to look at me like he can't believe I'm real. I'm shaking a little. And then he leans in again, and I'm grabbing his shirt, his hands are tangled in my hair, and our bodies are pressed together.

I thought our last kiss was intense—that kiss on his couch during my Very Bad Year—but it was nothing compared to this. Nothing compared to kissing him when I know him so much better and see him so much clearer. He shifts his weight, lowering me onto the bed and pressing my body into the mattress. I clutch his shoulders as his lips explore the sensitive skin on my jaw, my neck, behind my earlobe. His mouth finds mine again, and we kiss until my lips are swollen and my cheeks are marked from the stubble on his chin.

With every kiss, with every touch I want more. More of *him*. Desperately, I grasp the hard muscles of his shoulders and tug his shirt over his head. And it's cliché, I know it is, but the motion is a bucket of ice water dumped right over us. He freezes with his arms propped on either side of my head, blinking down at me in a daze, like he just woke up from a dream.

Or maybe it was a nightmare. Because the next thing I know, he's rolled off me, and the chilled air from the AC unit in the window blows across my heated skin. I shiver, and not in a good way.

Jacob slides to the edge of the bed and puts his head in his hands. "Shit. I can't do this."

I struggle to sit up. *"What?"*

He looks everywhere but at me. "I'm so sorry."

And just like that, all the oxygen goes out of the room. Oh my God. He's sorry. He's *sorry.* Is this really happening again?

"What the hell?" I stare at his back.

Finally, he turns to me, and the regret on his face is so agonizing that I have to look away.

"Sadie," he says. "You just broke up with your boyfriend of three years. You're upset about your parents. I came up here because you were crying and distraught. And then I made a move on you."

"I was *over* the crying when you made a move on me. I'm not crying now." Except I kind of am, but it has nothing to do with Alex or my parents, and everything to do with the humiliation I'm experiencing.

His head shakes back and forth. "Owen would *kill* me if he knew I took advantage of you when you were vulnerable."

My mouth drops open. "Excuse me? I do have some agency here. I don't need my brother to decide when I'm allowed to make out with someone."

"I know that. But I'm trying to be your friend."

I get off the bed and stomp to the other side of the room. *"Maybe I don't want to be your friend."*

Jacob slowly shakes his head. "I get it that this seemed like a good idea at the time, but I saw you crying out there on the street. This isn't—" He runs a hand through his hair. "We shouldn't start something like this. Not now when you're—"

"When I'm what?" Except I already know. I turn away, pressing a hand over my eyes. "Oh my God, I can't believe this is happening again."

"Again?"

How many times am I going to do this? What's it going to take for me to realize that Jacob isn't interested in me? He's Owen's best friend, and I'm Owen's pathetic, sad sister, and he feels sorry for me. And the worst part is that despite all of that, the sight of his messy hair and the broad chest that pressed me down into the mattress still has my heart turning to butterscotch pudding. "I think you need to leave, Jacob."

He hesitates, and then finally nods. "Can I call you tomorrow? To see if you're okay?"

I felt humiliated before, but that was nothing compared to the thought of him calling to make sure I'm not drowning my sorrows in a vat of raw cookie dough. I close my eyes. "Oh my God, please don't call me. Please just...go." I sink down on the bed, facing the wall.

Jacob moves toward the door and then pauses. *Please don't let him say anything to make this even worse.* A moment later, the door creaks open. As soon as it gently closes behind him, I'm crying again.

I reach up to wipe my eyes and a little furry head pops out from under my arm. Gio looks up into my face and meows. I pick him up and clutch him to my chest. "I'm done with men, Gio. Except you. You're the man of my dreams."

Gio purrs in agreement.

Chapter 23

September

"Sadie, can you come into my office?"

I look up in surprise from the peach cupcakes I'm decorating. My automatic reaction is that I'm about to be sacked, but... No. Xavier gets too much joy from firing people publicly, so it can't be that.

"Uh, sure." I leave my pastry bag on the prep table and follow him into his office.

He closes the door behind us and points to the couch. I sink down warily while he settles on the chair behind his desk.

"I've been hearing a lot of feedback about the restaurant's desserts lately." He pauses for me to react, but I'm honestly not sure what to say. Is the feedback negative? Positive? No doubt he's withholding that information because he gets a creepy satisfaction in leaving me off-balance.

"Okay...," I murmur.

"That feedback has been good," he finally deigns to tell me. "Very good."

I'm still not sure what he's looking for. Although I'd go

as far as to say the best pastries at Xavier's are all my concept, the executive pastry chef technically gets the credit.

"Uh, that's great."

There's another pause where he nods slowly. "It's not lost on me that the success of the restaurant's desserts should be credited to you." He presses a hand to his chest. "After myself, of course."

Of course.

But then I register the rest of his statement, and my eyes widen. Did he say credit? *To me?* "Oh wow. Thanks. I mean, the whole pastry team works really hard to ensure that everything that leaves the kitchen is the highest quality, but I do enjoy the process of creating new recipes, and obviously I'm a bit of a perfectionist when it comes to execution..." Oh God, not the nervous babble again. I snap my mouth shut.

"It's also not lost on me that you've become quite the leader. You've embraced your role in training Doug and the other new pastry staff, and you're making a real effort to help support the other divisions of the restaurant. Your willingness to focus on customer service with our VIP clientele is especially notable."

I sit up straight in my seat. Is it possible Alex was actually right when he argued Xavier wanted me to work in the dining room to test whether I was willing to be a team player? Maybe Xavier really didn't know that Rob was getting handsy. I mean, how would he know unless someone reported it? And since I didn't report it, it's likely nobody else did either.

I give Xavier my most magnanimous smile. "I'm just trying to do my part for the good of the restaurant, sir."

"It's appreciated."

"Well, I appreciate your...appreciation."

"Now." He shuffles some papers around on his desk. "I'd like to get to the point of why I called you in here."

Yes. Please get to the point.

I rub my sweaty palms on my pants.

Xavier holds up a paper that looks to be a letter of some kind. "This is from Dennis Petrucci." Xavier's current executive pastry chef. "It details Dennis's plans to end his tenure at Xavier's starting in the New Year."

Rumors have been flying that Dennis is considering job offers. But nobody has been able to verify that until now. I'm not about to blow this moment with my nervous babble, so I nod silently.

Xavier lowers the letter to the table and looks across the room at me. "I won't be making any announcements about the hiring of a new executive pastry chef until we tell the staff about Dennis's departure in a couple of months. But I wanted to let you know that I have my eye on you for the position."

I sit there frozen on the couch. Is this really happening? Have the long hours and hard work and caving to Xavier's ridiculous demands finally paid off?

"Thank you, sir," I manage to choke out. "I'm very interested in this opportunity, and I'm willing to do everything in my power to elevate Xavier's dessert offerings to the highest level."

Xavier nods. "I was hoping you'd say that."

"Absolutely."

"All right." Xavier goes back to shuffling papers. "That will be all."

I hurry out of his office and back into the kitchen, dying to tell someone about this, but Xavier made it clear that he wants to make the announcement in his own time. So I go back to icing my cupcakes, more determined than ever to make sure they're absolutely perfect. And if I have a huge grin on my face for the rest of my shift, well, I just can't help it.

On my walk home that evening, some of my joy dissipates. This promotion is the sort of thing that, in the past, I would have shared with Kasumi. And I would have talked to her about breaking up with Alex, and the mess I made with Jacob, too. But of course, I can't, because she's not speaking to me.

I pull out my phone and open it to Kasumi's Instagram page. I'm relieved to see that she seems to be doing much better than I was after being fired from Xavier's. She posts beautifully curated collections of photos promoting parties and events all over the city, and when I zoom in on her face, she seems really happy.

On impulse, I send her a message. *Hey, I just wanted to let you know I'm thinking of you. I miss you.*

I stop on the sidewalk to stare at the screen. Kasumi is constantly on social media, so maybe she'll see my message right away. Maybe she'll even respond. But a minute goes by, and then another one, and...nothing. I switch back to her Instagram profile, and just like I thought, she *is* online because at that moment, a photo pops up in her feed. It's a selfie of Kasumi grinning at the camera with Sonya and Marianne, the servers we used to be friends with at Xavier's, the ones who hated working with me in the front of the house. I'm not sure her message could be clearer.

Heart heavy, I sink down on the front step of a random apartment building.

Kasumi isn't going to give me a second chance. I blew it.

Since I'm already on Instagram, and I have no reason to hurry home, I switch over to Alex's profile. When I wasn't crying over sitcoms or eating chocolate chips straight out of the bag during my Very Bad Year, I was creeping on Alex's social media feeds. It was about this time that the blond woman showed up, the one I'm pretty sure he started dating after he broke up with me.

But this time around, *I* broke up with Alex, and instead of a blond woman, his Instagram feed is full of photos of expensive cocktails and the guys from work hanging out at their usual bar. He must not be dating her. If I scroll back farther, there are dozens of images from when we were together. I don't want to look, but my gaze is drawn there anyway. I focus on a photo of Alex holding two of my homemade strawberry rhubarb doughnuts up to his eyes like glasses.

I donut know what I'd do without you.

He's been calling me, wanting to talk, and there are times I badly want to pick up the phone. But the person I want to find on the other end is the Alex who would take silly photos with baked goods to make me laugh. The Alex who believed in my career and not just his own.

It took me two times around this same year to realize it, but Alex isn't that guy anymore.

Feeling more alone than I have in a long time, I haul myself off the stoop and keep walking. What if I called Owen to spill everything? Not about my second chance year, because my brother would definitely wonder if I'd fallen headfirst into a pot of dulce de leche when I started going on about wishes and fortune tellers. But I could talk to him about all the other stuff... Alex, and Xavier, and Jacob.

My shoulders slump. I can't talk to him about Jacob. I can't tell him his best friend tossed me aside like a fallen soufflé. Aside from the sheer humiliation I'd suffer, I do love my brother and wouldn't want to harm his friendship with Jacob. And I shouldn't break the news about the promotion at Xavier's until it's official, either.

As I approach Higher Grounds, the café glows from the pendant lamps hanging above each table, and their warmth spills out the picture window and onto the sidewalk. I peer in to see who's working tonight. José Luis stands behind the counter, smiling as he places a cup and saucer in front of a customer whose back is to me. I'm about to pull the door open when I realize I've seen that back before. It was in my apartment, and the man attached to it abruptly decided he wanted nothing to do with me.

It never occurred to me that our ill-advised make-out session would result in a joint custody arrangement, but apparently it has. Jacob quit stopping by Higher Grounds on the days I make pastries there, and I'm slowly backing away from the door now that he's inside.

It's fine. Everything is fine. I'll go home and celebrate my impending promotion with popcorn, Netflix rom-coms, and my cat.

There's nothing sad about that at all.

Chapter 24

It's not my usual day to bake at Higher Grounds, but Zoe texted to see if I'd come in and make another special order. We've been getting more customers who try my pastries at the café and then ask if they can place large orders for more. I'm a sucker for anyone who loves my baking, so I haven't been able to say no. But it means that I'm spending my days running back and forth between Higher Grounds and Xavier's, and when I finally fall into bed at night, I dream of pastry flour and confectioners' sugar.

The extra money is helping me to grow my Someday Bakery fund, and I can tell it's been helpful for Zoe, too. Right now, she's sitting at the front counter with her laptop open to a spreadsheet, and she looks like she's ready to tear her braids out of her head.

I slide a croissant in front of her, and she looks up from the computer. "Is there any possible way that two hundred and twenty-five minus three hundred and eighty-three isn't a negative number?"

I wrinkle my nose. "You're asking the person who scraped by with C-minuses in high school math. But I'm going to go out on a limb and say no?"

Her shoulders slump. "Damn it."

"I'm sorry." I top off her cup of coffee. "Anything I can help with?"

She sighs and rips off a bite of the croissant. "You're already helping— Mmmm. This is amazing. Is that apricot?"

I nod. "It's a new recipe."

Zoe slams the laptop shut and pulls the plate closer. "Thank you for coming in to do these special orders, Sadie. I don't want to put any pressure on you, but...they're really helping to keep this place afloat."

"I'm sure it's expensive to run a café like this." I've been saving to open my bakery for five years. If Zoe is struggling to keep Higher Grounds going, will it ever be possible for me to run a place of my own?

Zoe tears off another piece of croissant. "It was easier when I first opened about ten years ago. But my rent nearly doubled recently, and unless I increase my prices to match, it's harder to keep up."

"But if you raise your prices too much, people will just go to Starbucks."

"Exactly."

"Higher Grounds is so special, though." Unlike so many Brooklyn coffeehouses where, unless you have the perfect oversized flannel shirt, high-waisted jeans, and slouch in your beanie hat, you're an outsider from the minute you walk in. Here, Zoe makes everyone feel like they belong.

Even crazy cat ladies and lonely, gruff older women and shy musicians with a special place in their hearts for lonely, gruff older women.

"Thanks. I really wanted to create a space where people would feel welcome. And a community for musicians and poets and local artists."

"Well, you've definitely done that." There are packed performances like the one for the pink-haired singer-songwriter several nights a week, and a revolving display of artwork on the walls. But with Williamsburg real estate beginning to rival Manhattan prices, none of that probably brings in the kind of money Zoe needs to keep this place in the black.

My gaze slides around the room from the piano on the wood stage to the blue paint on the display cases rescued from an old five-and-dime in upstate New York. This place could easily be featured in a magazine. Zoe's wife, Natalie, is an interior designer, and she put careful thought into every little detail, like the whitewashed exposed brick walls that contrast with the dark wood furniture, the warm pendant lighting that gives each table an intimate feel, and the quirky orange and turquoise accents. There's even a wall of succulents growing behind the stage that I have no idea how Zoe keeps alive, but apparently, she has a magic touch with both people and plants.

"You know, Zoe..." I lean on the counter and look at her. "My ex-boyfriend Alex used to take me to swanky cocktail parties with his clients, and rarely were they in spaces as nice as this."

"It's all Natalie's doing," she says with more than a hint of pride in her voice over her wife's decorating skills.

"When you walk around Williamsburg, every coffee shop looks the same. They're either leather chesterfields and reclaimed wood, or they're mismatched furniture and..." I laugh. "Well, and reclaimed wood. This place is beautiful and unique."

"Thanks," Zoe says with her signature warm smile. "I really appreciate that."

"So, it occurred to me that on the nights that you close early, you could do private events here."

Zoe's eyebrows shoot up. "Yeah? Hmmm."

I nod, getting into the idea. "I bet there are hundreds of companies around Williamsburg that would love a space like this to host clients or parties for their employees."

Zoe gazes around the room. "You really think people would pay money just to host a party here?"

"Absolutely."

"What do you think I could charge for something like that?" Zoe flips open her laptop.

I name a price and she nearly drops her coffee mug. *"Really?"*

"That's just for the space. José Luis is always looking to work extra shifts. He could bartend, and if you apply for a liquor license, you could make a lot of money on wine and maybe a couple of signature cocktails. I could help you apply for one." Working in the restaurant industry, I have a little bit of experience with this. "And there's food, too. Cheese plates or—"

"Dessert." Zoe cuts me off. "We could offer Higher

Grounds coffee-and-dessert–themed parties. Cold-brew martinis with club soda and orange. Earl Grey old-fashioneds. And a spread of your amazing cakes and tarts."

"I love it!"

She starts typing on her laptop, jotting down all of our ideas. "If I could book some parties, would you be willing to make the pastries?"

"Yes!" I have no idea how I'll fit that in on top of the increasing demands at Xavier's and my gig making the regular pastries here. But I'll figure it out. Once I'm the executive pastry chef at Xavier's, I'll have an assistant and a whole team to help me execute my vision there.

Zoe looks up from the laptop and puts her chin in her hand. "How would we get the word out, though?"

I wish I could call Kasumi. With her social media skills, she'd know exactly how to promote something like this. But I keep calling, and she keeps sending me to voicemail.

If I were still with Alex, I'd try to get his firm to host a party here, but then I remember douchey Brett, aka Mr. "I don't leave Manhattan." I'm not sure the Wall Street–types would be willing to come out to Brooklyn anyway. But maybe—

"Zoe, I have a great idea. My brother's thirtieth birthday is coming up. I could throw him a party here. We'll invite all his friends at the tech company and that bar where he hangs out. They all have expendable income, and maybe some of them would be interested in a space to host parties." The fact that I still have my job means I can afford the cost of pastry ingredients and alcohol if Zoe can cover the staff.

I've celebrated my brother's thirtieth once before—during

my Very Bad Year. I took him to dinner and then to Blackbird for drinks. This is such a better idea. He deserves a big celebration, and Higher Grounds is the perfect place for it. The only problem is that I'll probably have to coordinate with Jacob. He *is* Owen's best friend after all.

And then, like he knew I was thinking of him, Jacob walks in.

We've managed to avoid each other for the past few weeks, but I've been coming into the café at less regular times, so I guess this was going to happen at some point. It's fine. I can be a mature adult about this. I am one hundred percent not thinking about how he's stroked my thigh or kissed my neck. And my body temperature is *not* rising at the sight of those beautiful hands that were all over my—

Nope. Not thinking about it.

I'm suddenly intent on rearranging the display of muffins in the case.

"Jacob, hey!" Zoe says, hopping off her chair to go around the counter and grab a cup for his café Americano. "Sadie was just telling me about an idea she has to use Higher Grounds as a space for private events on the nights we close early. As a way to bring in extra income."

I keep my head down and shuffle muffins from one side of the case to the other.

Zoe explains to Jacob about the desserts and coffee cocktails. When she's done talking, he glances in my direction. "I think it's a great idea."

"Thanks." My voice comes out breathless. "I thought we could hold Owen's thirtieth birthday party here. You know, to try it out."

"Owen would love that." Jacob gives me a tentative smile. "What can I do to help?"

I've stacked and restacked the muffins in perfect rows according to flavor, and there's no way to keep avoiding him. I look up into Jacob's eyes, and—*oh God*—my heart melts like butter. How can he seem so unaffected when I'm hyperventilating over here? Does he do a lot of yoga and meditation or something?

More likely, that night just didn't mean anything to him.

I pick up a pile of empty dessert trays. "I'll text you about the party." Before he can respond, I spin on my heels and flee to the kitchen.

Chapter 25

October

I'm standing at a prep table at Xavier's, placing cherries on top of a Black Forest gâteau, when Xavier calls my name from across the room. At the sound of his voice, I can't help but freeze up. I'm scheduled until close tonight. What if he asks me to work the front of the house serving Rob Thurmond again? I won't have any reason to say no.

While Xavier crosses the kitchen to stand in front of me, I frantically sift through a dozen possible excuses to get out of working with Rob. Maybe I could lock myself in the freezer. Or pretend to slip on a banana peel. How hard would it be to drop a sleeping pill in Rob's drink? Just as Xavier's shadow falls over the buttercream black-eyed Susans I'm piping onto a classic Victoria sandwich cake, I come up with my most far-fetched idea yet.

Maybe I should just be honest and tell him what happened the last time I worked with Rob.

"Sadie, I have a favor to ask you," Xavier says. I take a deep breath, ready to spill everything, but then I hear the next words that come out of his mouth. "I have a customer coming in on Saturday who specifically requested your mango and passion fruit cream puffs. Can you come in that morning and make them?"

My mouth drops open and I stare across the prep table. Not only is Xavier *not* demanding that I work with smarmy Rob, but he's not demanding I do anything at all. He's asking me for a favor.

One might even say he's being *polite*.

"I know you specifically asked for Saturday off," he adds. When has Xavier ever cared about a little thing like his employees' scheduling requests?

I nod dumbly. Saturday is Owen's big birthday bash at Higher Grounds, and I took off the entire weekend so I could spend every second baking for the party. I have an unbelievably long to-do list, even with all the tasks I've delegated to Zoe, José Luis, and Jacob. But—

I glance at Xavier. He's never asked me for a favor before. Or spoken to me in a calm, reasonable tone. Could this have to do with the executive pastry chef job? Maybe he really *is* considering me for the role, because otherwise, he'd definitely be barking at me right now. It's the only possible explanation.

I can't really make the cream puffs in advance, they'll go soggy and limp, so if I say yes, I'll have to come in on Saturday. I do some quick calculations in my head, cutting several hours from my birthday prep time line. If I finish all my baking for Owen's party on Friday, I'll have time to run over here to make the cream puffs on Saturday morning before I go back to help set up the furniture and change into my party clothes. It will probably mean an all-nighter on Friday, and I'll be exhausted for the party.

But if I say no, it could erase all the goodwill I'm building up with Xavier. I'll look like I'm not willing to be a team player, and that could be the end of the executive pastry chef job for me. I can't risk it, especially now that it's so close.

"Sure," I say, with as much enthusiasm as I can muster. "I'd love to help out."

Xavier gives me a long look across the prep table. "Thanks, Sadie. I appreciate it."

Friday morning, I arrive at Higher Grounds before dawn, and I've never been so thankful to work in a coffee shop in my life. Zoe greets me with a double latte, and I practically chug it while I run into the kitchen to organize my workspace and start the assembly line of mini pastries I've planned to cover the ten-foot dessert table.

The list is impressive: bite-sized lemon cheesecakes, chocolate cream puffs, and strawberry basil tarts. Orange Creamsicle macarons, rosemary shortbread, and salted caramel cookie sandwiches with espresso cream filling, just to name a few.

It's a monumental amount of work, but I'm determined to pull it off. Not just for my brother's birthday, but to help Zoe to keep the café afloat. At some point in the past few months, Higher Grounds became more than just a place where I work a part-time gig. It's a community.

My community, I realize as I slip out into the main room

to find that Mrs. Kaminski has turned into a full-on drill sergeant, barking orders at Jacob and José Luis as they attempt to hang a HAPPY BIRTHDAY sign over the coffee counter.

It's a bit early for decorations—the café is still open for regular customers today and tomorrow—but Mrs. Kaminski insisted. I think she's secretly thrilled to be included in our big project. I'm reminded again of the impression I had of her during my Very Bad Year, how I thought she was just a grumpy old bat. Now I know that she lives alone, her husband died years ago, and she's not allowed to have pets. Higher Grounds is where she found connection, the same way I did.

"Move that to the right. Over there." Mrs. Kaminski flicks a crooked finger in the general direction of José Luis's right hand.

"Here?" José Luis tugs at his end of the sign.

"No. That's all wonky." She waves to the left of Jacob. "It needs to go that way. Pull it to the left."

Narrowing his eyes in concentration, Jacob carefully slides the sign an inch to the left, and then looks to Mrs. Kaminski for confirmation. "How's this?"

"Too far now. Go right," Mrs. Kaminski snaps. But I notice a glint in her eye, and I swear now she's just messing with them. Jacob and José Luis play tug-of-war with the sign for a few more minutes until Mrs. Kaminski decides she's tortured them enough and orders them to climb down. In a graceful movement, Jacob braces his hand on his chair back and hops off, landing right in front of me. He shoots me a wink, showing he knows what Mrs. Kaminski is up to, and damn it, my heart slides sideways like layer cake on a hot day.

I quickly tear my gaze away from the man in front of me and take stock of how the rest of the setup is going. "Love the decorations, Mrs. Kaminski." Though she only growls a response, I can tell by the way the corners of her lips twitch for just a second that she's pleased with the compliment.

We've all been working on this party for weeks, and I can't believe everything is finally coming together for the big event tomorrow. José Luis practiced a dozen different cocktail recipes until we settled on our favorites, Zoe handled the food and special events liquor license, Mrs. Kaminski took charge of furniture arrangements and decorations, and Jacob pretty much did whatever I told him to do, including Ubering all over the city to pick up supplies and putting together a killer playlist to pipe through the café's speakers.

"How's it going with the desserts, Sadie?" Jacob asks, his gaze skimming over my chef's coat.

Suddenly, I remember that the ingredients for hundreds of mini pastries are covering the prep tables in back. "Oh my God. I have so much to do. I have to go." I spin on my heel and run for the kitchen where thankfully, I'm in time to pull two dozen gluten-free almond cookies out of the oven.

I fly around the kitchen setting the mixer to whip egg whites into stiff peaks and stirring choux pastry dough in a pan on the stove. I'm just starting to spread icing on an endless row of miniature dark chocolate cakes when someone slips through the door behind me. Immersed in my multitude of tasks, I only vaguely register that the person is at the sink washing their hands. I don't have even a second to look up and see who it is until suddenly, a strong male hand gently reaches over and slides the icing spatula from my grasp. Startled, I spin around to find myself staring up into Jacob's dark chocolate eyes, only inches from mine. I blush brighter than a red velvet cake.

"I'll ice them, you decorate," he says. "Does that sound okay?"

I nod, and the next thing I know, Jacob has swiped my tray of mini cakes along with my bowl of icing. "Zoe told me you're in a time crunch because you have to do some work for your boss tomorrow morning." He gracefully smooths chocolate buttercream over each delicate cake top, surprisingly good at this. I guess those piano-playing hands are pretty skilled with instruments of the nonmusical variety.

But let's be honest. I already knew that.

I busy myself with filling a pastry bag full of vanilla cream and not staring at his forearms. "Yeah. It looks like it's going to be an all-nighter for me."

"Not if there are two of us tackling it." Jacob glances up from the cupcakes and lowers the spatula to the table. "If you want my help, that is." His face flashes with uncertainty, and I realize this is the first time we've been alone together since that kiss in my apartment.

These past few weeks, Jacob and I have been too immersed in party planning to act weird about that night, and we seem to have come to an unspoken agreement to pretend nothing happened between us. But it's one thing to hang out with the group in the café while making lists about party supplies and talking about streaming my brother's favorite bands. It's entirely another to spend a whole day covered in sugar and cocoa powder while enclosed in a hot kitchen together.

Just thinking about it makes me want to wriggle out of this chef's coat to cool down.

But Jacob doesn't feel that way about me, I remind myself. So, instead, I say, "That's really nice, Jacob. Thank you."

Jacob shrugs it off. "I admire how hard you're working to make this Higher Grounds venture a success." He gives me a crooked smile. "But to be honest, I'm really just sucking up in the hopes that you'll let me cut in the long lines when you open your own bakery."

I laugh, and despite our messy interlude in my apartment, I'm reminded of how far Jacob and I have come this past year. It's almost unimaginable that he was around for most of my life, and I barely knew him. I certainly didn't appreciate him the way I should have. This friendship with Jacob is a second chance I'm truly grateful for. "You know you'll always be welcome in my bakery."

He flashes me a grin across the table, and with a flourish, gives the last cake on his tray a swipe of chocolate buttercream. "Now that these are done, what would you like me to do next? I'm at your service. There's just one thing I ask." He has a smear of chocolate on his cheek. It's killing me not to reach over and gently wipe it off.

Instead, I twist the pastry bag in my hands. "What is it?"

He laughs. "Please go easier on me than Mrs. Kaminski."

Chapter 26

It's the evening of Owen's birthday party, and Jacob and I are finally done with all the baking. So. Much. Baking. I'm coated in a fine layer of flour and powdered sugar that's going to take weeks to wash off. But it was more fun than I expected. And, thanks to Jacob's help, not only did I get everything done for Owen's party, but Xavier is serving up some beautiful cream puffs as we speak. I survey Mrs. Kaminski's decorations, José Luis's bar setup, and my pastry table. The café looks amazing, the pastries are delicious, and I'm really proud of us for pulling it off. We finish the last-minute details—lighting candles, polishing cocktail glasses—and the guests begin to filter in. I make the rounds greeting people, and when anyone compliments me on the great space I picked for the party, I hand them one of the business cards that José Luis designed for Zoe.

My brother arrives, and everyone yells "Surprise!" even though the party technically isn't one. I told him a time and place, but we didn't share the guest list or any of the details. So Owen does look genuinely stunned when he sees the crowd of people who came to celebrate him and notices the beautiful spread of cocktails and desserts.

Across the room, Jacob and I exchange a smile, and a warmth spreads through me. My brother really is lucky to have a friend who cares about him like family.

Owen wades through the crowd to come over and give me a hug. "Thanks, Sadie. I can't believe you did all this for me."

"It was a group effort," I tell him, glancing across the café to look for Jacob, who seems to have been sucked into the crowd now. "All of my café friends helped, and Jacob's around here somewhere, too."

Owen hitches his chin at someone behind me. "He's over there with Paige."

I turn around to find Jacob and Paige huddled by the dessert table. She samples a macaron and leans into Jacob as if it's so delicious, she might fall over. He laughs and takes her arm to catch her. I should have realized Paige would be here. She and Jacob seem pretty cozy, and from the looks of things, I guess they've been hanging out after all. Maybe she's the real reason he backed off from me.

I look away. "Come on, I want you to meet some people." I pull Owen to the table where José Luis is mixing cocktails. "José Luis, this is Owen."

José Luis's eyes light up. "Owen! We've heard so much about you." He leans across the bar to wrap Owen in an embrace, and Owen hugs him back like they're long-lost friends.

"Thanks for helping Sadie throw this party. It really

means a lot." Owen takes the orange rooibos old-fashioned José Luis offers him.

"We'd do anything for Sadie the Cat Lady," José Luis confides, giving me a wink.

Owen looks between José Luis and me. "So, I've been wondering how Sadie ended up with that nickname—"

Oh no.

Someday, I'm going to have to come clean and tell everyone at Higher Grounds that I never had a cat named Zoe. But today is not the day. Like so many things about this second chance year, I don't really have an explanation that won't make me sound like I've been spending too much time with my head in a hot oven.

"It's not important." I grab my brother by the arm before José Luis can say anything. "Come on, you need to meet Zoe." I tug Owen toward the dessert table and away from this conversation.

"Wait!" José Luis calls to us. "I didn't give Owen his birthday gift yet."

We turn back around.

"Gift?" Owen's eyebrows rise. "You didn't have to—"

"It's just a little something." José Luis shrugs, pulling a gift bag from under the bar and handing it to my brother.

"Aw, thanks," Owen says, pushing aside the tissue paper. He pulls a picture frame from the bag and turns it over in his hands. *"Whaaaat?"* His gaze flies to José Luis and then back to the picture. *"Wow."*

"Oh my gosh, José Luis!" I say, staring over Owen's shoulder. "It's gorgeous."

Similar to the sketch of me in the cake-dress and Jacob

in the piano-suit, José Luis has drawn my brother wearing a cartoony robot costume and skateboarding on a giant video game controller. It's so perfectly Owen that I stare at it in awe.

"This is amazing," Owen says, running a hand over the glass. "How did you even know what I look like?"

"Jacob gave me a photo." José Luis waves his hand like it's no big deal, but I can see he's pleased with our reactions. "And both he and Sadie talk about you all the time."

Owen cocks his head in my direction with a *you know you love me* grin on his face. I give him an exaggerated shrug like I have no idea what José Luis is talking about.

"Thank you so much." Owen nods at the gift in his hand. "I love it. It's going on the wall in my office, and all the other tech geeks at work will be jealous."

A couple approaches the bar looking for drinks, and José Luis picks up his cocktail shaker. "Guess I should get back to work."

We say goodbye, and I flash him a grateful smile as I tug my brother over to the dessert table. Zoe is setting out mini lemon shortbread cookies on a platter, and when I introduce her to Owen, she circles the table to give him a hug.

"Thanks for letting Sadie host my party here," Owen says after he's hugged her back.

"Oh, it's nothing. We adore Sadie," Zoe says with a smile in my direction, and again, I'm reminded of how lucky I am to be a part of Higher Grounds. Zoe and José Luis would have put equal effort into this party even if keeping the café afloat wasn't the motivation. Just because Owen's my brother and this party is important to me.

"She probably didn't tell you," Zoe continues, "but there are lines out the door for her pastries. Customers *love* them. It's been amazing for business."

"Sadie didn't tell me anything," Owen says, poking me in the ribs. "But Jacob's been raving about it."

I look sideways at my brother with the extremely childish urge to pull him aside and demand to know everything Jacob said about me. But instead, I blink innocently. "I'm sure Jacob hasn't been *raving*. He just likes my croissants."

Owen mutters something under his breath that sounds an awful lot like "if that's what you want to call them."

Zoe grins at us. "Owen, try a mini pastry."

Owen tosses back a lemon cookie. "Amazing," he says over a mouthful of shortbread and powdered sugar, and despite the caveman way he's eating, I'm ridiculously pleased he likes it.

He's polishing off his second cookie when Mrs. Kaminski shuffles over. "So, *you're* Owen." She peers at him over her glasses. "I have a present for you."

My brother looks at me quizzically, and I guess it *is* a tiny bit odd that an octogenarian he's never met is attending his birthday party, especially when I couldn't even bring myself to tell our parents about it. I make the introductions, and Owen brushes the crumbs off his palms so he can reach out and shake her hand. Mrs. Kaminski isn't much of a hugger.

"Mrs. Kaminski?" Owen cocks his head. "Wait. Aren't you the one who gave Sadie the cat?"

"Wasn't that so nice of her?" I say too loudly, before we can get into the cat lady thing again. "And look, she brought you a present, too. Open it!"

Mrs. Kaminski hands over a box wrapped in yesterday's edition of the *New York Times* and tied with a piece of yarn. Owen tugs aside the paper to reveal a beautiful knit scarf in heather gray with dark red detailing. "Oh, wow."

"It's gorgeous." I reach over to stroke the soft fabric.

"She made it herself," Zoe chimes in.

Owen wraps the scarf around his neck, and I hate to admit it because he's my brother, but it looks great with his white T-shirt and favorite maroon beanie.

"Oh, look." I reach up to tug on his hat. "It matches!"

Owen swats my hand away. "This is so nice of you." And then, before I realize what's happening, he's reaching over to give Mrs. Kaminski's shoulder a squeeze. She leans into him, and I stand corrected. Mrs. Kaminski *is* a hugger.

Owen's gaze sweeps out around the café. "It's so nice of you all to do this for me." He swallows hard.

I look closely, and I swear his eyes are a little red. "Are you *tearing up*?"

"No," he mutters, ducking his head and swiping at his eye with the back of his hand. "It's allergies."

"You *are* tearing up," I say with glee.

He gives me an exaggerated glare. "I'm *moved*, okay? My friends are here, and you did all this for me, and… *Jeez.* Can't I be a little sentimental on my thirtieth birthday?"

"Oh, Owen." This time I give him the *you know you love me* grin. "You can be sentimental about what a great sister I am anytime you want."

He laughs, bumping his shoulder into mine. I elbow him in the side in return. Zoe smiles, shaking her head at us, and excuses herself to go and help José Luis with the line that's forming for drinks. Mrs. Kaminski follows.

Once they're gone, Owen turns back to me. "Thanks for all of this," he says.

"You know I love you." I elbow him in the side. "Even though you're gross."

He jokingly pushes me away from him again.

Chapter 27

For the rest of the party, I alternate between mingling with Owen's friends and restocking the pastry table. Everyone seems to be having a great time, and it's well past midnight before the guests start trickling out. Eventually, only a small group remains, and we sit around a cluster of tables telling embarrassing stories about Owen. He's glowing, surrounded by his friends and holding the hand of a cute red-haired girl named Nora who leans into him whenever she laughs.

Across the table, Paige shares a bench with Jacob and does a lot of leaning into him, too. I pour another drink and try not to think about the muscular arm she's pressed up against, or how it felt when it was wrapped around me. I'm stupidly glad when Paige gets up to grab a bottle of wine, leaving Jacob alone on the bench.

On her way back to the table, Paige pauses in front of the stage. "You guys," she says in that extra-loud tone of someone who's a little tipsy. "We never sang 'Happy Birthday' to Owen." Her gaze settles on Jacob, and she gestures at the piano. "Jacob, come and play the piano for us!"

"Please no." Owen shakes his head with a laugh. "I just turned thirty, not three."

Paige cocks her head. "Okay, not 'Happy Birthday.' But play something for us."

Jacob's gaze swings in her direction, and I'm pretty sure his ears are turning red. "Oh..." He shakes his head.

Nora claps her hands. "Yes! Let's hear you. Owen says you can play *and* sing. What songs do you know?"

The flush is making its way across Jacob's face now. "This is Owen's night. Nobody wants me to get up and perform."

"Of course we do!" Paige says, grabbing his hand and trying to pull him in the direction of the stage. "Don't we?" She turns to the guy on her left.

"Sure, let's hear it," the guy says with a shrug.

Jacob shifts in his seat and tugs his hand away from Paige. "I don't think so. I'm not really a performer."

"It's just us, it's not like it's Carnegie Hall or anything! Besides, I can't believe you've never so much as played 'Mary Had a Little Lamb' for me on that piano in your apartment. Please?"

Jacob drags his hand through his hair, and I can tell he'd rather cut off a finger than get up in front of everyone. But Paige is starting to get a little loud, and he probably doesn't want to cause a scene. I glance at Owen. He must know this is mortifying to Jacob, but from the slight lack of focus in his eyes, I can tell he's tipsy and not really paying attention. Oblivious, Nora leans over and whispers in his ear.

I'm tempted to snap at Paige to quit pushing, but I don't want to embarrass Jacob with a scene, either. I look around the room, and my gaze settles on the bin full of empty liquor bottles next to the bar.

"We should take the recycling out to the alley," I announce, jumping to my feet and making a show of walking over to the recycling bin. Bracing my feet and cringing like a powerlifter in my final heat at the Olympics, I bend to pick it up. "Oh, it's too heavy to carry by myself." I stand, stretching my back like maybe I pulled something. "Jacob, can you grab an end?"

He's watching me, lips twitching like he's trying not to laugh. "Sure."

Before Jacob can stand, José Luis hops off his stool by the bar and waves me away. "Relax, Sadie. I've got it." He lifts the bin without any effort and carries it under one arm toward the kitchen.

Sighing, I go back to the table and drop into my chair.

"Come on," Paige says, still laser-focused on the idea of Jacob performing. "Play something. It'll be fun."

"Paige," he says quietly, but firmly. "No."

By now, I've had it. I take a sip of my mostly full cocktail, then put it back on the table, deliberately setting it at an angle. And— Oops! It tips over, sending green tea–infused vodka and cucumber garnish splashing across the table and dripping to the floor. I jump to my feet again. "Oh my gosh, I'm such a klutz."

Owen shakes his head and tosses a handful of cocktail napkins in my direction. Jacob stands and hurries over to the bar to grab a couple of dish towels. Back at the table, he slides up beside me and hands me one. We lean in to mop up the mess at the same time, and our shoulders collide.

His cinnamony scent drifts over, and a flush makes its way across my cheeks. I grab the overturned glass and carry it into the kitchen.

Jacob follows with the wet towels. The door swings shut behind him, and the conversation out in the café fades to the background. "Thanks for the diversion," he murmurs.

I shrug. "Paige didn't seem like she wanted to let that one go."

Jacob glances through the small round window on the kitchen door to where Paige and the others sit. "I get it that people find out I'm a musician and can't imagine why I *wouldn't* want to get up and play for everyone." He shakes his head. "It's probably a little strange."

I set the glass in the sink and turn to face him. "It's not strange. You share your music with millions of people. You're not obligated to personally get up and sing a Tom Petty song for them."

He gazes across the narrow space at me, and behind his glasses, his eyes are dark and intense. "It means a lot that you understand."

It feels like someone turned the oven to a thousand degrees. I look away and busy myself with stacking the clean baking sheets lying in the dish drainer. When I reach over my head to put them on a shelf above the sink, they start to slide. Before I can react, Jacob moves behind me, taking the pans from my hands and placing them neatly on the shelf. I spin around and find myself encircled by his arms, my face inches from his chest.

"Thanks." My mouth is suddenly dry, and it comes out like a whisper.

He lowers his arms but doesn't back up. "Is this another diversion?"

"A diversion from what?" But I know exactly what. From the way he makes me feel cold and then hot, solid and then liquid, like chocolate melting on the stove.

"Sadie," he says in a low voice. "Can we talk about what happened that night at your apartment? I don't think I did a very good job of explaining myself."

I stare at the buttons on his shirt, so I don't have to look him in the eye. "I think you explained yourself pretty well." We might have a physical attraction, but he made it clear, not once but *twice*, that he's not into me. "That night was a mistake. I'm not really sure why we need to rehash it."

"That's what I'm trying to tell you." He blows out a frustrated breath. "That *I'm sorry*—"

"God, please *stop*." I press my hands to my burning cheeks. "If you apologize for kissing me one more time, I'm going to scream." Pushing past him, I head for the door.

"Sadie." He whirls around and grabs my arm before I can escape. "I'm not saying I'm sorry I kissed you. I'm saying I'm sorry I *stopped* kissing you."

I freeze, and he slides his hand up to my shoulder, gently turning me so I face him. "Can we please talk about this?"

Before I can answer, the distant voices of Owen and his friends grow closer out in the café. Jacob lets go of me, and I hurry to the other side of the kitchen just as Owen pushes open the door with a handful of dishes.

He pauses, looking back and forth between me and Jacob. "Am I interrupting something?"

"No." I lift an innocent shoulder. "Of course not."

Owen's brow furrows like he knows I'm lying. "Right, well, everyone's heading out." He glances in Jacob's direction. "You coming? Paige is waiting for you."

"Uh…" Jacob clears his throat. "I should stay and help clean up."

"It's fine," José Luis says, breezing in from the back alley. "We're almost done here. Sadie and I can finish up, and I'll walk her home."

"Great," Owen says, his voice buoyant. "Thanks, man." I'm not sure if he's extra-chipper from the alcohol or because he's trying to shut down whatever's going on between me and Jacob. Maybe Jacob wasn't wrong to consider how Owen would feel about the two of us getting involved. This could get as sticky as toffee pudding, and my brother would be stuck right in the middle.

I put on a bright smile. "Yeah, thanks, José Luis."

Owen crosses the room to give me a hug. "This was great, Sadie. You're the best."

"Happy birthday." I give him a squeeze in return. "Have fun with *Nora*," I add in a sing-song voice, because as his sister, I'm contractually obligated to take every opportunity to tease him. "You'd better call me tomorrow and tell me if there's anything serious going on between you two."

"No call necessary, then." Owen gives me a cocky grin. "This is purely friends with benefits."

"Ew!" I cover my ears. "Don't say another word about the benefits."

The kitchen door swings open, and Paige and Nora walk in.

"You guys ready to go?" Paige asks, sidling up next to

Jacob. "So convenient that our apartments are in exactly the same direction." She gives him a flirty smile.

Jacob pauses and, even though I'm looking anywhere but at him, I feel his gaze on me. "You sure you don't need help cleaning up?"

For a second, I'm tempted to ask him to stay. But most of the dishes are in the dishwasher, José Luis has already taken the bottles out to the alley, and Paige is clinging to him like caramel on an apple. What would be the point?

"I'm sure." I meet his eyes now.

"Okay." He pauses for another moment before turning and following Paige through the kitchen door.

Chapter 28

November

I arrive for Thanksgiving dinner at my parents' house with homemade pies, and Owen arrives moments later with store-bought chocolates. Naturally, my mom swoons over the chocolates so wildly you'd think Godiva stuffed those truffles with opium. On the subject of my pies, she gives me a distracted "oh, thanks," and heads to her office to finish up some emails.

I leave the desserts in the kitchen where my dad is rushing around swearing at whatever's burning in the oven while green beans boil over on the stove. He's always enjoyed cooking as a break from the wretchedness of *Oedipus* and *Antigone*, but to be honest, his dried-out Thanksgiving turkey is always a bit of its own tragedy. I'd offer to help, but he doesn't like my method of mashing potatoes with the mixer because it's not *traditional*. Instead of pointing out that the ancient Greeks wrote on parchment scrolls but that doesn't mean my dad has any plans to ditch his laptop, I wander to the living room to watch football with Owen. On the way, my mom calls to me from her office off the hallway.

"Sadie, can you stop in here for a minute?"

I take slow steps, feeling like I've been caught sneaking in after curfew. I've only been home for ten minutes; what could I have possibly done to warrant being summoned to my mom's office?

"How was your train ride?" my mom asks after she's sat on the opposite end of her office couch from me.

"Uh, fine." Did she call me in to chitchat?

"No problems with the connection?"

"Nope."

"And—" She examines her nails without looking at me. "How's Alex?"

I flinch. *Oh, here we go.* "How would I know? We broke up."

"Of course." My mom turns to arrange the pile of books on the coffee table. "I just thought maybe you still talked once in a while."

"No." I don't tell her he's called a couple of times and I stared at the screen, debating whether to answer until the phone eventually stopped ringing. "We don't talk."

She does a headshake-shrug combination like, *I'm just asking, why are you getting so defensive?* "Okay."

We both stare at the opposite wall. Is Alex the only reason she called me in here? Am I dismissed now? I should make a run for it before she pulls out the college brochures, but something holds me back. We never sit on the couch and talk. "So, uh. How's work?"

My mom blinks like she's surprised I asked. "It's fine. I'm spending most of my time prepping my presentation for the National Conference of Language and Literature." She feigns a shiver. "It's in Minnesota. In January."

"Oh wow. That sounds…unpleasant. Is Dad going with you?"

"These days, your father prefers to hole up in his office writing textbooks. He doesn't present much at conferences anymore. And you know." She rolls her eyes. "He can get away with it."

"He can? Why?"

"He's a full professor with three decades at the university."

"So are you." I wrinkle my forehead. "You're the dean of the whole department. So why do you have to risk losing a limb to frostbite while Dad gets to stay home?"

"Oh." She waves a dismissive hand. "Men always get away with things like that." My mom gives a resigned shrug, and my memory snaps to Xavier insisting Doug could finish making my cakes despite his lack of experience. To the executive pastry chef taking credit for my lemon tarts when his tasted like hand soap.

"You're dealing with sexism, even at your level?"

"I've dealt with sexism at every level. I don't know any woman in my field who hasn't."

I don't know any woman in my field who hasn't either. But for some reason I thought it would be different for someone who'd made it all the way to the top of a "respectable" field like hers. Someone with so much power. "But you're in charge of everyone. Why don't you stand up and demand that things change? Refuse to go to the conference in the North Pole and tell one of those dudes in your department that they have to go instead."

My mom sits up straight. "Because going to that conference is exactly how I ended up in charge of everyone. I publish papers and rack up presentations for the most prestigious professional organizations. I play the game and work twice as hard as any man in my program. And now, I'm one of the few women in the entire country at the head of a university literature department."

I sink back against the couch cushions. "Wow, I had no idea."

She gives me a pointed look. "You end up at the top of your field by working within the system, not making a scene every time you feel you've been wronged."

Gazing around her big, fancy office with its wall of diplomas and shiny mahogany desk in the middle, I have to admit, nobody could argue that my mom's not a success. "But don't you ever feel uncomfortable about it? I mean, you know the system is messed up. You know it's not fair that dad can do what he wants, and you can't. Aren't you making it harder for the next woman by smiling and going along with it? Shouldn't you use your power to speak up?"

My mom sighs. "What good would that do? I'd be branded as hysterical, and the department would be wary of hiring the next woman. Is that really any better for anyone?"

I let my mom's words sink in. Are her actions any different from how I've spent my second chance year? I've gone out of my way to be agreeable at work, to go along with Xavier's demands, and to deliberately bite my tongue. It's not like I don't know that if I were a man, Xavier would treat me differently. And it's not like I don't know it's wrong. But I've tried speaking up and look how well that worked out for me. Was I really better off getting fired? Losing my apartment? Getting blackballed from the entire industry? Or am I better off grabbing that executive pastry chef job and running with it? Maybe making a space for the next woman?

"I'm up for a big promotion at Xavier's." I blurt it out before I can stop myself. "He'll be announcing it any day now. *Executive pastry chef.* It's kind of a big deal."

I'm not supposed to say anything, it's not even official yet. But when my mom's eyebrows raise, and she says, "Really?" in a voice that sounds maybe a teeny-tiny bit interested, I don't regret a thing.

I nod, leaning into my story. "You know Xavier is a frequent guest judge on *Top Chef*, and he's written several best-selling cookbooks."

"I remember you mentioned he's a TV personality. I didn't realize he's also an author."

"This job—it's not just about baking cupcakes. I'll be Xavier's right-hand person, in charge of design and execution of all the desserts at the restaurant. I'll really make a name for myself. Maybe even end up with a publishing deal for my own cookbook, too." Now I'm really getting ahead of myself, but I can't seem to stop talking. Especially when my mom cocks her head and not only looks in my direction, but for the first time, it's like she actually *sees* me.

"It does sound like a very promising opportunity."

I grab her hand, seizing the moment. Now that she's offered a tiny slice of approval, I want the whole damn pie.

"Mom, come into the city and have dinner at Xavier's. I'd love for you to see what it's really like there. I think you'd be impressed."

She nods slowly. "Maybe I will. Let me wrap up this semester first, and we can look at our calendars over winter break."

"Okay! That would be great. Anytime you can make it."

"I'll look forward to it." She smiles.

The doorbell rings, announcing the first guest arriving for dinner. I jump up to answer it, glowing like a brioche bun browning in the oven.

Chapter 29

We always have at least three or four of my parents' wayward graduate students and the literature department's visiting professors at our holiday gatherings. When I was a kid, there was nothing more boring than sitting at the Thanksgiving table through two hours of conversation about the social commentary in Austen compared to Brontë. Don't ask me which Brontë. Apparently, there were several.

Let's be honest, I still find it really boring, but at least now there's alcohol. Plus, I'm still feeling cautiously warm and fuzzy after my conversation with my mom earlier, so I'm willing to nod along.

When we've exhausted the Janes—both Eyre and Bennett—the conversation moves to Owen's new job, but there's only so much the literature crowd can say about self-driving vehicles. Across the dining table, a gray-haired Shakespearean scholar named Angela is starting to look a little cross-eyed. When she leans across the table toward me, I brace myself, hoping she won't ask my thoughts on *Macbeth*.

"Sadie," she says. "I don't believe I know what you do for work."

I reflexively glance at my mom, waiting for her to interrupt before I admit to her academic friend that I'm just a baker. But as my mom makes her way around the table pouring coffee, she gives me a little pat on the arm. "Sadie is a pastry chef at a restaurant called Xavier's in the city."

My eyes widen at her tone. Maybe there isn't quite pride in her voice, but there's not disapproval either.

"I admit," Angela confides with a smile, "the Food Network is a bit of a guilty pleasure. I'm very familiar with Xavier's reputation. Fran, why didn't you tell me your daughter is in charge of desserts at a famous restaurant?"

I hesitate. Technically, I'm not in charge yet. And I don't want to lie. "Well, I'm really an assistant. But a lot of the recipes are mine, and I do most of the work of executing them."

"Sadie's up for a big promotion," my mom says. "So, she'll be in charge soon."

My mouth drops open because this might be the first time in decades of Thanksgiving dinners that my mom has volunteered anything about my baking to her friends and colleagues.

"You are?" Owen calls from the other end of the table. "Nice work, Sadie."

"What's the new job?" my dad inquires, and his unexpected interest leaves me a little uneasy about this entire conversation. I really shouldn't have said anything until the offer is official.

"Executive pastry chef," I mumble.

It all sounds so terribly glamorous." Angela gives me a wink. "I'll look out for you to judge *Top Chef* someday."

"There might even be a publishing deal for a recipe book," my mom announces, and truly, who is this woman bragging about me? If I had the job and book deal in hand, I'd be thrilled by her sudden interest in my career, but instead, my stomach churns.

"Well, it's not official or anything."

My dad's eyebrows raise as he takes it all in. "Keep us updated," he instructs.

"Yeah. Sure." Grasping for a subject change, I shamelessly throw my brother under the bus. "So, Owen, how's Nora? Are you two still dating?"

My mom stops with the coffeepot in hand, her gaze swinging to my brother. "Owen, you have a girlfriend?"

"Who's Nora?" my dad chimes in.

Owen glares at me over his THERE'S NO PLACE LIKE PEMBERLEY coffee mug. "She's just a friend."

"Friend with *benefits*," I mouth at him across the table. Out loud, I say, "She's super pretty and really, really into Owen. And *so* nice, too."

"Shut *up*," Owen mouths back.

Most mothers would be happy to hear that their thirty-year-old son has met a nice girl, but not mine. No woman will ever be good enough for her baby. "Well, don't let her distract you from your work," my mom advises.

"But," I chime in innocently, "isn't it a thing in your circles that a man with a big pile of money must be looking for a wife... or something like that?"

My mom's graduate student slaps her hands on the table.

"It is a truth universally acknowledged that a single man in possession of a good fortune must be in want of a wife!"

I've been around the block enough times to know she's quoting Austen. "See?" I nod and point in agreement. "Owen's on the marriage track."

"Are you serious about this girl?" my father asks.

Lucky for my brother, the doorbell rings.

"I'll get it!" Owen jumps up, intentionally knocking into me as he rounds the table and makes a break for the foyer. "Jacob's here!" he announces when he returns a minute later.

I sit up straight, and my head swings to the dining room entrance where Jacob is standing. He always stops by on holidays, of course Jacob's here. And, oh look…Paige came, too. She's leaning really, really close to him, and… Wow. That doorway is narrower than I remember.

Jacob and Paige move into the room, and my dad pulls up two more chairs. Somehow, Jacob ends up next to me, with Paige across the table.

"Thanks for letting me tag along with Jacob." Paige smiles at my parents. "He was raving about Sadie's pies over dinner. I had a chance to try a few of her pastries at Owen's birthday party, and they were amazing."

I shoot her a grateful look.

"Where are you from, Paige?" my dad asks.

"I grew up in California and came to the East Coast for grad school a few years ago. I love it, but it's hard this time of year without any family nearby." She flashes Jacob a smile. "I appreciate Jacob's parents welcoming me. And now your family, too."

"Which grad program?" my dad asks, because of course he does.

"I did my PhD at Johns Hopkins," Paige says. "Then I moved to New York for a job at the Institute for Public Health Policy."

"That sounds very prestigious."

My dad and Paige launch into a conversation about her work. I try to follow along, but Jacob's cinnamony scent drifts toward me, and the tender, spiced apples in my pie smell canned in comparison.

"So," I murmur in his direction. "Paige seems really great."

"Yeah, we've been hanging out recently." Jacob shifts in his seat so he's facing me. "I lived next to her for a few years, but we really never said more than *hi* in the elevator until I sent her that wine and chocolate like you suggested."

Oh, lovely. A reminder that Paige and Jacob's relationship is all my doing. Just what I needed. "Well, I'm really happy for you."

"Are you?" He gives me an odd look.

Of course not.

"Of course." I smile broadly. "She's lovely. Smart, obviously. And really pretty, and super-fun. Very outgoing." I can't seem to stop babbling. "I really like her. She seems great." Pretty sure I already said that. "And if you're happy, I'm..." *I'm what?* I have no idea. I wave my hand in the air. "...you know."

"Happy?" Jacob prompts.

"Exactly." I give him a friendly little punch on the arm, and God, if someone could please stop me before I humiliate myself further, that would be super. My only consolation is that I didn't call him "buddy."

Yet.

He definitely looks like he's trying not to laugh at me.

"Okay, well. Nice chatting with you." I pick up an empty pan and head for the door.

In the kitchen, I put away the leftover food and scrub the pots and pans until Martha Stewart herself couldn't find anything to criticize. But once the kitchen is sparkling, something holds me back from going out into the dining room. Maybe it's my dad's admiration of Paige's degrees that leaves me a little depressed. For once, my parents seem vaguely interested in my career, but it's not like the promotion is official or anything. And now I really need it to happen, or I don't know what I'll tell them.

Maybe I'm bothered by the fact that Jacob brought Paige. I can't seem to stop thinking about that night in my apartment. And he can't seem to stop showing up with his pretty, smart, and outgoing neighbor, proving that he's absolutely *not* thinking about that night in my apartment.

I grab my dad's old coat from the hook by the back door and head out into the November chill. Maybe a walk will clear my head. I circle the neighborhood a couple of times, but when an icy rain begins to fall, I head back. As I turn the corner onto my parents' block, I slow my steps. There's a man standing alone in the driveway. He's just outside the dim pool of the streetlamp, and from this angle, he doesn't resemble my dad or Owen, or—as far as I can tell—any of our Thanksgiving guests. I can't decide if he looks menacing. Either way, it's late, and dark, and I'm alone. I reach in my pocket for my pepper spray, but my hand comes up empty except for a crumpled tissue and an ancient Halls Mentho-lyptus. I'm not in the city and this is my dad's coat.

I take a deep breath. My family is right inside the house, and this is a nice, safe neighborhood. Surely, freaking out over a strange man lurking in the rainy darkness is totally an overreaction, right? I inch closer, trying to peer over the shrubbery to see if I can get a better look at him. He looks tall and lean, but that tells me exactly nothing about whether or not he intends to murder me and bury my body in the woods behind the New Brunswick mall.

The man turns and takes a couple of steps in my direction. As he draws nearer, I open my mouth to scream. But at the last second, something stops me. There's something familiar about the shape of him. And... *Wait a minute...*

He steps into the light and gives me a smile. "Hi, Sadie."

"Alex?" I say, right before I trip over a crack in the sidewalk.

Chapter 30

I manage to catch myself on the neighbor's white picket fence before I fall ass over teakettle into the rhododendrons. "Jesus, Alex," I say, after I've righted myself. "Didn't your mother ever tell you not to lurk on dark streets at night? You nearly gave me a heart attack."

"Sorry." He takes a step toward me. "I just had to see you."

"You didn't think texting first might be a good idea? *Hey Sadie, I was thinking of hanging out on your parents' front step in the dark. If you come home, don't mace me.*"

"I was afraid you'd tell me not to come."

"And you thought scaring me half to death was the way to convince me otherwise? Why didn't you ring the doorbell like a normal person?"

Alex smiles sadly. "I got nervous."

I let go of the neighbor's fence and slowly make my way onto my parents' front porch. "What are you doing here, Alex?"

"I miss you. I've been miserable without you."

I gaze up at him standing there in jeans and his old

fraternity hoodie. He was wearing that hoodie on the day we met. I've rarely seen him like this lately. In the months before we broke up, we got together after work when he was in a suit and tie, or at his place where he hung out in shiny workout shirts and expensive track pants. I didn't even know he still had that old sweatshirt. I look away before he can see me react to that. I'm not sure if what I'm feeling is for the Alex standing in front of me, or if it's nostalgia for what we used to have.

"I don't know what to say to that."

"Say you'll give me another chance."

"Why? Because you need a good Wall Street wife, and you think with a little grooming, I'd fit the bill?"

"I deserve that." Alex looks down at the pavement. "I'm so sorry I said those things about your job not being important." He holds his hands out, fingers spread wide. "I'm an ass."

"You are."

"How can I make it up to you?"

"I don't know."

He cocks his head at me. "I talked to Dave about hiring more women at the firm."

My head jerks up. "Really?"

"Yes."

"Yes, you really did, or yes you're just *saying* you did so I'll get off your back?"

"Yes, I really did." He takes a step in my direction. "He commended me for my commitment to diversity."

I can't hide my skepticism. "Well, I mean, it's one thing to blow smoke about diversity and another to create a culture where there are real opportunities for people who aren't a bunch of white guys."

"Sadie." He sighs. "I'm trying."

And I can see that he is. Why am I always so all or nothing?

"I'd give anything to make it up to you," he continues.

He's so forlorn, standing there with his shoulders slumped and his hands in his pockets. So completely opposite from the cocky investment banker making the rounds and shaking hands and lecturing me about not understanding *the culture*. Again, I'm reminded of the Alex I used to know. Before the new job and money and expensive watches. *And he's trying.* Shouldn't I meet him halfway?

When I hesitate, he grabs my hand. And at that moment, the front door opens.

"Sadie?" My mom peers into the darkness. "We heard voices out here. Is everything . . . ?" She trails off as her head swings from me, to Alex, to my hand still clutched in his. "Oh, my goodness. *Alex!*" The door flies open the rest of the way, and she rushes out onto the porch in her socks. "It's so good to see you."

As my mom envelops my ex-boyfriend in her arms, my dad appears in the doorway. "Did you say Alex is here?"

"Yes, look, Jim." My mom pushes Alex toward the front door. "I found him and Sadie holding hands on the porch."

"Wait. We weren't—" But nobody is listening to me.

My dad reaches out to shake Alex's hand and clap him on the back. My mom insists he come inside. And before I know what's happening, he's sitting at the dining table with the rest of the guests, in the chair next to mine. Everyone stares awkwardly as they wait for an explanation for Alex's sudden reappearance, and a flush creeps across my skin. I peek at Jacob, who's been displaced to a seat across the table next to Paige. In a gesture that couldn't be more indifferent to the fact that my ex-boyfriend just crashed our holiday meal, Jacob picks up his fork and takes a bite of pie so enormous, I don't actually know how he manages to cram it in his mouth.

"So," Owen says, getting right to the point. "Are you two back together or what?"

Alex clears his throat. "Well, that's why I'm here. I'm hoping Sadie will take me back." He turns in his seat to look at me, face earnest. "I know I don't deserve you, and I was a thoughtless jerk, but—"

"Alex." I press my hands to my hot cheeks. "This isn't really the place... Maybe we should go back out on the porch to discuss this."

"No, I want your family to be here. I want them to know how important you are to me." Alex shoves his chair back and takes my hand. "Please, Sadie. I love you. Please give me another chance."

And—*oh my God*—he drops to one knee.

My eyes widen. My mom gasps. From somewhere far away, Owen mutters, "Whoa, dude." I stare at Alex. Is he really doing this right now, in front of everyone?

"Sadie," Alex says, gazing into my eyes. "Will you marry me?"

Yep. He's really doing this right now, in front of everyone.

Alex pulls out a ring that gives Jacob's colossal bite of pie a run for its money, and my mom makes a choking sound in the back of her throat. My eyes dart around the room at the surprised expressions on the faces of our Thanksgiving guests, who probably weren't expecting quite such a show when they RSVPed to dinner. Eventually, it lands on my parents.

For the first time in as long as I can remember, they're looking right at me with matching expressions of pride and happiness. And it's startling, because I'm used to seeing them gaze distractedly over my shoulder as if we're at a party and they're checking to see if someone more important walked in. I'm used to their disinterest, their nods and shrugs, their not-quite-listening to what I have to say. And I'm used to them not having much to say to *me* unless it's to tell me what to do or criticize something I've done. For my whole life, I've been a disappointment, a failure. I've screwed up everything with my rash decisions, my big mouth, and my terrible career choices.

But today...something amazing happened. Today, I'm no longer a stale, store-bought Twinkie. I'm homemade angel food cake with Chantilly cream and fresh strawberries. Today, I finally have my parents' love and approval. All I have to do is open my mouth and say *yes*.

Just say yes.

My gaze jerks to Jacob and, for one brief moment, our eyes lock. And then he looks away, and I deflate like an over-proofed bread loaf.

"I can't."

Alex blinks. "Excuse me?"

My dad flops back in his chair, and my mom hisses, *"Really, Sadie?"* like I'm a toddler who's gotten into the sugar and dumped it all over the floor.

"I can't marry you, Alex."

Alex goes pale. "You're serious?"

I look down at my hands. "I don't think we're a good fit for each other. And once you have a little distance, once you meet someone who *is* a good fit…" I remember that woman in Alex's Instagram photos, the one he started dating after we broke up during my Very Bad Year. I hope he'll run into her somewhere. He looked happy in those photos, and maybe she can be what he wants. "I think you'll realize that we're both better off."

"Sadie, I think we should talk about this. If you'll just *listen*—"

I shake my head. I have no idea what I'm doing with my life. But I know this isn't it. "I'm sorry, Alex." And with that, I stand up and run out of the room.

Chapter 31

December

December at Xavier's is always a busy time of the year with private parties and holiday gatherings, and this year, I'm working overtime to make sure everything is perfect. I'm expecting the announcement about the executive pastry chef any day now, and I *need* that job. My parents are still mad about the scene I caused at Thanksgiving, and I can't go home this Christmas and tell them I lost the promotion, too.

That's why it's after eleven o'clock at night, the rest of the staff has gone home, and I'm still at Xavier's prepping pastries for the Christmas parties that start a couple of days from now. After weighing and measuring out my dry ingredients into lidded containers, I carefully label each one so all I have to do is add them later to the mixer with eggs, milk, and butter. I'm stacking them in the pantry, just about ready to head home, when Xavier appears in the doorway. I jump about a hundred feet in the air, knocking into my tower of Tupperware, but I manage to straighten it just before it topples.

"Oh my gosh, you scared me." I press a hand to my heart. "I didn't know anyone else was still here."

"I was doing some paperwork in the office." His gaze slowly sweeps down to my feet and then back up.

I cross my arms over my chest. The kitchen was hot from the ovens and woodfire grill burning all day, so I'd ditched my chef's coat a while ago, and now I'm standing here in a tank top and leggings. I definitely would've stayed covered up if I'd known anyone else was here. We're not even allowed to wear chef's coats without the name of the restaurant embroidered on the pocket. Is Xavier annoyed that I'm out of uniform? In the lead-up to this promotion, I've been extra careful not to do anything that could be viewed as unprofessional, and I really hope I'm not screwing this up when I'm working so hard to do everything right.

"You're here late," Xavier finally says.

"Yeah, I'm getting some ingredients prepped for the holiday." I flash him an overly bright smile and give one of the canisters a shake. "Just trying to be prepared."

Xavier takes a couple of steps into the pantry so he can read the labels I've taped to the sides of the containers.

"Very good. I appreciate your hard work."

Whew. He's not mad. Still, with Xavier's roller-coaster moods, it could have gone either way. "Just doing what I can for the good of the restaurant." It can't hurt to suck up a little more.

Xavier takes another step toward me, and I'm aware that he's standing awfully close. It's a narrow space, and two people don't usually come in here at the same time. Despite the heat in the kitchen, goose bumps pop up on my arms. I try to inch backward without it looking obvious.

"I wanted to let you know that I'll be making the announcement about our new executive pastry chef next week," he says with a smile. "I think you'll be *very* happy to hear the news."

For a moment, I forget the awkwardness of the two of us crammed into this closet. *It's happening next week.* "Oh wow, thank you. You know I'll always work hard, and I won't let you down."

"I know you won't." He reaches toward me, and I think he's going to shake my hand, to make it official. But instead, his fingers lightly brush my arm from my elbow to my shoulder and back again. My eyes widen and my body stiffens like vanilla meringue.

"You had a little flour there," he explains. Except it's not really an explanation at all, because the flour is gone and his cold, clammy fingers are still pressed against my rapidly heating skin.

Is he—?

This isn't—?

Is it?

No, I'm sure he doesn't mean it the way I think he does. I'm overly sensitive because of Rob. If I make a big deal out of this, it will embarrass us both.

And then Xavier's hand slowly wraps around my upper arm and his mouth inches closer to mine. I want to pull away, but it's like I'm frozen here.

"Don't worry," he murmurs. "We can keep this between us."

And—*thank God*—his voice knocks me out of my stupor. I push past him, and my shoulder lands squarely in his chest. Xavier goes careening backward from the force of it, directly into my carefully portioned canisters of dry ingredients. They tumble off the shelf and crash to the floor. The lids pop off, and flour billows through the air like an East Coast snowstorm. Xavier slips in the smooth powder and grabs on to the shelf to keep from falling over.

And I run. Out of the pantry, across the kitchen, and into the break room. I grab my purse and my coat and keep going, straight through the restaurant and out the front door. On Bedford Avenue, I nearly crash into a group of people walking past on the sidewalk, probably heading for one of the bars. They're joking and laughing together, and I'm jealous of how carefree they are.

"Whoa, girl. You okay?" one of them asks, and I nod, extracting myself from their group and heading in the opposite direction.

I turn the corner onto a side street, and a gust of wind blows through my thin black tank top. Suddenly, I'm shivering uncontrollably, and icy tears stream down my cheeks. But I feel strangely detached from my body, like the whole sordid episode happened to someone else.

I stop in front of one of the brownstones lining the street and pull on my coat. The house is dark, the occupants probably asleep, and I'm jealous of them, too. My apartment is only eight blocks away, but now that Xavier's is behind me, my legs have turned into jelly. I sink down on the front step of the house and dig into my purse for my phone. I try my brother, but he's usually in bed most weeknights by ten thirty. I know he'd come in a second if I could reach him, but when his voicemail clicks on, I hang up.

The cold, damp step beneath me is seeping through my thin leggings, and the bitter wind is picking up speed. I should get up and go home, but I'm crying too hard now. I pull my knees to my chest and wrap my arms around them.

And then I remember Jacob and his late-night café Americanos. If he's working on a project, he could still be awake. The teeny-tiny bit of pride that's left in me insists that I absolutely should *not* dial Jacob's number, but rock bottom wins out, and I hit the button next to his name.

He picks up on the first ring. "Sadie, is everything okay?"

The concern in his voice has my heart folding up. I can't imagine what he must think with me calling him so late like this. "Yes," I whisper because I don't want to worry him. Except this is Jacob, and I can be at my worst with Jacob. "Actually, no." I wipe my eyes on my sleeve. "Can you come?"

"Where are you?" I hear thumping on his end, a door opening and slamming, a key jingling.

I tell him the cross streets.

"I'll be there as soon as I can." His voice sounds worried. Urgent. "Stay on the phone, okay?"

"Okay."

I huddle on the steps listening through the phone to the rhythmic beat of his feet on the pavement, and in less than five minutes, I hear them in person, running down the block toward me.

"Sadie?" Jacob skids to a stop and kneels down in front of me. "What happened?" He's panting so hard he can barely get the words out. Taking me by the shoulders, he looks me over like a child who fell off the swing set. "Do I need to take you to a hospital? Or call an ambulance?"

I shake my head. "No, it's nothing like that."

Jacob leans back to meet my eyes. "Do I need to beat someone up for you?"

At the image of shy, reserved Jacob giving Xavier the smackdown, I manage a watery smile. "Thanks. But no."

His gaze roams over me. "Tell me what you need."

At the gentleness in his voice, I'm crying again. Because I didn't know it until this exact second, but what I needed was him.

Jacob slides his palm to my cheek. "Let me take you home."

I nod, and he holds out a hand to help me up off the step. Back on Bedford Avenue, Jacob flags down a cab, which is probably overkill considering I live less than half a mile away, but I'm grateful for the warmth of the backseat and the darkness where I can close my eyes and lean into him.

When we arrive at my apartment, I flip on a lamp in the corner. Jacob must think I'm either the world's worst drug mule or I've lost a fight with a powdered doughnut, because every inch of me is covered in the flour Xavier spilled all over the pantry. I'm reminded of the fortune teller's red potion raining down as I asked for a second chance, for a do-over of my Very Bad Year. I hold back a bitter laugh. What's that saying about being careful what you wish for?

I take a quick shower and put on a pair of drawstring

pajama pants and a T-shirt. When I come back out into the main room, Jacob hands me a steaming mug. "I looked for tea, but all I could find was cocoa powder and sugar. So, this is my attempt at hot chocolate."

I take the mug and inhale the scent. "I'm a pastry chef. Cocoa powder and sugar are my love language." And then I blush. "I mean. I didn't mean that you made me hot chocolate because you're, because we're— Oh God. Never mind. Thank you for the hot chocolate, Jacob."

Jacob's mouth slants into a smile that's almost sad. "I know what you meant."

I wrap my hands around the warm mug and sink down on one end of the bed.

He hesitates for a moment, and then sits on the opposite end. "You want to talk about what happened tonight?"

I don't want to talk about it. I don't even want to think about it. I want to open the trash can and toss the whole episode in. When I close my eyes, I'm back in that pantry with Xavier leaning closer. And when I open my eyes, I'm crying again.

Jacob takes the hot chocolate out of my hand and sets it on the side table. And then he grabs a blanket from the bottom of the bed and wraps it around me. With him leaning in close like this, my old blanket smells just like the plaid throw on his couch, the one I practically lived in during my Very Bad Year. I never thought I'd feel nostalgic for a blanket, but *The Golden Girls* and a jar of Nutella are looking pretty good right now.

I never thought I'd wish to have that year back, instead of this one.

Jacob settles me against his chest, and I close my eyes, feeling the gentle rise and fall of his breath. I reach for his hand. "Thank you for being here, Jacob."

"You don't need to thank me." He weaves his fingers through mine. "There's nowhere else I'd rather be."

And in that moment, there's nowhere else I'd rather be, either.

Chapter 32

I wake up alone. The sun is slanting in through the window, and Gio is crawling all over me, meowing to be fed. At some point last night, I fell asleep with Jacob leaning back against the headboard of my bed, and me leaning against Jacob. But now the space beside me is empty, which feels like a pretty good metaphor for my state of mind.

Body aching, I climb out of bed. As much as I'd like to lay here all day, avoiding my life, I'm supposed to be at work in a couple of hours. Xavier has planned a special prix fixe dinner, and I've got four dozen mini bûche de Nöel cakes to ice and decorate. I don't know how I'm going to face him, but I don't feel like I have much choice. I still need this job to pay my bills. And thanks to my big mouth on Thanksgiving, I still need this promotion, too. How would I explain to my parents that I blew it?

I get dressed, gulp down some coffee, and shuffle the eight blocks to Xavier's. The kitchen is buzzing with sous chefs and servers prepping food and tableware for today's dinner service, so I manage to slip in the back door without any dramatic confrontations or ingredients flying through the air. Right now, that's all I can ask for.

Grabbing my apron, I tiptoe into the pantry, half expecting to find a pile of white powder and toppled containers strewn across the floor like an arctic crime scene. But the room is sparkling, the floor mopped, and the shelves wiped down. Maybe Xavier cleaned it up last night in an effort to pretend nothing happened today. Burying my head in the sanding sugar seems like an excellent coping strategy, so my plan is to get my work done and avoid any more scenes.

I grab the ingredients for a batch of chocolate icing and carry it to the prep table. Xavier flits in and out, barking orders, but I keep my head bent over my cakes. He doesn't acknowledge me, and I don't make eye contact.

About half an hour before the first reservations of the night, Xavier calls the staff into the kitchen for a meeting. The prix fixe menu is a departure from our usual service, so he probably wants to go over the details. He gathers everyone around, clapping his hands and speaking in a booming, overly jolly voice, as if Santa popped in to wish us a Merry Christmas. It's so weirdly unlike him that I look up from my cakes and, from across the room, his gaze locks on mine. His eyes narrow for just a second, and despite the heat from the ovens, a shiver runs up my spine.

Xavier slowly turns back to the staff, clapping his hands. "Everyone, I have an announcement to make. As you know, Dennis will be leaving us soon, and I'm sure that you've all been eagerly waiting for me to name the new executive pastry chef."

A murmur runs through the staff, and I wipe my sweaty hands on my chef's coat.

"Well." He pauses for effect, as if this is the Oscars and we're waiting to hear who won the award for Best Pastry Chef. "I'm happy to announce that Charles Pascale will be coming to us from The May Fair in London, starting on January first."

My body goes hot, and then cold, and my vision blurs. I grip the prep table in front of me for balance. Xavier didn't hire Charles Pascale overnight. Which means that yesterday, when he was dangling the promotion and trying to make out with me against a shelf of canned goods, he knew Charles was coming. And he probably knew it for months.

Xavier never intended to give me that job. He'd been lying all along to keep me sucking up to him and pandering to his VIPs. Lying and waiting for just the right time to make a move on me. And somehow, I convinced myself that I was the problem. That I shouldn't speak up, I shouldn't choose my own feelings. That I should shut up and smile.

I spent the last year shaping myself into someone pleasant and agreeable, someone who went along, who didn't rock the boat. And somewhere along the way, I threw the old Sadie overboard. The old Sadie who was strong, and confident, and who stood up for herself. The old Sadie who would have never taken this shit.

She's somewhere out there. Adrift.

And I have no idea who the hell I am anymore.

I drop my icing bag, and slowly push away from the prep table, my movements slow and labored, as if I'm slogging through caramel sauce. And right there, in front of Xavier and the entire restaurant staff, I turn and walk out the door.

Chapter 33

My parents' house is quiet when I let myself in, and I hope it's because everyone is asleep. I deliberately put this off, waiting until the very last train was about to pull out of Penn Station before I got on. Once I hopped off in downtown New Brunswick, I decided to walk the two miles home rather than call my dad or an Uber to pick me up. I know I'm just prolonging the inevitable. The first thing my parents are going to ask me tomorrow morning is if I got the promotion.

I guess it wouldn't be a Thatcher family gathering if I didn't let my parents down. It turns out that massive disappointment pairs well with festive holiday beverages. *Merry Christmas, your daughter is still a disaster. Eggnog, anyone?*

No doubt, Owen will come home for the holidays having invented a robot that can cure cancer, casually announce that he's been promoted to president of the world, or have accomplished something equally impressive that my parents can hold up as a shining example of how well it *could* have gone for me, if only I'd gotten a proper education.

Tiptoeing into the hallway, I hang my coat on a hook by the door. Then I turn around and—

"*Jesus, Owen!*" I spring backward.

My brother is standing there, arms crossed, leaning against the doorframe to the living room.

"Quit lurking like that!" I whisper-yell.

"I'm not lurking, I'm calmly standing here."

"You're standing there in a lurking manner."

Owen rolls his eyes. "You're the one creeping around in the middle of the night." He looks at me sideways. "And don't take this the wrong way, but you look like you slept in an alley. Make that in a dumpster in an alley."

"How could I possibly take that the wrong way, Owen?" I huff past him, but when I do, I catch a glimpse of myself in the hall mirror. And well, he's not wrong. It's impossible to miss the black mascara smears underlining my bloodshot eyes or the fact that my nose is still red and puffy from crying. Oh, and look, my shirt is on backward. I pull my arms through the armholes and spin it around.

My brother squints at me. "Seriously, what's the matter?"

I shrug, looking over his shoulder at the family photos lining the wall that my mom used to insist we take every year. I'll never tell anyone what really happened at Xavier's. It's the most mortifying thing that's ever happened to me, and I'd love to erase the memory from my own head. What a complete idiot I was, staying late, cheerfully organizing ingredients in the pantry, and making an extra-special effort to earn a promotion Xavier never intended to give me.

I really was nothing but a nice face and a perky pair of tits after all.

"I didn't get the promotion." I try it out on Owen, practicing for my parents tomorrow.

"Shit. I'm sorry. What happened?"

Maybe I'm just being sensitive, maybe it's my parents' voices humming in my head, accompanied by a rousing chorus of my own insecurities, but what I hear is: *What did you do?*

"I don't know. He just gave the promotion to someone else." I move into the living room and flop onto the couch.

Owen follows, sitting on the chair opposite of me. "I really thought you had it."

I did, too. But looking back, Xavier never said the job was mine. He said he had his eye on me, that I'd be happy with his choice, and I was doing a great job. But it was *how* he said those things. I know I didn't read into them.

Did I?

Somehow, Xavier is still gaslighting me, and he's not even here.

"Well, you deserved that fucking job," Owen says, and I feel bad for all my unkind thoughts about him earlier.

"Well, now I have to tell Mom and Dad." I prop my feet up on the coffee table and accidently kick over a pile of books. Sophocles and Euripides tumble to the floor, but I don't have the energy to rescue them. "And they're already devastated that I turned down Alex's proposal, so they can add this to the list of ways I disappointed them."

"That's the dumbest thing I ever heard."

"What is?"

"That not agreeing to spend the rest of your life with someone who was incredibly wrong for you means you're disappointing Mom and Dad."

I look up. "Alex was incredibly wrong for me?"

"Yes? Obviously? I mean—" He holds up a hand like he's about to count off the ways on his fingers, but then he hesitates. "Wait a minute."

"What?"

"Well, are you one hundred percent sure you're done with him?" He leans forward in his chair. "I'm only asking because I don't want to shit-talk him and then have you turn around and get back with him later. That never ends well."

I wave my hand in a have-at-it gesture. "Shit-talk away."

Owen opens his mouth and then closes it. He frowns. "Well, now that I know I'm allowed, I don't really feel like it. I mean, he *was* incredibly wrong for you, but he was an okay dude."

I sit up straight. "If you thought he was wrong for me, why didn't you say something when we were dating?"

"Seriously?" Owen shakes his head. "Please refer back to *it never ends well*."

"Well, you're right. Alex *was* incredibly wrong for me." I slump back against the couch cushions. "But Mom and Dad are still devastated."

"Are *you* devastated? What do you care if they are?"

I raise my eyebrows. "Says the son who literally never devastates them."

He gets up out of his chair and goes into the kitchen. I

hear the refrigerator door open and glass clinking around. A minute later, Owen is back holding two bottles of beer. He hands me one and takes a long swig of the other.

"It's not all it's cracked up to be, you know." Owen drops back into his chair.

"What are you talking about?"

"Being the good son. I realize it's obnoxious to be like, *Woe is me, my parents love me too much*, but...you've met them. It's a lot of pressure."

"Really?" I squint at him across the room. "It never seemed like a lot of pressure. They've always been thrilled to support you to do all the computer-y stuff you like."

Owen takes another gulp of his beer and sets it on the side table on top of a hardback copy of *Middlemarch*. "Well, that's only because I did the computer-y things they approved of."

"Wait." I blink at him. "So, you don't want to be doing...whatever it is that you do? I thought you loved AstRoBot."

"I mean, I like it. It's good. It's fine. But..." He sighs. "When I was a kid, I wanted to design video games."

"Yeah...I figured that was something you grew out of. Or..." I trail off. *Or what?* I remember how he was always inventing games on that old basement Mac. And how his eyes lit up with excitement when he described a new idea to me and Jacob over brunch that one day. Gaming has always been a passion for Owen, but I guess it never occurred to me that he might like to do it as a career. His ascension to CTO of AstRoBot has been so meteoric that it's all anyone ever focused on. "Do Mom and Dad know?"

"Do they know I'd prefer to be designing video games? Yes." He runs a hand through his hair. "Do they acknowledge or care that this is something that would make me happy?"

This question is about my parents, so therefore, rhetorical. "Right."

Owen drains his beer. "I've always admired your ability to basically say, *Screw it* and be who you want to be. I tell myself I'm going to quit and give this game idea a chance, but I keep getting all these promotions, and Mom and Dad are so damn *proud*..."

I get it. When your role has been clearly laid out for your entire life, it's not easy to pivot to being someone else. This past year has been a big, fat lesson for me. "Well, for the record, *I'd* support you one hundred percent if you wanted to torch your job and follow your dream, Owen."

"Thanks."

"And Jacob would, too," I add. "He's a really good friend."

"Is he?" Owen narrows his eyes at me. "How would you know?"

And to my great mortification, I blush. "Well, uh—"

Owen leans forward, resting his elbows on his knees. "What's with the two of you? You guys never even spoke for years. And all of a sudden, you're planning birthday parties together and bonding over your mutual friendship with some old lady, and, like"—he waves a hand at me— "saying stuff like that about each other."

My heart seizes on that last part. "Is *Jacob* saying stuff like that about me, too?"

Owen crosses his arms over his chest and gives me a death stare. "Why do you care?"

"I—" Why *do* I care? With a sharp inhale, I picture Jacob at the piano playing that beautiful, haunting song. Making me smile when I was upset with my parents. Jumping in to help me decorate piles of cupcakes for Owen's birthday. Breaking the world speed record to come and get me from the steps of a Brooklyn brownstone just because I called and asked him to.

Tangled up with me on the couch.

I close my eyes.

And in that moment, I know, without a doubt, exactly why I care.

Chapter 34

My eyes fly open, and I stare at my brother. "Oh my God."

"What?"

I get up and pace across the room and then back. Pausing in front of Owen, I open my mouth and then close it again. And then I spin on my heel and pace back and forth again.

"Sadie. *What is it?*"

"I—" I stop pacing and press my hands to my flushed cheeks. "*I'm in love with Jacob,*" I half-mumble, half-blurt out.

Owen's mouth drops open, and at first, no sound comes out. He blinks a couple of times and then drops his head into his palms. His shoulders begin to shake, silently in the beginning, but soon, I can hear little jagged puffs of breath from beneath his hands.

"Owen?" I ask cautiously. *What the hell?*

My brother's shoulders shake harder, his whole body rocking now. The gasps grow louder. And all of a sudden, it dawns on me.

"Oh my God. *Are you laughing?*"

He lifts his head from his hands, nodding vigorously, but he can't actually get any words out thanks to the fact that he's practically in hysterics. He grips the arm of the chair really roaring with it now.

"What is the matter with you?" I demand. "Get it together."

"I'm—" He gasps. "I'm trying."

I stand in front of him with my hands on my hips. "Try harder."

"I am, I am. Okay." He coughs. "Sorry, it's just…" And then, *Seriously?* He's laughing again. Finally, after a couple more minutes of this, he sucks in a deep breath and gets it under control.

I smack him in the arm and then cross the room to flop back on the couch. "I can't believe I just *bared my soul* to you, and this is how you reacted."

"I'm sorry. I'm sorry. It's just—" His lips twitch, and if he laughs again, I'll kill him. "Jacob's been low-key in love with you for years. For practically forever."

"He what?" I sit up. "Jacob has not been in love with me."

"He has." Owen nods. "Truly, madly, deeply."

"What? Since when?"

"I think it started when we were in fourth grade, and you were in fifth. Some jerk on the school playground stole Jacob's saxophone and threw it in a dumpster. And you came along and told the kid that if he didn't climb in there and get it, you'd crush him like a bug under your shoe. That was it for Jacob." He throws his hands into the air like *I don't get it*. "Goner."

"I vaguely remember this." I squint at him, searching my memory. "And," I have to acknowledge, "it does sound like something I would've done."

"You think?"

Jacob, in love with me. And all of a sudden, my heart is aching with longing and hope. Is it really possible? He must feel *something* for me. Friendship, attraction. He showed up all those times. And you can't fake the intensity of those kisses we had. But I don't want only attraction or friendship. I want...

Everything.

"So, if I'm in love with him, and he's felt the same for years..." My gaze swings to my brother. "Why were you *laughing*?"

Owen gets to his feet and heads into the kitchen. A minute later, he comes back with a bottle of whiskey and two glasses. "This might call for something a little stronger." He hands me a glass, splashes in some amber liquid, and then takes the bottle and the other glass back to his chair.

I take a tiny sip, and the whiskey burns all the way down. I set the glass on the coffee table next to my untouched beer. "So?" I demand. "Tell me."

"Well." Owen takes his time pouring himself a drink. "Jacob loved you for years, and you were totally oblivious. And now you have all these *feelings* for him..." He shakes his head slowly. "And Jacob finally met someone else."

My stomach lurches. *Paige.*

"How was I supposed to know he felt that way? He never did anything to make me think..."

"Are you kidding? How is it possible you never noticed him constantly hanging around you?"

"He was constantly hanging around *you*. You're his best friend."

"Wrong. *I* never hung out at that bakery where you worked in high school."

What? I mean, sure, Jacob used to sit in the back of the café where I worked. But lots of kids hung out there. And Jacob always had his head bent over a textbook and barely looked up when I brought him his order. "He wasn't there for me. That bakery was a good place to study. Or maybe he just really liked my muffins."

Owen snorts. "Oh, he liked your muffins all right."

If we were sitting closer, I'd smack him again. "You are a gross person."

My brother smiles like he's proud of it. "How many times was he there at the end of the night to drive you home?"

I bite my lip, trying to remember. If Jacob was studying at the café at closing time, he'd offer me a ride. But half the time, he was coming to our house anyway. And those rides were so painfully silent. I couldn't wait for Jacob to pull the car in our driveway so I could jump out and run into the house. "I thought it was because otherwise, *you* would have had to come and get me. Remember, you were the only one who got a car in high school so you could drive to Trenton for those weird Mathletes events?"

"Fine," Owen concedes, tapping his fingers on his whiskey glass. "But our junior year of high school, Jacob wrote an entire album of songs for you. He burned them to a CD, and I swear it took him a whole month to work up the nerve to give it to you."

"He never gave—" But a half-formed memory settles over me. A skinny, flannel-wearing Jacob hovering in my doorway with a CD in his hand. When he gave it to me, I assumed he was Owen's musician friend who liked making mixtapes. I didn't know he *wrote the songs for me.* But maybe I wasn't paying attention. My cheeks burn. I think I thanked him and then put the CD on my shelf.

"You never even listened to that CD, did you?"

I shake my head slowly.

Owen looks at me with his eyebrows arched, like I'm the dumbest person on the planet. Which, maybe I am. Because when I think back on this second chance year, the one constant, the one person I could count on was Jacob. When I needed him, Jacob was there, over and over. And if I really think about it, I see that in his friendship with Owen, too. The way they're like brothers, the way they'll do anything for each other.

That's how Jacob shows he cares. He doesn't make wild declarations. *He shows up.*

I take a sip of whiskey, for courage. "So, what do I do now?"

"Nothing. Unfortunately, I think you do nothing."

"Wait. What? This is the part of the evening where we craft a plan to remind Jacob he still loves me. What am I supposed to do with *nothing*?"

"Listen, Sadie." Owen stands up now, and paces across the room. "Jacob is the best guy I know. And while this may feel like a big revelation to *you*, he's spent a lot of time wrestling with feelings that you didn't reciprocate. And now, he's finally met someone else. Paige is smart, and fun, and she draws him out of his shell." He stops in front of me. "You know I love you. But..." He cringes, pulling off his hat and running a hand through his hair. "That's why I need to tell you that I think Jacob is finally moving on. And I just don't want him to get hurt again."

I can see Owen is really serious. All traces of his laughing fit from earlier are gone, and it's clear this really matters to him. And—I look down at my hands—I'm a mess. I've screwed up every single thing I've touched this year, and I'd probably screw this up with Jacob, too. And he deserves better.

"Okay," I whisper. "I totally understand." I get up from the couch, but my legs are wobbly. Now that my feelings for Jacob are so glaringly obvious, my heart is lurching for the door. It's straining to go and find him and tell him how I feel. To beg him to love me back.

But I can't. If he's happy with Paige, I have no right to interfere.

"I think I'm going to bed." I force a smile. "Good night, Owen."

"Wait." He grabs my arm as I walk past. "Are you okay?"

"Yep. Super."

"You're upset." Owen looks me over, and luckily, my face was already puffy, and my eyes were already red, so it's not like he'll be able to tell the difference. "We can talk about this more. I don't want you to get hurt either."

"No...no. It's all been kind of a shock. But I really am

fine." I tug my arm away from him. All I want is to go upstairs so I can stop smiling this stupid fake smile.

He hesitates, and then finally says, "Okay, if you're sure."

I head upstairs to my childhood bedroom, closing the door as quietly as possible so I don't wake up my parents. A couple of years after I moved to New York, my mom packed up my books, movie posters, and other remnants of high school into boxes in the closet and turned it into a guest room. I sit on the bed, staring at the wall that's now painted neutral gray instead of the pale pink of my childhood. The queen replaced my old twin-sized canopy bed, but the matching white dresser and bookcase are the same. My gaze locks on that bookcase, on the shelf that used to hold my rows of CDs.

I jump up off the bed and fling open the closet door. In the back corner, behind the camping gear my parents haven't used in twenty years, sits a pile of cardboard boxes labeled with my name. I haul them out into the room, one by one, and slice open the packing tape. There's really no rhyme or reason or much organization. My mom wouldn't have considered my keepsakes from high school to be very important.

In the first box, I find a stack of old yearbooks, a jewelry box of mostly tarnished silver necklaces given to me by old high school boyfriends, and a folder of recipes I'd cut out of magazines. Another box holds the young adult novels I used to love and that my parents never considered to be quality literature. I'm surprised my mother didn't burn these in the backyard firepit. Another box holds more stuff: framed photos and old journals and sparkly pens. I open the final box to reveal a haphazard pile of old CDs. I dig through them until my hand closes over the one I'm looking for.

When I read the words carefully written on the cover in black Sharpie, my eyes burn. *Songs for Sadie by Jacob Gray.*

How was I so thoughtless? So stupid?

I run my hand over Jacob's neat script. I remember those *d*s and *b*s from when I lived in his apartment during my Very Bad Year, when he'd scrawl his grocery list on a notepad on the fridge. Small round circles with long tails, sort of like backward- and forward-facing half notes.

I turn back to the box of keepsakes. Now that I've found the CD, how am I going to listen to it? It's not like I keep a CD player lying around. I wouldn't even know where to *buy* a CD player, at least not in person, and definitely not in New Brunswick on Christmas. I bet Owen would have some ideas—maybe he left an old CD-ROM drive in the basement that he could hook up to a laptop—but then I'd have to tell him why I need it. Defeated, I'm about to stuff the CD in my suitcase to figure out when I get home in a couple of days, when inspiration strikes.

My mom's car. She drives a twelve-year-old Honda. My parents are always talking about replacing it, but it still runs well, so they're too practical to justify the expense. I'm almost positive it has a CD player.

I tiptoe out of my room and back down to the entryway. My mom's keys are hanging by the door on a nail next to the coat hooks. I slip my feet into my shoes and open the door. At some point in the hour since I arrived home, it started snowing. Our ordinary suburban neighborhood has turned into a magical sparkling wonderland with snow dusting the lawns and Christmas lights blinking on houses. My spirits lift, just slightly. I didn't used to believe in miracles, or second chances but, well, here I am living this year over again. So, maybe there could be a chance for me and Jacob.

Out in the car, I back out of the driveway and head down the street. When I'm around the corner and out of sight of the house, I pull over and park. If anyone in my house wakes up, I don't want them to find me in the driveway listening to Jacob's CD. I can tell them I forgot my toothbrush and ran to the twenty-four-hour pharmacy or something.

I leave the car running, and with shaking hands, I carefully pull the CD from the case. After a bit of trial and error, I figure out how to open the player, and a little plastic tray comes sliding out. I lay the CD on the tray and the dashboard sucks it back in. There are a few clicks and whirs, and then the digital display blinks the words *Track 1*. And suddenly, the car fills with the first gentle chords of a piano.

It takes me a second to register what I'm hearing. But when I do, my heart bursts open like molten chocolate cake.

Chapter 35

I'd know that haunting melody anywhere, the beautiful chords of the song Jacob played on the piano that night in his apartment.

That song was for me? He wrote it for *me*?

Tears well in my eyes, and I'm filled with an overwhelming longing to be there with him again, on that night, on the couch in the semidarkness. He loved me then, I know he did. Before I screwed it all up, before I wished away that year and wished for this one instead. I'd wanted Alex and my job and so many things that I can see with such clarity were wrong for me. When what I really needed was right there in front of me. If I could go back, I'd do it all differently. I'd never let him walk out thinking everything that happened between us was a mistake.

I turn up the volume as the music swells around me.

I'd never let him walk out at all.

A few more bars of the music play, and then—*Oh God, what's happening?*—the player starts to rattle. I lean in, searching for a power button to switch it off. But there isn't one, and the noise grows louder, sort of a creaking now.

I frantically hit the eject button to get my CD out. The disk stays in the machine, but now it's making a horrible, scratching, metallic whir. I try the eject button again, over and over. *Oh please.*

Finally, the CD player jerks open with another terrible screech, and my disk comes flying out with a pop. I grab it, and when I do, it cracks into two pieces.

"No!" I shriek.

Noooooooo.

I clutch the halves in my hands, trying to piece them back together. But even if I could somehow make that work, the whole disk is marked with wide scratches, as if it were clawed by a lion who hates me.

It's toast.

It's gone, and I'll never get it back. And maybe that's a metaphor for everything that mattered before I stupidly tanked my old life and chose this one instead. Maybe Kasumi is gone, and Jacob is gone, and my dream to be a pastry chef is gone. And the old Sadie—the one who was pretty great but talked herself into not believing it—maybe she's gone, too.

I flop my head down on the steering wheel with a low moan.

Thump. Thump.

My head flies up and swings toward the noise on the driver's side window. I let out a scream. All I can see is a gloved hand and an arm in a blue coat, but it's clearly a man—tall and broad—standing next to the car, knocking on the glass. I reach for the gear shift so I can peel out of here. But right before I do, the man calls out, "Sadie?"

It's muffled through the window. How does he know my name? And then—"It's Jacob." Ah, okay, that explains it. He takes a step back and holds his hands in the air as if to show me he's harmless.

I roll down the window. "Jesus, Jacob, you scared me to death," I yell. My heart bubbles like doughnuts in hot oil.

"Shhh. Don't wake the neighborhood," he whispers. "What are you doing here?" Jacob bends down to peer into the car, and little droplets of melted snow sparkle on his dark hair. What if I got out of the car and threw myself in his arms? But then I remember the CD on my lap. I quickly shove the pieces onto the floor mat to hide the evidence.

"What are *you* doing here?" I ask. Maybe my longing for him somehow sent a wish into the universe and he appeared? Believe me, stranger things have happened. But next time, the universe and I need to work on our wish-delivery system. I can't take this kind of excitement.

Jacob hitches his chin toward the Craftsman bungalow across the street from where I'm parked. "That's my parents' place."

Oh right. Jacob grew up only a couple of blocks from Owen and me. I probably would have recognized the house in the light of day, but tonight, I had my mind on other things.

"I tried calling when I saw you sitting out here, but you didn't answer," Jacob continues.

I look around the car. "I think I left my phone at home."

"So, are you here looking for...me?" he asks.

"Yes." *Yes, I'm here looking for you. I will be looking for you for the rest of my life.* "Uh, I mean, no. I mean, I was just out for a drive. You want to come?" I kick the CD farther under my seat.

He hesitates, and I'm seized with wild hope. Finally, his shoulders droop, just a little. "I can't. Paige is here, and we were in the middle of a movie. I just came out when we noticed your car."

"Oh." I look back toward the house, and Paige is standing in the doorway now. I mean, of course Paige is here. That's how it works. When you're dating someone, and they're important to you, you invite them home for the holidays. It's not like Owen didn't warn me. She waves, and I lift my hand weakly in return. "That's so nice that Paige is here with you for Christmas."

"Well, her family is in California, and she couldn't get the time off to fly out there. I didn't want her to be alone."

"She's lucky to be with you." *So lucky.* "I'll let you get back to your movie." I shift my body so I'm facing the front windshield.

Jacob takes a step back, away from the car. "Merry Christmas, Sadie."

"You too, Jacob." I put the car in gear and drive off.

Chapter 36

It's amazing how much heavier your body feels with half of your heart missing.

I drift through the rest of the holiday in a daze, which, in the end, is a blessing. When I make the announcement to my family that I didn't get the promotion, I have a new level of detachment that I've never been able to achieve with my parents before. I guess they're upset, but you know what? That's their problem. I'm dealing with my own heartbreak over here, and I don't have the energy to suffer through theirs.

Back in the city, I spend my time lying in bed, staring up at the ceiling with Gio curled up on my chest. I'm going to have to figure out a job soon, because I only have a couple of months' cushion before I'll have to dip into the money I've been saving to start my bakery. For now, I can't face it, though. New York might be a big city, but the restaurant industry is a small town, and I'm sure Xavier has trash-talked me to everyone he knows. If I end up losing this apartment, it's not like Jacob is going to take me in again.

I try not to dwell on Jacob, but he's everywhere in this tiny apartment. Standing in the middle of the room, filling up the space. Smiling at me from my couch, a plate of chocolate cake on his lap. Wrestling with my cat and suggesting the perfect name.

Walking across the room, sitting on the bed, and kissing me.

The worst part is that I did this to myself. Jacob loved me. I know he did. All through my Very Bad Year, and long before that, he loved me in the most generous, thoughtful, the most *Jacob* ways. If I hadn't been so self-absorbed, I might have looked up from my own misery to see it. To see him. And if I had, I'd probably be with him right now. But I wished that year away. I wished that chance away. And when I did, I set a whole new year into motion. One where Jacob met Paige, and he fell in love with her instead of me. It's all my fault. And there's nothing I can do to change it.

By the time the morning of New Year's Eve rolls around, Gio and I are three seasons of *The Golden Girls*, six pints of Ben & Jerry's, and a packet of cat treats into my epic moping marathon. I really, really, really don't want to go out and face the world, but Zoe is planning a New Year's party at the café, and she needs me to make the pastries. As miserable as I am, I can't let Zoe down, so I drag myself out of bed and head for the shower for the first time in...Well. Let's not talk about how long it's been.

Six hours later, I'm at Higher Grounds arranging a tray with macarons while José Luis and Zoe bustle around, moving tables and hanging decorations, once again at the direction of Mrs. Kaminski.

"Come on, Mrs. K," José Luis says, shimmying across the dance floor to the music playing through the speakers. He holds out his hand. "Don't we deserve a little break? Why don't you show me your moves?"

Mrs. Kaminski swats him away, and I can't help but laugh. I have to admit, I'm feeling a teeny, tiny bit better. This place always seems to do that to me. I go back to my pastries, and a minute later, as I'm wrestling with an industrial-sized box of plastic wrap, I hear the front door jingle.

"I'm sorry, we're closed for a private party," Zoe tells the customer who walked in.

"Oh, I just wanted some coffee," the customer says.

My head jerks up. I'd know that voice anywhere.

"Kasumi?"

My former best friend stands at the counter, staring at me with wide eyes. "Sadie? Wow, I didn't expect to see you here."

She's wearing a black coat, but underneath, I can see the edges of a tulle skirt peeking out. It's New Year's Eve, she's probably off to a costume party, one that she'll photograph beautifully and get a hundred billion likes on Instagram. The ache in my heart comes back in full force. I miss Kasumi. I miss her energy and the fun we had. I miss talking to her.

She eyes my tray of cookies. "Do you work here now?"

I nod. "Yeah, I make all the pastries."

"What happened to Xavier's?" There's an edge to her voice, and I can't blame her. I put Xavier's first and blew up our friendship over it. But at least Kasumi's talking to me;

she hasn't turned and walked out, which is major progress from all my other attempts to reach out to her. Is this my chance to apologize and finally fix this?

Suddenly nervous, I drop the box of plastic wrap and fumble to pick it up. "Could we talk for a minute? I really want to explain what happened. And apologize to you."

Kasumi hesitates, but she doesn't say no. I seize on this opening, tilting my head toward a table in the back of the room. "Please? We can sit over there."

"I have to work tonight..." She trails off, looking at me across the counter, and then she finally nods. "But I guess I have five minutes."

I blow out a relieved sigh. "Thank you."

We make our way to the table in the back, and Zoe swings by to drop off two cups of coffee. I clutch the mug, grateful to have something to do with my hands. "Thanks, Zoe."

"Let me know if you two need anything else, okay?" Zoe must have overheard our conversation at the counter because she rests a hand on my shoulder, showing she's here for me, before she walks away.

Kasumi watches Zoe head back behind the counter, and then turns back to me. "So."

I take a deep breath and look at her across the table. "I want to apologize for throwing you and Samantha under the bus at Xavier's. I knew she didn't leave that tray of food out, and I should have backed you up."

"I just don't understand why you didn't. I mean, what happened to you?" Kasumi's eyes narrow, and she levels an accusing glare at me. "You used to be such a strong person, and you'd stand up for people and have their backs. And then all of a sudden, it was like you were a different person, and I didn't know you at all."

I look down at my hands wrapped around my coffee mug. "You're right. And I'm so sorry."

"So, what changed?" Kasumi leans back against her chair and crosses her arms.

"I don't know how to explain it, exactly." Again, the *I'm living this whole year over for the second time* explanation really isn't going to cut it. But it's not really about that anyway. I let my friend down. That was a decision I made. "To be honest, I guess I just started listening to the voices in my head. The ones saying that if I want to be a success, I had to play the game." I stare into the dark liquid in my cup. "You know, don't be so loud or opinionated, or..." I shrug. "I got scared that if I didn't tone it down, I'd lose the things that mattered to me... Like my job. Or Alex."

Kasumi looks at me sideways. "So, how did that work out for you? You know, not being so loud, or opinionated, or whatever?"

"Really, really badly." A laugh bubbles up before I can stop it. "And—" My smile fades. "It turns out that I did lose things that mattered to me. That *actually* mattered." I meet her eyes. "Like you."

She looks at me for a moment, her face softening now. And then she nods like maybe she kind of gets it. "To be fair to you, it probably wasn't just the voices in your head you were hearing. It was also the voices of your parents, and Alex, and you know..." Her lips curve into a tentative smile. "Society."

I look up at her. She *does* get it. Why didn't I just talk to her about all this months ago, when we were still friends? Maybe I wouldn't have felt so alone. Maybe I could have saved us both so much heartache. "That's not an excuse, though. I made my own decisions."

Kasumi takes a sip of her coffee. "So, what *did* happen at Xavier's? Why don't you work there anymore?"

I open my mouth to give the same explanation I've been spouting to everyone, the one that sounds like the pack of lies it is. *I decided Xavier's wasn't a good fit, I'm looking for new opportunities, it was time to move on, blah, blah, blah.* But instead, what comes out of my mouth is, "Xavier sexually harassed me."

Kasumi's eyes widen. "Oh my God, Sadie. I'm sorry."

"Yeah." I stare out across the café. It still makes my skin crawl to remember it. "He dangled a promotion in front of me to try to get me to sleep with him." *It never ceases to be mortifying, does it?* "One that he never intended to give me."

Kasumi is silent for a minute, and then finally, she pulls her coat off, like she's decided to stay for a while. And then she leans in. "He did that to me, too."

My gaze flies to hers. "What? When?"

"A couple of different times. He'd reach across me while I was chopping vegetables and get a little too close. Or he'd make an uncomfortable dirty joke when nobody else was around." She shakes her head. "And then one day, he called me into his office and tried to back me up against the desk..." She cringes. "I was lucky that one of the servers—Ethan—walked in, or I don't know what I would have done."

"Why didn't you tell me?"

Kasumi stares at her coffee, sliding her finger around the lip of the cup. "It was so embarrassing. I mean, I'm someone who stands up for herself, who works with her best friend to unionize her culinary school classmates..." She gives me a sad smile. "I just couldn't believe it was happening to me, and I didn't know how to stop it."

I nod because I *get it.* "Even though you know rationally that it's not your fault, you wonder if maybe you did something to lead him on. Because otherwise, why would he ever think..." I trail off, remembering all the times Xavier complimented me on my pastries, all the times he dangled that promotion in front of me, and I'd been so grateful. Had I given him the wrong idea?

"Right, and you can't help but think, he's a world-renowned chef, and I'm just...me." Kasumi shakes her head. "Who was going to believe me?"

"I would have."

She meets my eyes now. "A year ago, I would have believed that unconditionally. But then all of a sudden, you started sucking up to him, going along when he wanted to parade you in front of those VIPs, and backing down when he bullied people. I...I didn't know anymore."

"I'm sorry." I reach out and grab her hand. "I'm so sorry you went through that, and I wasn't there for you."

"To be honest, I probably overreacted when I stopped talking to you for so long." Her expression is pained. "I just wanted someone to blame, and it was easier to blame you than it was to blame Xavier, or you know...the whole fucking patriarchy."

"I wish we'd just talked about this back then."

"Well, I'm glad we've both gotten away from that place. And honestly, it's probably for the best." She gazes around the room. "This place is gorgeous, and that woman you work with seems really nice." She hitches a chin in Zoe's direction. "And I found a new job working with Devon."

"Your social media influencer friend?"

"Yeah, he's been planning these huge parties, and I'm working with him to promote them. It's going really well, and I'm thinking of starting my own business."

"Kasumi, that's amazing!"

She pulls out her phone and shows me an Instagram post about a carnival-themed party tonight. I gasp. My gaze flies to her outfit, a sparkly red-and-white–striped T-shirt tucked into a black tulle skirt with suspenders. I've seen that outfit before. Oh my God. The carnival party is *tonight*.

"Kasumi," I say, my voice shaking. "Will there be a fortune teller at the party?"

"Yes, why?" Her brow furrows. "What is it with you and fortune tellers?" But she sounds more curious than mad.

"I, uh." What am I supposed to say to that? "I'm just curious. You know, it seems like fun to have your fortune told."

"Well, I can put you on the list. I'll be pretty busy running around at the party, but..." She flashes me a smile that's almost shy. "Maybe we could hang out later this week?"

My chest swells like sourdough in the proofing drawer. "I'd really love that."

She smiles and stands, pulling on her coat. "I have to go, but if you come tonight, just give the guy at the door your name. And I'll text you about getting together later this week." Kasumi pauses for a moment, and then she leans in and gives me a quick hug. "I'm really happy to see you, Sadie."

"I'm really happy to see you, too."

After Kasumi leaves, I break records mixing cake batter, piping choux pastry, and rolling out pie dough. I need to get to that party and find the fortune teller. We have some unfinished business.

Chapter 37

There have been a lot of moments over the past year where I've experienced that déjà vu feeling of having had a conversation or been in a certain place before. And, for the most part, I've gotten used to it. But nothing prepared me for walking into that carnival-themed party for the second time. I feel like I've stepped into a movie that's playing on repeat, one with trapeze artists, sword-swallowers, and a low-key lion furry as a DJ.

And, oh shit. Clowns.

Bozo moonwalks across the dance floor, an actually pretty impressive feat considering those massive shoes. I'd stop to watch, but I don't have a death wish, so I quickly scurry in the other direction. I grab a frothy buttered pop-corn martini and down it for courage, realizing mid-chug that I didn't like these things the first time around, and they've only gotten worse since my Very Bad Year. Still, I finish it because I've already committed.

I locate the fortune teller's tent—not really an enormous challenge considering it's in exactly the same place as it was the first time I found it—and I stay on the periphery of the room, edging around the bodies pulsing on the dance floor. As I draw closer to the panels of purple velvet, I try to swallow down the ball of spun sugar that seems to have lodged itself in the back of my throat. Last time around, I barreled inside the enclosure with a clown in hot pursuit. But now, I cautiously pull aside one curtain and slip inside, standing as straight and rigid as the tent poles holding it up.

The same tiny old woman with the same shiny red scarf tied over her long gray hair sits behind her table. Her crystal ball rests in exactly the same spot as it did during my Very Bad Year, and her scarlet-and-gold peasant dress rustles as she moves. I'm soothed by the familiarity of it all. She might be the only person in the world who understands this strange time loop I've gotten myself into, and I'm hoping for a moment where I'm not the only one holding the secret.

The fortune teller glances up from her crystal ball, takes one look at me, and mutters, "Oh, it's you," in a flat, disinterested voice.

I take a couple of stumbling steps into the middle of the room. "So, you know who I am?"

The fortune teller gives a small nod. "You're one of the ones who wanted to go and change the past." She looks at me straight on. "I knew you'd be back."

"How did you know?"

"Because you people are always back." She waves a dismissive hand. "You think if you can just go into the past and change yourself, change the people around you, you'll win some golden ticket to your image of a perfect life. And then a year later, you realize it's all smoke and mirrors, and you end up standing here—*wah, wah, wah*," she moans in a baby voice. *"I want to switch it back around again."*

"Can I do that? Can I switch it back around?" Somewhere in the far corners of my consciousness, I realize I'm probably missing the point. But after the year I've had, it's too hard, it's too much work to go there, and I'm too tired to try. So, I seize on what I want to hear.

She sighs deeply, rolling her eyes as if she expected better of me, and I'm nothing but a massive disappointment to her. *Join the club, lady.* "No."

I take that in. *No?* "Um, no isn't really going to work for me."

She gives me a bored shrug, examining her manicure.

"What if—?"

"No."

"But—"

"Final sale, no returns or exchanges."

I throw my hands in the air. "But you sold me a defective year! Nothing turned out the way it was supposed to. The job turned out to be horrible, the guy was all wrong for me, and the right guy fell for someone else."

She looks up at me, her eyes wide and bright, mouth twisted with pity. "Wow, that really *does* sound like a problem."

I breathe out a sigh of relief. Finally, she gets it. "Thank you. So, can we fix it?"

The fortune teller leans back in her chair. "Still no." From under the table, she produces a hardback book with a royal-blue cover and a title in embossed gold. *Spells and Curses for the Self-Employed Practitioner, Volume IV.* She slides a pair of reading glasses on her nose and opens the book.

"Are you kidding me?"

She licks her finger and flips the page.

I stand there, incredulous, while she ignores me, nodding along with the bass from the hip-hop song playing out on the dance floor and studying her book. I throw up my hands. "So, what am I supposed to do then? You're the one with the crystal ball and..." I wave at her book. "...*potions*. You tell me what I'm supposed to do."

"You want to know what to do?" she asks, keeping her eyes on the page.

"Yes. Yes, I want to know."

The fortune teller slams the book down on the table so hard the crystal ball rattles, threatening to pop off its stand and roll away. She pulls her glasses off her face, and then looks up at me. "Quit fiddling around in the past. Quit trying to change things that don't need to be changed. Figure out what you want. *And go get it.*"

I'm silent as her words sink in. *Figure out what I want.*

When I wished for this second chance year, I thought if only I could tone myself down and smooth out all the rough edges, I'd land the perfect job, the perfect guy, and finally, my parents' acceptance. But it turns out that in pursuit of those things, I twisted myself into someone I don't recognize. And I lost all the best parts of myself.

I shake my head. "I've spent the last year molding myself into this person I thought I was supposed to be. The one who's not too loud or opinionated or not such a big mouth. And somehow along the way—" I wave my hand with a bitter little laugh. "That girl who stood up for kids on the playground and people at work...and who stood up for *herself*...I don't know where she went. She's gone."

The fortune teller huffs in annoyance. "She's not *gone*." But then she pauses, cocking her head and meeting my eyes. "Maybe she got lost along the way, but"—she flicks a bejeweled hand in my direction—"she's still in there."

"How do you know?" I whisper over the lump in my throat, slowly lowering myself on the stool across from her.

"Because," she says. "You get to choose." Like it's that simple.

"What if I choose wrong?"

"Listen, honey," she barks at me like a grumpy grandma, and for a moment, I wonder if she and Mrs. Kaminski are related. "If you need to be anyone other than exactly who you are—for a shitty restaurant job, for some Wall Street doofus, or to win your parents' love—"

My mouth drops open, because how did she know about all that stuff at Xavier's, and Alex, and *my parents*? I never told her any of that. She gives me a narrow-eyed stare, looks down at the crystal ball, and then back up at me with even more contempt, if that's possible.

Oh right. *Fortune teller with actual magic*. Forgot about that little detail.

"Anyway, *as I was saying*," she continues. "If you need to be anything other than exactly who you are—for *anyone*— then the problem is with them, and not with you."

I bite my lip, as the past year rolls past me like a movie trailer of my life. The poop-emoji cakes and Rob Thurmond's hand on my thigh. Brett and Zach and the designer clothes. My parents' disappointed faces. It turns out the job and the guy weren't so perfect after all. And maybe I don't really want my parents' acceptance if I can't earn it by being myself.

But then there's Zoe and José Luis and Mrs. Kaminski. My chest swells with pride over everything I've built at Higher Grounds. The success of our private events, the buzz over my pastries.

And Jacob.

I falter a little when I think of Jacob. Because maybe I do know what I want. The problem is that I'm terrified I figured it out too late. I turn back to the fortune teller. "What if what I want is gone? And I can't get it back?"

"Well." This time, all traces of annoyance are gone. Her gruff exterior has softened, face lined with compassion. "I guess you won't make that mistake again."

And with that, I know that she's not going to look into her crystal ball, and I've used up all my wishes. I'm planted here, for better or for worse, on this day, in this year. I can choose to stay stuck, to keep looking back at yesterday, at what could have been. Or I can move forward. *To tomorrow.*

"Thanks," I say, standing up and slowly making my way to the door.

The fortune teller clears her throat and hitches her chin at a glass jar on the table. TIPS, the sign says. I laugh for the first time in a long time and stuff a twenty into the jar.

"Good luck," she calls to me as I make my way out of the tent and back onto the dance floor.

Without the thick drapery muting the sound, heavy bass

from the dance music reverberates through me. I stand at the edge of the crowd as bodies kaleidoscope around me. Near the lion's cage, I spot Kasumi taking a selfie with the sword-swallower, and I smile, making a mental note to like the photo on Instagram later. The strong man dances past in his red bodysuit and I give him a wave. He shakes his Styrofoam barbell at me and shimmies onward. And then, out across the dance floor, I spot another familiar face. It's—

Paige. And she's not alone.

She's here with long-haired Brandon, the bike messenger. And by *here*, I mean *making out.* And by *long-haired Brandon*, I mean *not Jacob.*

Did Paige and Jacob break up?

I wade into the crowd until I reach them. And then, because her mouth is still attached to Brandon's, I tap Paige on the shoulder.

"Hiiiiiii!" she says, whirling around and leaning in to give me a sloppy hug.

"Is Jacob here with you?" I yell over the thumping bass.

"What?" Paige tilts her head to the side, trying to hear me over the beat of the music. "No. Jacob is with Owen, I think." She shrugs. "This is Brandon."

"Hi, it's so nice to meet you." Brandon throws his arms around me, even though I'm pretty sure he has no idea who I am.

"So, you two are dating?" I wave my finger between them.

Paige nods happily.

"And you're not dating Jacob anymore?"

She shakes her head.

"Okay." That's all I really need to know. "Good to see you, Paige," I yell. She hugs me again.

With a wave, I turn and make my way toward the exit, my heart swirling like peanut butter through brownie batter. Somehow, Paige is dating Brandon. Which means that maybe . . . Jacob isn't dating anyone?

Near the coat check I notice one of the bars scattered around the periphery of the warehouse, and . . . there's that wave of déjà vu again . . . the line is short. In the same spot as my Very Bad Year, the Grey Goose and Absolut bottles are lined up on the shelf. I order a shot and carry it to a darkish corner where I have absolutely been before. Just like last time around, beanbag chairs and couches are scattered around on the floor and a few couples are talking or making out. Nobody even glances in my direction.

In one swift motion, I toss back the vodka, feeling the burn all the way down. And then, before I can lose my nerve, I dial my phone. It rings once, twice, three times, and—*Oh come on, universe, I'm trying here. The least he can do is pick up.* But he doesn't pick up, and after three more rings, the voicemail clicks on, and Jacob's voice comes through the line telling me to leave a message. I grip the phone tighter, aching from the sound of him, and when the phone beeps, I consider calling back, just to hear it again.

Instead, I start babbling.

"Jacob, it's Sadie. I probably shouldn't be calling you. I've messed a lot of things up this year. But I'm not sure I could live with myself if I didn't tell you that . . . Well." I take a deep breath and then blurt it out. "I-think-I'm-in-love-with-you."

I hesitate now because I'm not sure that's quite right. "No. I *know* I'm in love with you. And I'm sorry that I didn't see it—didn't see *you*—sooner. I wasted so much time. But for once in my life, I know exactly what I want, and it's...you." I pause again, running out of steam now and not sure what to say next. How are you supposed to end a call when you've just confessed your love to someone's voicemail? I really didn't think this one through, but I guess I wouldn't be me if I thought things through. Finally, I settle on an extremely awkward, "Okay. Well...Goodbye." And then I hang up.

I close my eyes, but this time, no warm breeze blows through the warehouse, and there are no magical clouds of sensation. It's just me, standing in a dank warehouse, hoping a boy will love me. Is it possible I could change my life, not by wishes and potions, but just by being...me?

The throbbing beat of dance music rattles me to my core, and I open my eyes slowly, adjusting to the darkness.

I take a deep breath in, and then—

I scream at the top of my lungs.

The clown. The clown is standing in front of me, his too-wide painted-on eyes only inches from my face. I freeze as terror envelops me. *Anything but the clown.* His creepy gloved hands wiggle in my direction, and I back up, right into a table. I'm pinned. Trapped.

Again.

And then, like a trapeze artist sailing in, I remember who I am. I am Sadie Thatcher, and I don't take shit from anyone. I am loud, and opinionated, and yeah, maybe some people would call me abrasive, but those are words they use for women who won't go down without a fight.

And I'll own them.

"Leave me alone!" I yell, rushing the clown like a defensive end and smacking my palms squarely into his shoulders. The clown teeters on his ridiculously large shoes, his arms windmilling in slow motion before he sails backward and lands on his padded clown-butt.

He stares up at me from his place on the floor, a stunned expression on his face, red gloves raised in surrender. I brush off my hands, take my time stepping over him, and then slowly walk out of the warehouse.

Chapter 38

I ride the subway back to my neighborhood, and, once again, I find myself swimming upstream through crowds of revelers carrying New Year's party hats, noise blowers, and bottles of champagne. Out on the street, the buildings create a wind tunnel, but this time, instead of a flimsy bolero jacket and minidress, I'm in jeans and my warm winter coat, and the cold December gale doesn't faze me. I should head to Higher Grounds; it's after nine and the party will be in full swing by now. But I have one more thing to take care of, so instead, my feet turn right instead of left down Bedford Avenue.

Ten minutes later, I slip into the kitchen door at Xavier's. The staff bustles around me, plating dishes and calling out orders, deep in the chaos of the New Year's Eve service. A few people give me odd looks as I cross the kitchen toward the hallway leading to the office, or nudge each other and gesture in my direction, but nobody tries to stop me.

As I leave the safety of the crowded kitchen behind me and draw nearer to seeing Xavier for the first time since I rejected his advances and he gave my job to someone else,

I start to sweat in my heavy coat. I still have dreams about that night in the pantry, still wake up shaking and wondering what I could have done differently. I haven't really thought through what I'll do when I find Xavier, but I'll never put that night behind me until I face him again, on my terms.

And then, before I can spend any more time going over it in my head, I turn the corner and run into him right there in the hallway.

His eyes widen and he takes a step backward, almost as if he's afraid I'll give him another shove like the one in the pantry. And believe me, I'm tempted. He wouldn't be the first clown I knocked on his ass tonight. But I'm not here to assault him, as much as he deserves it. So instead, I say in a cool voice, "Hello, Xavier."

He's silent for a moment, looking me up and down, and then he huffs in disgust. "So, you're slinking back here to beg for your job back," Xavier sneers. "You think you can just walk out on one of the busiest holidays of the year and then show up like nothing happened?"

I should be angry at the nerve, the ego of this man, thinking I'd ever beg for this job back. Except that a year ago, I *did* beg for it back. I went and changed my entire life, relived an entire year, because I thought this man's job, his recognition of me mattered more than my own pride and self-respect. I've come a long way since then. And as my friend the fortune teller says, *I'll never make that mistake again.*

And with that, the tension leaves my body. I don't need this confrontation. I don't need to tell Xavier off, to make a speech, to make a point that he's not evolved enough to understand anyway. This isn't about him. It's about me realizing I deserve better than this.

But before I can spin on my heel and walk away, he keeps talking. "Well, it's your lucky day because we're short-staffed, and Rob Thurmond is here with a large party. For some reason, he seems to like you—" He follows that with another huff of disgust. "So, if you get changed and get your ass out there, I might not have you blackballed from every respectable restaurant in the city. And maybe if you do a *very good job*, I'll let you come back to work."

My skin crawls at the innuendo in *very good job*. And the absolute last thing I ever want to see again in my life is Rob's florid face and beady little eyes.

But then I think of Rob's hand on my leg and Xavier's lips coming toward me. Of Kasumi enduring the same thing in silence. Of all the women out there in the dining room right now, serving Rob's party or needing to stay late after work. I'm not special. If I walk out of here, it will be someone else who leans over to pour a glass of water and ends up with a hand on their ass. Or who goes in the pantry to refill the saltshakers and ends up cornered.

It turns out that a little confrontation isn't looking so bad after all.

"Of course, sir," I say with a smile. "I'd absolutely love to."

An hour later, I'm in my server's blouse, circling Rob's table with a pitcher of water. I splash some into each glass and not a single person thanks me. I don't think anyone even notices I'm there. It's like their glasses magically filled themselves.

Rob is the exception. "Over here," he demands with a wave of his hand. I approach cautiously, like he's a burned pie I left in the oven, and quickly fill his glass. I can feel his eyes on me, sizing me up, and I brace for what he's about to do, tightening my hand on the water pitcher in case I need a weapon. But then someone across the table calls to him, and he turns away to respond. I head to the bar to pick up a drink for one of the other diners.

As I stand at the bar waiting for the bartender to mix up my drink order, someone walks up behind me and grips my ass with a firm hand. "Hey, sweetheart." Rob's hot breath blows in my ear. "Get me a martini, will you?"

My entire body tenses, and I whirl around to face him. He's standing so close I have to back up against the bar to keep his crotch from pressing up against my stomach. Rob rests one arm on the bar so I'd have to duck under it to escape. And even though I've been in this position before, even though I was expecting it this time, I'm horrified that it's actually happening. I'm in shock that a man would have the audacity to treat a woman like this in a room full of servers, restaurant guests, and his friends. But he believes his power allows him to behave like this.

A sense of calm comes over me. I take a deep, cleansing breath and let it out slowly. "Did you say you wanted a martini?" I ask sweetly. I reach for the cocktail the bartender has just placed on the counter. "Here you go." And then I pick up the glass, and I dump the contents all over his head.

And who would have guessed, but that's all it takes to get his crotch out of my navel and his garlicky breath out of my face. He staggers backward, sputtering, right into a two-top where a couple is celebrating their first anniversary. The table tips backward, taking Rob down with it, and he lands with a crash in a pile of plates and glasses and three-tiered lemon raspberry cake. The anniversary couple spring to their feet as the entire dining room goes silent, all eyes on Rob flailing on the floor like an upended turtle in a puddle of lemon curd.

"Help me," Rob croaks at the anniversary couple, holding out a sticky hand to the man towering over him in shock and awe. The man reaches out to help Rob to his feet as I approach.

"If you ever even *think* of groping me or anyone else at this restaurant again," I say, my voice rising sharply. "I'll have you arrested."

The anniversary man's wide eyes fly from Rob to my angry face. And then his gaze darkens as it swings back to Rob. In the next second, the man opens his hand and lets Rob go crashing back down to the floor. I'm delighted to see his ass land right on a dessert fork.

At this point, Xavier has come running into the dining room. "Sadie," he hisses. "I should have known you'd be involved in this. What do you think you're doing?"

Before I can tell him that what I'm doing is refusing to smile and look pretty while someone tries to sexually assault me, he turns to the crowded restaurant. "Folks," he says in a booming voice, clapping his hands together. "I apologize for my employee's unprofessional behavior. I'd like to offer dessert to everyone, on the house."

"*Unprofessional?*" I push past him until I'm standing in the center of the dining room. "You know what's unprofessional? Letting your customers casually grope the women who work for you because they throw their money around. You know what else is unprofessional? The owner of a restaurant trying to coerce his employee to have sex with him in exchange for a promotion." I level my gaze at him so it's clear exactly who I'm talking about.

Several people in the dining room gasp.

Xavier comes over and grabs my arm. I jerk away from him as one of the servers—Ethan—runs to my side. "Get your hands off her," he barks.

I flash him a smile because I appreciate his help, even if I no longer need it.

"This woman is lying," Xavier announces to the customers. "She's bitter that she didn't get a promotion, and she's making this up."

"Am I making it up, too?" a voice calls from the back of the restaurant. It's Sonya, one of the servers. "Because you cornered me in the break room one night and implied I'd lose my job if I didn't do what you wanted."

"The same thing happened to me." The bartender steps out from behind the bar.

Now Xavier is the one sputtering.

The woman from the anniversary couple turns to her companion. "This is disgusting. We're leaving." She marches away from the table, and I notice with great satisfaction that the heel of her shoe lands directly on Rob's foot.

Across the room, another group stands up and tosses

their napkins on the table. As they head for the door, several other tables of customers follow.

"Wait!" Xavier calls to the rapidly emptying room, but one by one each table gets to their feet and walks out. He turns to me. "You're going to regret this."

I shrug because Xavier can't hurt me anymore. "Why?" I ask innocently. "Because I'll never work in this town again?" I shrug. "I have a feeling I'm not the only one."

And with that, I take a step over Rob—*another clown on the floor, thanks to yours truly*—and for the last time, I turn and walk out the door.

Chapter 39

*B*ack at Higher Grounds, José Luis is making cappuccino and Kahlúa cocktails behind the bar, and Mrs. Kaminski is sitting in her usual spot at the counter. In front of her is a large glass with a straw, and José Luis keeps topping it off with whatever is left in the bottom of the mixer after he pours the customers' drinks. When I arrive, he produces another glass and straw, and now I'm downing my own leftover cocktail.

From my perch on the seat beside Mrs. Kaminski, I take it all in. The café is bright and festive, packed with people mingling around the dessert trays, chatting in small groups at the café tables, and dancing to the band onstage. At some point in the evening, José Luis dug up a couple of gold feather boas and plastic New Year's headbands, and both he and Mrs. Kaminski are wearing them proudly.

Customers come by to rave about my pastries to José Luis, and he points to me. "The *artiste* is right here!" he declares in a voice loud enough to make me wonder if he's also been hitting the Kahlúa.

My phone buzzes on the counter, and I grab it like it contains the secret to the universe. Which, at this point, it does. My universe anyway. Midnight is approaching, and I haven't heard a word back from Jacob about my rambling message. I check my texts, and my shoulders slump. It's a message from Owen, wishing me a happy New Year and asking me what I'm doing.

At Higher Grounds.

Cool.

What are you doing? I'm shamelessly hoping he'll mention Jacob.

The usual, Owen replies, telling me exactly nothing. Or maybe it's telling me everything. If Jacob and Owen are together, Jacob would have said something about my message. The fact that my brother is completely silent on the subject doesn't seem like a very positive development. I drop my phone back on the counter.

Zoe, who's been absent since I arrived, pushes open the front door of the café with an armful of milk jugs balanced in her hands. I run over and grab two of them to lighten her load.

"Thanks, Sadie." Zoe hefts the rest of the plastic containers onto the coffee bar, handing one to José Luis to mix up another batch of cappuccino cocktails. "I had to run to the deli down the street. With the mad rush for your pastries over the holidays, we've been selling out of drinks, too." She gives me a grin, her white teeth contrasting against her dark skin. "Not that I'm complaining; you've been amazing for business. In fact, if there was any chance you could come in and bake a couple more days a week..."

I turn to look at her, shaping the idea in my head like a ball of focaccia dough.

Zoe holds up a hand, probably taking my silence for lack of interest. "Sorry, I don't mean to pressure you. I know you're stretched thin already. And," Zoe gives me a rueful smile, "baking at Higher Grounds isn't exactly your dream."

And suddenly, it's so clear, I can't believe I didn't see it.

"Actually, Zoe, what if it *is* my dream?"

Zoe rounds the counter so she's standing on the other side, facing me. "What do you mean?"

"I love this place, you give me tons of creative freedom, I make my own hours, and I work with the best people in the world." I lean on the counter, my excitement building. "What if I want to work here full time? Or...even better. What if we were partners? I have some money saved. Why would I open my own place when everything I need is right here?"

Zoe's mouth drops open. "I— You'd want to do that?"

"You're selling out of everything I make. What if I could really focus on increasing the pastry offerings and building our private events? And we haven't even *talked* about catering. I know some really hardworking people who unfortunately might be out of a job soon—" I think back to the customers marching out of Xavier's restaurant. We could hire the chefs and servers to cater our events. "There are so many possibilities."

"Sadie," Zoe says, looking a little dazed. "I completely

love this idea. But, what about your dream of opening your own bakery?"

I think about that dream. Of *all* the dreams I've been chasing during my Very Bad Year. I was so wrapped up in what I thought I wanted I didn't stop to recognize what I actually had.

I'll never make that mistake again.

By some miracle, I've been given a second chance on my second chance, and I'm not about to blow it.

"Zoe, I don't really want my own place. I want to work with people I care about, who care about me. And that's you." I grab her hand and squeeze. The combination of caffeine, alcohol, and adrenaline leaves me a little light-headed, filling me with emotion. I turn to José Luis. "And you." He blows me a kiss. "And you, too, Mrs. Kaminski." I smile at the older woman. Her eyes are glassy from the cocktails, her HAPPY NEW YEAR's headband askew, and she smiles back at me for maybe the first time ever.

Finally, my gaze slides back to Zoe. "So, what do you say?"

Across the room, the band pauses the music and the singer steps up to the mic. "Only one minute until midnight!" he announces. And suddenly, we're swallowed up by the crowd jumping to their feet. Noisemakers rattle, José Luis pops corks on bottles of champagne, and the band plays a drumroll.

"Ten..."

Someone slides a bubbling glass into my hand.

"Five..."

Someone else wraps a gold feather boa around my neck.

"Three..."

And then Zoe is back in front of me, clutching my hand.

"*Yes.* Let's do this." She flashes me a grin. "*Partner.*"

"One..."

I throw my arms around her.

"*Happy New Year!*"

Chapter 40

The party carries on for hours, and I'm swept up helping José Luis make drinks and refilling pastry trays. I jump in to restock bar supplies, arrange piles of chocolate-dipped profiteroles and lemon shortbread stars on the dessert table, and mingle with the crowd, handing out dozens of cards and talking up Higher Grounds' special orders and private events.

The last partygoers don't trickle out until sometime after 4:00 a.m. Mrs. Kaminski is nodding off in her chair, but she insisted on staying until the end, and she rallies when José Luis pops open one more bottle of champagne to toast Zoe's and my new partnership. We crowd into a corner booth, lifting our glasses and talking about ideas for the future of the business. I toss back the champagne with a wide smile, but inside, I'm starting to lose a little bit of steam.

Jacob should be here tonight. He's a part of Higher Grounds too, and it doesn't feel right for us to celebrate this new chapter without him. My phone hasn't buzzed since my brother texted hours ago, and Jacob must have gotten my message by now. His silence can only mean that he'd rather pretend nothing ever happened between us, and I guess I have to accept that.

I guess I have to be happy with the fact that I gave it my best shot.

Zoe slides in next to me and puts an arm around my shoulder. And then it's like she can read my mind, or maybe it's all over my face, because she says, "Jacob should be here, shouldn't he?"

It hits me at once, and my eyes fill with tears. It's going to be a long, long time before it stops hurting. I guess maybe I deserve a little hurt, because Jacob felt this way about me for years, and I was clueless. But he moved on, and someday I will, too. But today is not that day. My throat tightens, and all I can do is nod. "Shit," I mutter, wiping my cheeks with the heel of my hand.

Zoe gives me a comforting smile. "Don't give up on him yet. I bet he'll come around."

My head swivels in her direction. "How do you know how I feel about him? *I* didn't even know until..." My voice cracks. "Until it was too late."

"Well, he's a great guy. Who wouldn't be a little bit in love with him, and I say that as a happily married lesbian, mind you." She hitches her chin at Mrs. Kaminski, dozing again with her cheek on José Luis's shoulder. "I think he's the first man to turn Mrs. Kaminski's head since her husband died two decades ago. And when he's around, you both get that..." She waves a hand up and down in my direction. "...*glow*. I was almost afraid to go in the kitchen when the two of you were baking for your brother's birthday for fear I'd find you doing it on the prep table."

My body heats as I imagine Jacob lifting me up onto that metal surface and leaning in to kiss me. Dropping the pastry bag and putting those beautiful musician's hands on my...

God. I press my hands to my heated cheeks. "Well, this is just great, Zoe. I will never be able to go into that kitchen again without blushing."

She laughs. "I'm just saying. Don't write him off yet."

At that moment, the front door swings open and a cold breeze blows into the café. I spin in my seat. Maybe it's Jacob, and Zoe really *is* a mind reader.

But the person standing in the doorway in a cloud of black tulle and red glitter isn't Jacob. It's Kasumi, and if there is one person other than Jacob I want to see tonight, it's her. This night feels like the start of something new and special. Something important. I want her to be a part of it.

"Sadie, I'm so glad you're here!" She runs to our table and drops into the seat across from me, waking Mrs. Kaminski up from her nap. "I went to your apartment, but you didn't answer the door, and then I remembered that you"—she points at Zoe—"said there'd be a party here tonight. This is *not* news I could share over text."

"What kind of news?" I sit up straight.

Kasumi holds out her phone, open to her Social page. "Press play," she says, gesturing at the video pinned at the top.

We all crowd around Kasumi's phone, and I gently tap on the video. A few shaky seconds go by before I realize what I'm looking at, and then the video comes into focus. It's me, shot on someone's phone from across the room at Xavier's. I'm standing over Rob as he flops around on the floor like a fish, and my voice cuts in sharply, demanding that he never grope anyone again. The video follows me crossing the room to tell off Xavier and ends with the other staff members chiming in with their own experiences of harassment and the diners walking out.

"Marianne sent it to me, and I had to post it." Kasumi points to the bottom of the screen where the likes and retweets are in the hundreds of thousands. "Look how many people are talking about this. Everyone is saying what a badass you are, and there are calls to revoke Xavier's James Beard Award."

"I—" For once in my life, I'm stunned into silence.

"Are you mad?" Kasumi asks, looking at me cautiously. "I know I should have asked you first. But you're so freaking amazing, and I admit, I just really wanted Xavier to get what's coming to him. This felt…bigger than just us, you know?"

I nod because I do know. That's exactly how I felt when this scene was playing out in real time. Like it was my chance to do something that really mattered. "No—I'm not mad." It occurs to me that now there's video evidence of my big, loud, opinionated mouth all over the internet, and my parents are going to see this. For some reason—maybe it's the alcohol or sheer exhaustion—it strikes me as hilarious, and suddenly I can't stop laughing. My friends cackle along with me.

"Girl, you're a hero," José Luis declares once we've calmed down a bit. "I'm so proud of you."

"Good for you, Sadie," Zoe says, bumping her shoulder into mine.

Even Mrs. Kaminski nods in appreciation. "At my first job as a nurse, the doctor I worked for used to squeeze my behind when I walked by. Back then we didn't call it 'sexual harassment,' we just called it 'being a woman.'" She pats my hand. "I wish I'd had someone like you to give him a good kick in the you-know-what."

"Me too, Mrs. Kaminski."

Zoe holds up her glass. "This venture is going to be such a wild success, you'll never have to work for a man like that again."

Kasumi looks around the café glittering with silver Christmas lights and candles flickering on the tables. "So, what is it that you guys do here, anyway? The space is really pretty." Kasumi gestures at Zoe. "You own the place?"

"I do." Zoe flashes me a grin. "But I've got a brand-new partner."

I smile back. "We're branching out into high-end retail baked goods, catering, and private events."

"Oh wow. I need more info," Kasumi says.

I sit up in my seat, remembering that this is exactly the kind of thing Kasumi is good at. Look at how many hits she got on my video in just a couple of hours. "Any chance your soon-to-launch social media marketing business is looking for its first client?"

Kasumi holds up her phone and waves for me and Zoe to lean in. She snaps a photo. "Let's see..." Her thumbs fly over her screen. *"The restaurant employee who took down Xavier for sexual harassment is launching a brand-new woman-owned venture."* She waves her hand in a give-it-to-me gesture. "And the website is...?"

"HighergroundsNYC.com," Zoe supplies, eyes wide as she watches Kasumi in action.

"Okaaay..." Kasumi continues typing. Then with a dramatic tap of her finger, she looks up at us. "Set to post tomorrow at nine a.m. Then we sit back and let the magic happen."

"Wow, Kasumi. Thank you."

"Anything for a friend." She cocks her head and gives me a smile, and my eyes well up all over again. I'm reaching across the table for a napkin as I hear the front door swing open again. Behind me, my brother's voice bellows, "Happy New Year, everyone!"

A moment later, Owen slides into the booth next to me. "What's up, Sadie the Cat Lady?" he asks, drumming his hands on the table.

Mrs. Kaminski peers at him over the top of her glasses. "Nice of you to finally show up."

"Mrs. Kaminski, I love you," I say, cracking up.

My brother gives me an exaggerated glare. "We sat on a broken-down F train for hours to get here tonight, and this is the thanks I get?"

My head jerks up. *"We?"*

"Yeah, Cat Lady. After your voicemail confession—which, by the way, I notice you didn't listen to a word I said at Christmas, did you?—we hopped on the subway to come over here, but the damn train broke down on us."

The *F train*. It broke down during my Very Bad Year, and of course it broke down the second time around, too. Is that why I didn't hear from Jacob? Because he was on the train? But if Owen is sitting across from me... *Where's Jacob?*

Chapter 41

I spin around in my seat to find Jacob standing on the stage in the front of the room. My breath hitches at the familiar sight of him: dark hair tousled from the wind, right hand tapping out a nervous rhythm on his thigh, those glasses that do all kinds of things to my insides. He dips his head before looking up, and then his eyes connect with mine. I shove on my brother's arm until he moves out of my way and lets me climb out from the booth. Making my way toward the stage, I keep my gaze glued to Jacob's, and when I'm about ten feet away, I stumble to a stop.

"Hi, Jacob," I whisper, terrified and full of hope.

"Hi, Sadie," he says softly. "I got your message."

"Yeah? What did you think?"

He pauses, tilting his head to regard me across the distance. "I think," he says. "I think I've loved you so long in silence, and it's time for me to say it out loud."

And then...

And then.

He sits down at the piano.

He takes a deep breath.

He lifts his hands.

And his fingers begin to move across the keys.

I gasp. My eyes widen and my head swings to my brother and friends in their booth, and then back to Jacob. *What is he doing?* Jacob doesn't *perform* in front of people. *Ever.* I can see he's nervous, I can see his hands shake, just a little, but he gives me a half smile, letting me know it's okay. And before I can react, he leans into the mic and starts to sing. And I swear in that moment, my heart cracks like crème brûlée. Tears well up in my eyes at his beautiful, textured voice, and those dark, intense eyes focused directly on me.

I don't recognize the song at first because the original is an up-tempo rock song played on the guitar, but Jacob has completely transformed it, stripping it down to simple piano chords and a beautiful, slow, sad melody. When it dawns on me, I let out a startled, teary laugh.

He's singing a Tom Petty song.

I stand there, tears dripping down my cheeks, as the final chord rings out on the piano. He lifts his fingers from the keys and turns on the bench to look at me, scrubbing a hand across his forehead. And it's so familiar. It's déjà vu again, except last time, we were alone in his apartment, and it was the first time I'd ever heard him play. Last time, it was the moment I'd started to fall in love with him, and now, I've well and truly fallen.

Jacob stands, and I run up the stairs to the stage and into his arms. He crushes me against him, and I fist his shirt in my hands, holding on tight. And then he leans down and kisses me. From somewhere far away, a cheer goes up, echoing through the café, and a champagne bottle pops. Laughing, Jacob and I break apart and turn to find our friends standing and clapping and yelling.

Jacob looks at me, his smile open and unrestrained, without a hint of shyness. "I love you, Sadie." He takes my face in his hands and kisses me again.

From somewhere far behind me, I hear Owen ask Mrs. Kaminski if he can try on her feather boa, and I smile, grateful to my brother for the distraction, for giving us this little bit of privacy. I have so much I want to say to Jacob, so much lost time to make up for. I pull him down on the piano bench next to me. "I found your CD, the one with the songs you wrote for me. That's what I was doing in the car in front of your parents' house that night. I was listening to it, and then it broke. I never got to hear past the first song. But that song is beautiful. It's perfect, and I can't believe you just *did* that right now. That you played and sang for me in public—"

"Sadie." Jacob cuts me off mid-babble, which is probably the right move on his part. He smiles. "I've been waiting about two decades to have you in my arms and to hear you say something to me, and I'm wondering if maybe you could just—"

I clutch his shirt, pulling him closer. "I love you."

He exhales a deep, shaky breath filled with so much emotion, it's like he's been holding it for all these years. I say it again, and then again. "You know," I tell him, "it's hard to shut me up once I get going. You might get sick of hearing it."

"From that day you stood up to a bully on the playground for me—" He gazes out across the café as if he's picturing it play out. The dumpster, the saxophone case, and me telling some kid I'd squish him like a bug. "I thought you were amazing." He turns to look at me now, admiration burning in his eyes. I remember the two of us on his couch during my Very Bad Year. I was lamenting my big mouth, wishing it didn't get me into so much trouble. And Jacob said...

I wish you could see yourself the way I do.

So, *this* is what it's like to be loved by someone who appreciates who I am, not just who I could be or should be. Not just who they *want* me to be.

"After that," Jacob continues, "there was never going to be anyone else for me." He gives me a lopsided smile and shrugs. "I waited two decades to hear you say you love me, and it's going to take a lot more than two to get tired of it."

"But what about Paige?" I ask. "Owen said you were happy."

Jacob shakes his head. "Owen and I talked about it after you left your message. I think I led him to believe Paige and I were more into each other than we really were. I think I *wanted* us to be more into each other than we really were. But the truth is, both Paige and I were trying to get over other people, and it was convenient to hang out with someone who lives next door. But our hearts weren't really in it."

"But you kept bringing her home for the holidays."

Jacob shrugs. "Her family lives in California. I didn't want her to be alone."

He was being a good friend. *Of course he was.*

"So, you and Paige are over?"

His lips tug into a lopsided smile. "She didn't even like me enough to spend a couple of weeks playing Olivia Rodrigo on repeat. It took her about three days to start dating a guy named Brandon who she met on a dating app."

I choke back a laugh. "Paige and Brandon met on a... dating app. Wow. That's—" *Some serious cosmic intervention.* "That's amazing. Good for them." I have a feeling Alex is going to meet that Instagram woman any day now.

Somehow, despite my meddling, everything worked out exactly as it was supposed to. Out across the café, Owen is wearing Mrs. Kaminski's feather boa, and she has his beanie hat pulled over her gray bob. José Luis leans over to adjust their poses so he can sketch their portrait on a napkin. Kasumi and Zoe are giggling over Kasumi's phone, no doubt playing my tell-off video again, counting how many retweets it's gotten.

I turn back to Jacob. By some miracle, Jacob is here with me. "I love you," I tell him again. And then I grab his hand and we hop off the stage, making our way over to everyone who matters most in the world.

Epilogue

January

I wake to the sun slanting in the window and the events of the night before on my mind. Telling off Xavier. Partnering with Zoe at Higher Grounds. *And Jacob.* My heart melts like icing on a cinnamon roll when I think of Jacob onstage, playing the piano and singing just for me. I still can't believe he performed in front of everyone, and it almost feels like a dream.

The star-shaped midcentury chandelier above the bed sways gently, as if it's nodding along to this assessment. A breeze from the window ruffles the curtain in agreement. It's the one I always leave open a crack because otherwise, the old radiator in the corner will leave me roasting when I wake up.

I roll over, my eyes still adjusting to the sunlight, and gaze at the man sleeping next to me. A year ago, who would have ever guessed that Jacob and I would be...

I flush at the memory of what happened when we came home last night. Let's just say that some combinations go perfectly together, like chocolate and peanut butter.

His back is to me, rising and falling beneath the covers.

He's pulled the duvet all the way up to the crown of his head, and I reach out to tug it down so I can wake him with a kiss. But something stops me. Something familiar about this moment.

I've woken like this before, with a man sleeping next to me. Just like the last time, it's January first, and just like last time, his face is obscured by the duvet.

I bolt upright.

Was last night a dream? Or—*oh no*—even worse. Have I gone back to the start of my second chance year...*all over again*? Panicked that I'm stuck in a horrible *Groundhog Day* loop, I grab the duvet and fling it aside, exposing the man's bare shoulders and back.

He slowly rolls over. "Sadie." The man's eyes drift open. "What are you doing?"

I reach over and squeeze his arm to make sure he's real. "Jacob? *Oh, thank God*."

He smiles. "Were you expecting someone else?"

"No." I flop back against the pillows, a laugh rumbling in my chest. "No, absolutely not."

Jacob snakes an arm around me, pulling me close. "I can't believe I'm here with you."

"I can't believe it either." And with my pulse still stuttering, I roll over so I can see his face. "Jacob, what day is it?"

He blinks. "Thursday, I think."

"No, I mean the date."

"Um." He looks at me sideways. "I think New Year's Day generally falls on January first."

Of course it does. But— "*What year is it?*"

"Really?" he asks with a laugh.

"Just tell me."

Jacob says the year, and I smile broadly, settling back against him as his familiar scent drifts over me. I feel movement at the foot of the bed and look down to find Gio carefully making his way across me to curl up on Jacob's chest. He turns on the purr, and Jacob smiles and scratches his head.

It's a new year. One I've never lived through before, one with endless possibilities. The past is behind me, and I'm finished with trying to change things that don't need to be changed.

I couldn't be more excited about what will come next.

Acknowledgments

I'm so thrilled this book found a home with Forever/Grand Central Publishing. Thank you in particular to Estelle Hallick, Alli Rosenthal, Stacey Reid, Daniela Medina, and Justine Gardner for working so tirelessly to get this book in front of readers. To Sabrina Flemming, thank you for all of your feedback that helped take this book to the next level. And a *very* special thank-you to my editor, Junessa Viloria, for championing this story, for sharing your amazing insights, for believing in this book's message, and for falling in love with Jacob. It's been truly wonderful to collaborate with you.

To Jill Marsal, I am endlessly grateful to have you as my agent. This book has been in the absolute best hands with you every step of the way. Thank you so much for believing in it and in my writing career.

To Sarah Congdon, thank you for creating the most beautiful cover that ever existed. It makes me happy every time I look at it.

I am fortunate to have some of the best writer friends

in the world. This book, and my writing career, wouldn't be what it is without two incredibly talented groups of women. To my "local" friends, Lainey Davis and Elizabeth Perry, I value our coffee shop chats so much. I'm so grateful for your advice, your incredibly spot-on and sometimes tough-love feedback, and for always answering my text messages. To my "GH" friends, Anna E. Collins, Megan McGee, Sharon M. Peterson, and Katy James, just about the best day of my writer-life was when I walked into that conference room in NYC and met you all. Your friendship and support throughout my career—from unpublished writer to *The Second Chance Year* (and beyond!)—has meant everything.

Thank you to Lauren Kung Jessen and Meredith Schorr for your enormous generosity in sharing your time and wisdom with a brand-new Forever author! I adore both of you and your books! I hope to pay it forward someday.

I couldn't write a comedy without acknowledging Jennie, Amie, Monica, and Mandy, the other four members of the "Fab Five." I'm so glad we were awkward teenagers so we were forced to develop a sense of humor.

Thank you to my amazing kids, Anjali and Indy, for looking out for your father when your mother disappears for days at a time to write books.

To my husband, Sid, thank you for your endless, endless support of my writing career, from reading my very first, very badly written manuscript to encouraging me to finally quit my day job. From celebrating my successes to letting me talk in circles during the challenging times. And a special, extra huge thank-you for cheerfully wrangling the monsters when I'm on a deadline.

To the Brusoski/Wiesner family, it takes a village to raise children, and apparently to write books, too. Thank you for the unflagging support you've given me in both of these ventures.

Letter from the Author

Dear Reader,

Thank you so much for choosing to read The Second Chance Year *with your book club! I hope you found the book funny and entertaining. At the same time, I hope the themes of this story spark some interesting conversations among your group.*

My inspiration for this book began with the idea of the do-over. I imagined that all of us have something in our past—a conversation, an event, maybe even an entire year—that we'd love to go back and change. We think that maybe if we knew then what we know now, we could fix our mistakes and life would be perfect.

But if we actually had the chance to go back and change the past, would we be happier? Or would we find that things had actually worked out for the best the first time around?

Do we sometimes second-guess ourselves when maybe we shouldn't?

Sadie is someone who rarely second-guessed herself until, in one Very Bad Year, everything fell apart.

Or so she thought.

As I began to dig into Sadie's Second Chance Year, I happened to read about several incidents during the

#metoo movement where high-profile chefs were accused of sexual misconduct by women working in their restaurants. I imagined how women in those situations might have second-guessed their own instincts, maybe to hold on to their job, for fear that they would be blamed, or maybe because on some level, they blamed themselves for what happened. These #metoo stories inspired Sadie's career as a pastry chef and her job in Xavier's restaurant.

Ultimately, in writing this book, I wanted to explore Sadie's journey through second-guessing and self-doubt until she finally came to understanding the value of believing in herself and trusting her instincts.

I hope you enjoyed Sadie's story! I'd love to hear more about your book club discussion, so please reach out over social media! And thank you again for reading.

Best wishes,
Melissa

Discussion Questions

1. When Sadie meets the fortune teller and asks about a do-over, she says about her Very Bad Year: "I can't help thinking if I'd known what was coming, I would have made different choices." Is there a year of your life you look back on and wish you could do over? What choices would you make differently?

2. Sadie worked with Zoe, José Luis, and Mrs. Kaminski at Higher Grounds during her Very Bad Year, but she doesn't grow close with them until she goes back there during her second chance year. Why do you think she didn't appreciate them the first time around?

3. When Jacob goes to Sadie's apartment to share the desserts Sadie baked for her parents, Jacob tells her he's never been able to reach out and grab the one thing he's always wanted in life. What factors were holding Jacob back from confessing his feelings for Sadie for all those years?

4. Sadie has a very difficult relationship with her parents throughout the book. But at one point, her mother reveals that even as a university dean, she still has to work harder than the men in her department. Sadie is surprised to learn that her mother is still dealing with sexism at her high-level job. Did this conversation change your opinion of Sadie's mother? What about Sadie's father? Why or why not?

5. As the #metoo movement has shown, many women who experience sexual harassment keep quiet about it. Throughout the book, Sadie deals with unwanted advances from Rob Thurmond and her boss, Xavier. Yet, she doesn't tell anyone about it until she opens up to Kasumi at the end of the book. Only then does she learn that Kasumi had similar experiences. Can you relate to why Sadie and Kasumi kept quiet? Why or why not?

6. On New Year's Eve of Sadie's Very Bad Year, she tells Jacob, "I'm too old to let my big mouth ruin my career and my relationships." So, in her second chance year, she stops speaking up, even in situations she believes are wrong—such as when Alex's coworker Zach makes sexist comments or Xavier blames a line cook for ruining a pan of food. What did you think of Sadie's first approach (loudly calling people out) compared to her second approach

(staying silent)? What would your approach be in similar situations?

7. Later in the book, we learn that Owen would rather be inventing video games than working for a robotics company. Why do you think Sadie was able to go against her parents' wishes and Owen wasn't? Sadie tells Owen that she'd support him if he decided to give up his job and follow his dream. Do you think Owen will ever decide to do this? If so, how do you think their parents will react?

8. At the end of the book, when Sadie learns that Paige and Brandon met on a dating app, she thinks, "Somehow, despite my meddling, everything worked out exactly as it was supposed to." She calls it "*some serious cosmic intervention.*" Do you believe that everything works out as it's supposed to? Or do you think we're able to control our own destinies?